TALES OF THE
HEXAGONVERSE

3. THE OTHERS

OTHER HEXAGON COMICS
NOVELS & COLLECTIONS

TALES OF THE HEXAGONVERSE

3. THE OTHERS

Translated by
Michael Shreve

Edited by
**Romain d'Huissier
& Jean-Marc Lofficier**

Stories by
**Cédric Burgaud, Julien Heylbroeck,
Travis Hiltz, Romain d'Huissier,
Jean-Marc Lainé, Jean-Marc Lofficier,
Ghislain Morel, Eric Nieudan,
Philippe Pinon, Olivier Vignot**
and **Jean-Hugues Villacampa**

BLACK COAT PRESS

Visit our website at www.blackcoatpress.com
and
www.hexagoncomics.com

TABLE OF CONTENTS

Jean Girodet by Luciano Bernasconi

Introduction

For the uninitiated, this is a collection of short stories featuring characters from the Hexagon Comics universe.

All stories are pretty much self-contained, and you do not need to have read any of the comics to enjoy them— although, of course, you might experience more fun if you are already familiar with the characters.

A short introduction before each story provides all the basic information about who the characters are, and what their powers are. We have also included pin-ups from the comics to help the reader visualize what they look like if you have not encountered them before.

These stories do not violate the established continuity of the comics. They fit within the "empty spaces" existing before, between, and after the comic book stories.

A short biography of each writer is provided at the end of this book; the great majority of them are distinguished French science fiction or fantasy writers who have had many other works published. I do not like the term "fan fiction," and this anthology, just like *Tales of the Shadowmen*, relies on established talent.

Romain d'Huissier, who edits the original French series (published under the name "*Dimension Super-Héros*"), is himself not only a popular and prolific author, but a major creator of role-playing games—including one devoted to the Hexagon Comics universe. Romain has also penned two novels featuring the Hexagon Group of heroes, *Dark Matter*, already available, and *War of the Immortals*, which will be available later this year.

Michael Shreve is one of Black Coat Press' most distinguished translators. If you like pulp heroes, we strongly recommend his translations of Leon Sazie's classic, *Zigomar*, or of André Caroff's *Madame Atomos* series.

Finally, readers interested in delving into the history of Hexagon Comics, France's oldest shared comics universe, are encouraged to buy a copy of our illustrated book, *Hexagon Comics: The First 70 Years*, available from our catalog.

Hexagon began in 1950 as Editions Lug, and published a great number of digest-sized comic magazines until 2003. During its first four decades, it published many original stories, as well as translations of popular Italian and Marvel series—they were, in fact, the very first publisher to translate Marvel Comics for the French market.

The company was relaunched in 2010 under the brand new name "Hexagon Comics" by the undersigned, with a line of reprints of the classic stories, as well as the launching of new series such as *Strangers* and *Guardian of the Republic*.

Now, read on…

Jean-Marc Lofficier

Jean Girodet works for the secretive and private French think tank "LION", led by his father, whose purpose is (allegedly) to preserve world peace. Dave Kaplan lives in New York and is a photo-journalist working for the New York Examiner *(owned by the Wilson Group). He is a friend of Sibilla. This story mixes truths and lies, manipulations and deceptions...*

Jean-Marc Lainé: *The Others*

The hurried footsteps of a few travelers echoed off the large gray paving stones of the Rome train station where a warm, summer breeze blew through the columns of the vast hall. Behind the glass doors lurked the tumult of the *piazza della Repubblica*, blaring horns and screeching tires of the Italian drivers overheated by the August sun. The phrase "road rage" seemed to have been invented just for them.

Turning his back to the Eternal City and its streets packed with revving engines and shouts, Dave Kaplan put his suitcase down with a sigh and took a minute to look at the departure board. The 7:45 p.m. for Paris was still not posted. He had some time yet, but no desire to take one last stroll through the city. He could feel the exhaustion setting in after the week he had spent running between Milan, Bologna and Rome.

He picked up his suitcase, sighed again, and made a tour of the station, glancing wearily at the store windows and bars. Then he went back to the board. From the end of the platforms the tracks stretched out to the horizon like long, straight scars gashed into the urban tissue of the Roman metropolis. His train would be announced any minute now...

Kaplan walked a little farther and stopped at one of the stalls selling piles of mismatched *fumetti* – Italian comics. He took one and thumbed through the black and white pages about a beautiful, blond detective of the supernatural and her ape-like bodyguard. He smiled. Vague memories of his childhood reading floated up in his mind. Snatches of esoteric mysteries, cryptic investigations, wild chases and gunfights came back to him. Conspiracy theories, secret societies, buried cities, apocalyptic weapons and men in black, with long series of explanations in speech bubbles filled up like bloated wineskins. The memory of these childhood pleasures relieved his fatigue and, for a second, he thought of buying a few copies to read on the train. He looked at the cover with the gorgeous blonde and her ape-like bodyguard walking into an obscure landscape surrounded by ghostly shapes. But it reminded him too much of his work, so he put it down. It would be better to use the fifteen hours on the night train to catch up on all the sleep he'd missed over the past few days.

The announcement of his train shook him out of his reverie. The 7:45 for Paris was ready to leave. Kaplan checked his car number, stuffed the tickets into his hip pocket, and walked onto the platform.

Meanwhile, *the other man* wove through the passengers and hurried into a car.

Kaplan was speechless for a moment. The man he had just seen seemed familiar, but he could not place him. An old acquaintance? A former colleague? Someone whom he had interviewed during one of his many investigations? He usually had a faultless memory for names, but the other man remained stubbornly nameless.

He was surprised, then he looked at the car number where he had stopped. It wasn't his. He kept walking to his car and quickly found his seat. He put his suitcase on the luggage rack and looked at the other seats. They were all reserved to Paris, but he was the first one there. Leaning against the window in the corridor, he watched the ballet of rushing passengers, the men in dull business suits, the couples exchanging goodbye kisses, the tourists loaded with baggage. He stepped back into the doorway to let a lady with her hair in a bun pass, wheeling her suitcase behind her. He glanced down the aisle.

The other man was entering a nearby compartment.

Kaplan furrowed his brow. He told himself that the man might have gotten in the wrong car and had made his way through the rest of the train to reach this compartment.

He sat back down and tried to forget the strange coincidence. He needed rest: he had to sleep. The speakers announced the imminent departure and, within seconds, the train started moving while Rome went on with its summer life.

Kaplan's mind started racing along with the rising speed of the train. Like a persistent itch, the image of the other man kept coming back, like a guest you can't get rid of after the party is over. Suddenly, like a forgotten memory returning after many years, he remembered the other man's name.

With some reservations and little self-confidence, Kaplan watched the Italian suburbs fly by his still empty compartment. The industrial districts, speckled with hangars and parking lots, faded into an anonymous scenery, sneering and forgetful. He stood up, changed his mind, shook his head, then went into the corridor. He walked down to the compartment where he had seen the other enter and glanced inside.

The man was sitting alone. He was looking at some papers and seemed absorbed in his reading. On his knees was spread out the various elements of a file: photos of destroyed buildings and crime scenes and press cuttings that looked like anthropometric illustrations.

"Girodet?"

The brown-haired man continued reading as if he had not heard the voice talking to him.

"Jean Girodet?"

The other looked up and quickly stuffed the papers into the briefcase sitting next to him.

"It's me, Dave Kaplan."

Still sitting, the man smiled at Kaplan, but looked confused.

"We met at the Sorbonne fifteen years ago."

"Kaplan? Ah! Dave Kaplan!"

"That's right. It's good to see you, Girodet. I saw you on the platform, but I didn't recognize you right away. It was only after the train started off that it all came back to me. I wouldn't have expected to meet you in Rome."

"What a funny surprise, eh? I, too, never thought I'd see you in Rome. What are you doing here?"

"I'm coming back from a job. I'm a reporter now. I work for the *New York Examiner*. I was on a week-long investigation all over Italy. I went through Milan, Bologna and Rome, and last week, I spent three days in Paris, meeting people and gathering information. Now, I have to get all my notes together and write a coherent article. And believe me, it won't be easy."

Girodet motioned to Kaplan to sit across from him in one of the empty seats.

"Complicated subject?"

"Complicated, no. It's just that no one will believe me, Jean. I'm working on the supernatural for a big spread in a cultural supplement for the Sunday paper. The supernatural is always a big hit. You tell stories of ghosts and phantoms, doors slamming by themselves, photos of winged angels and the public eats it up. And I get to visit the Old Country on the paper's ticket. Pretty cushy."

"The supernatural? That's interesting."

"You must be kidding. Haunted houses, ghosts, secret societies that live in the abandoned tunnels of the Metro, reincarnation of famous people, witches and wizards trying to raise the Antichrist, magic weapons and grimoires holding secrets that will drive you mad if you read the wrong verse... All these stories of magic words, conjuring, mass hypnosis and the end of the world, seriously, it's shocking that people still believe in that stuff. Nothing is ever proven, even the things that people think they've seen."

"You shouldn't take such things so lightly, Dave."

Kaplan looked at him. "Don't tell me you believe in all that nonsense, Jean?"

Girodet gave him a look that carried all the weariness of the world. "If only you knew what I think of it all, Dave..."

In the silence of the empty compartment, the two men stared at each other.

Kaplan was discovering a Girodet who was nothing like the shy, thin young man sitting in the back of the auditorium at the Sorbonne. Before him sat a tired man with weary gray eyes. The former student looked like one of those old soldiers sitting stock still, his gaze wandering, dreams full of pain and sorrow that do not fade when the alarm clock rings. Like them, his movements were slow and measured, his hands grazed the bench without leaving a trace; he seemed always on the lookout, lying in wait for a sound, a movement, a bad surprise, like a hunted animal ready to jump at the faintest unexpected noise.

Kaplan smirked and pointed to the briefcase lying on the seat next to Girodet. "Does that have something to do with what you're hiding here? You've seen things that no human being should ever see?"

Girodet looked at Kaplan. With sadness. As if something had happened and it was too late now. "Have you seen the documents?"

"You were looking at them when I came in. You were so absorbed in them that you didn't hear me. I called your name a couple of times. I almost thought you didn't recognize your own name.."

"Maybe that's because it's not my real name.

For the first time in weeks, Kaplan was at a loss for words. He covered it up with a little laugh and then. "We've known each other since what… since we were 20, right? You've always been called Jean Girodet. That's your name."

The old friend from the Sorbonne sighed. "Let's say instead that it's not the only name I use. I feel like it's not really my true name."

"You feel like? Don't you remember?"

"I… For years now, Dave, I've worked for LION. Often under a pseudonym. Undercover. I've switched identities many times before. I gather information. I dig and search and nose around. I've gotten data on the activities of all the major government agencies, including yours. And yes, I've seen things that nobody should have seen. Things that make your ghosts and haunted houses sound like children's stories."

The staccato of the wheels on the rails beat more loudly.

Dave Kaplan stared at his old friend as if he was seeing him for the first time. And behind the layer of weary sadness he thought he recognized a determination and assertiveness that scared him for a moment. Then his journalistic instinct took over again.

"How did you...?"

"Sorry, Dave, it's my job to know. And I do. I know where you've been, who you met in Rome and Milan. I know you worked with that columnist for *Flash* in Milan, Sibilla, on a story of demonic possession in the suburbs there. I know you were at a ceremony to invoke Otar, and that without Morgane's intervention, the Sons of Shivar would have loosed their hellish divinity on Earth. I know you met Doc Zarbi and you explored the Rue des Morillons..."

For the first time, Girodet smiled.

"Don't look at me with those big, bewildered eyes. I have a file on you. It's one of the thickest."

Girodet opened his briefcase and took out a file full of dog-eared folders. The worn cardboard bore witness to frequent handling. He had consulted these archives a lot, added new material regularly, sorted and classified the photos, reports and notes. Paper clips and staples bundled the papers together. Out of the corner of his eyes, Kaplan noticed a few rolls of film and several diskettes in the briefcase.

Girodet took a pack of folders and put them on the top of the briefcase after shutting it. He pulled out one and showed Kaplan the title. The journalist saw the six letters of his own name and that it was, indeed, stuffed full.

"Now you know I'm not making this up, Dave. Everything weird you've seen is recorded in here. Really. You just have to read through it to see for yourself. But I'm sure you trust me now."

Girodet put the file on the seat next to him.

"And I trust you, too. I know that you understand. That you will believe me."

The secret agent handed a folder to the journalist. On the cover was a white sticker with the words *Homicron File*. Kaplan undid the string that was keeping sealed all the secrets of the file and started thumbing through the documents. He recognized the pages that he had glanced when he had first entered the compartment. He stopped at what he had thought was an anthropometric illustration. It was a copy of a military file. The man with stars on his shoulders in the photos was General Hartland. His life was laid out, his service record in foreign countries, his slow climb up the military hierarchy... The other documents, including a lot of photos taken with a zoom lens, were about various projects that he had been in charge of. One could see fenced-in areas, hangars in the desert, flashes of light behind rocky peaks, the charred ruins of what looked like a huge airplane or a gigantic helicopter...

Dave Kaplan went through the file. He lingered for a moment over the photo of a man suspended in the air, floating over the ground in a bluish halo of light. Someone had written the word "*Homicron 1*" above the image in black ink. He looked at the next image: a woman also hovering in a bluish light. Another handwritten caption read "*Homicron 2*". Kaplan raised his skeptical, almost amused eyes, to his friend.

Jean Girodet waved his hand at the file to indicate to his friend to keep reading. Kaplan turned the pages. Tables and graphs showed the fluctuations of energy and the peaks of activities of the "*Homicron subjects*". Official reports on letterhead from the Army General Staff had been photocopied and stuck in the file. Most of them were stamped with a big *CONFIDENTIAL*. He scanned the rest of the file with his journalist instinct whispering that things were getting more and more mysterious.

He stopped at a picture that he did not understand at first. Men in chem suits were leaning over a corpse with its chest opened and organs revealed. Other photos showed different steps of the same autopsy, men in hazmat suits cutting out and weighing the viscera. Kaplan spread out the photos in front of him. The dissected man was unusually tall, his muscles were slender, his hands too long, even for his height. His fingers looked very flexible and on closer inspection Kaplan could have sworn there was an extra phalanx.

The journalist recoiled. He mumbled something, then leaned over the pictures again for a closer look. He turned them over and read what was on the back: *Kyrosian Autopsy* followed by the time and date.

Kaplan put down the photos and with a wry smile asked, "What kind of joke is this?"

"It's no joke, Dave. The photos are real."

"Get outta here! It's a hoax. Like the Roswell story and the little gray men, the alien autopsy…"

"Little gray men exist, Dave, although that's not what they call themselves. And their autopsy was real. Just like this Kyrosian. But we have to put it out on TV like it's all a prank so nobody takes it seriously."

"Don't tell me that Area 51 exists and they're using alien technology to develop all our inventions."

"Area 51 exists, but it's a prison. However, there is an R&D section that works on confiscated materials and some-times even extraterrestrial corpses. But the prototypes are test-ed and commercialized in Area 102."

"You're just messing with me."

"Coming from the guy who investigates ghosts, immortal beings and magic gloves?"

David Kaplan took one last look at the autopsy and then carefully slipped the photos back into the folder and closed the file on all the little secrets of the US army. He turned to the window hoping to see familiar territory, to get lost in the dis-tant horizon, but it was already night outside. The train had no doubt crossed the Italian border into France but the window was jet black and he saw only his own tired reflection with darker circles around his eyes.

"A Kyrosian?"

"It's a race from a hostile galactic empire that was trying to conquer Earth."

"If I hadn't seen that file, I'd probably tell you to watch fewer of those Roland Emmerich films…"

"I think I'm not explaining it very well. That's not my specialty, explaining things…"

"So start from the beginning."

"The beginning was the Apollo 19 mission."

"There never was an Apollo 19 mission. The last one was Apollo 17 and Congress never approved the budgets for any after that."

"That's the official version. The truth is that the two missions were failures. Apollo 18 had trouble with the Moon landing and Apollo 19 was caught in a magnetic storm on its way back to Earth. The table with the energy fluctuations is about that. Alphan energy made up of particles held in isolated magnetic fields. A bunch of stuff I don't really understand, but it's all in there, in those reports. NASA made contact with the Alphans, who are able to inhabit material objects, a body for example."

"You mean these… Alphans are inside people?"

"Not all people, but yes. The two individuals you saw in the photos, *Homicron 1* and *Homicron 2*, are two Earthlings who encountered Alphans. The energy field that surrounds them is a protection mechanism to defend their physical body. It generates an energy that allows them to defy gravity and they can pump out excess energy in the form of rays, by emitting light…"

"And where do the Kyrosians come in?"

"The reports don't say exactly what the relationship is between the Alphans and the Kyrosians. As far as we can tell, we might be in the middle of a space war. Or a diplomatic dispute. We might also think that since the Alphans don't have their own bodies, they are a threat to the Kyrosians. In short, we don't really know which side is the good guys and which is the bad. We just know that Earth is in the middle, and they landed on American soil. Moreover, they're not the only extraterrestrials we've identified. There are also... the *others*. They've got a few specimens in Area 51."

"And General Hartland is in charge of the the autopsies of these... specimens?"

"I'm not really sure Hartland is his real name. His file has many gaps. He has a background in intelligence. I turned up a few foreign missions. I know that he's used weapons and material that the military-industrial complex had not officially developed. He's not much for scruples. He figures the ends justify the means. He's the ideal man to build an American super-soldier."

"A super-soldier?"

"What do you think Homicron 1 and 2 are except an attempt to create a superman at the beck and call of the US government? Did you see the wreck of that plane? The biggest carrier in the US fleet and Homicron 1 did that. Imagine what an army of soldiers with his powers could do."

Kaplan's eyes narrowed suspiciously. "Is that your job, Jean? Discovering the secrets of foreign governments and giving the information to the French? So that they can copy the Americans and make their own super-soldiers? Is that your great mission?"

"Don't worry about the French, Dave. They already have their own super-soldier – the Guardian of the Republic."

Kaplan laughed loudly, which provided a much needed relief.

"Don't laugh, Dave. The Guardian program is coming along just fine. According to my sources, the French have turned to genetic experiments to make a superior athlete – something called A.S.T.R.A. And they're not the only ones... All those scandals about sports doping can't be for nothing. Where do you think Big Bad Ben and Hazel Toff come from?"

"Hazel Toff? And our governments finance this kind of madness?"

"Not officially, of course. But considerable sums have been allocated to these research programs and when the scientists achieve something concrete, there's never a problem finding money. Especially in the present cases where some of the funds are coming from private sources."

"Private?"

"They called it sponsorship. Do you know who's behind most of it? You met him in Paris last week. It's Count Saint-Germain."

"That fraud? You don't believe in his immortality, do you? It's just a legend, a lie, a carnival trick so the old playboy can strut his stuff among the high society."

"Nobody knows if he's truly immortal, but his file stretches back centuries. There aren't too many ways to explain his unnatural longevity…"

Kaplan frowned skeptically. His brain was working fast, maybe too fast, like an empty mill whose momentum is not slowed down when grinding away at the grain. He needed something more substantial to sink his teeth into if he were to believe Girodet's hare-brained ideas.

"You're talking about all this like an outsider, but you work for LION, right? Aren't they part of French intelligence? Are you spying on your own people, Jean?"

"Information is power. Being a journalist, you can't disagree with that."

"Who do you work for, Jean? Really."

Girodet stared at his old friend for a moment, then he looked down, opened the briefcase and straightened out the files inside before closing it again and clicking the latches. He put the briefcase on the seat next to him and looked up at the ceiling for a long time. Then he sighed.

Kaplan waited patiently for Girodet to deign to reply. But the agent stayed silent. *Well*, Kaplan thought, *a journalist must ask questions.*

"You're not going to tell me that there's a global conspiracy behind all this?"

Girodet smiled wearily across at him and held up his index and middle fingers. Unintentionally he was making the "V" for victory sign for a war that nobody knew about.

"There is not *a* global conspiracy behind all this, Dave. There are two."

Kaplan snorted, almost. Neither the pleasure of seeing an old friend straight out of his memories of youth, nor his taste for a good, fantastic story, nor the fatigue from too many investigations and too much travel, were any excuse for the crazy plots that were unfolding before him since he had left Rome. He sank back into his seat with a smug smile on his face.

"On one side, there are all the people who finance the secret projects," the spy went on.

Girodet was unaffected. The secret agent paid no attention to the mocking look in his old friend's eyes. He was eager to explain everything, to throw light onto all the darkest corners. As if he had already said too much, as if the secret was already out and was going to disperse its mysterious scents to the four winds before the journalist could get a lead to follow.

"You can call them the *Insiders*. They're in every country all over the globe. They include Hartland, Count Saint-Germain, the Sullivans, the Sauternais, the Rostands, Wilson's conglomerate…"

"The Pope, too?"

"I don't have proof. For now, there are only rumors. Still, it's this international network that's pouring out astronomical budgets to build up defenses and manufacture weapons."

"For what?"

"To defend us. To protect us"

"But protect us from whom, damn it?"

Girodet sighed, not so much from weariness but more to give himself the courage to go on.

"Dave, I told you that Earth is surrounded by extraterrestrials. The Alphans and Kyrosians are just the beginning… There's another race that's threatening our world. A race of strange beings coming from outer space. They're already here. They can take human form. They can copy the appearance of anyone and replace them. That's the other conspiracy. That of the *Others*."

"That's what you call them?"

"No one's found a better name. Some witnesses have identified one of these things which called itself *Wampus*. So, we also refer to them as *Wampoids*. But we don't even know if Wampus is a name, a rank, a species or maybe even a concept. We just know how to spot them."

"All the better. Because if what you're telling me is true, your… *Others*… well, you could be one of them. Or me! How can you be sure that you're talking to the real me and not a copy?"

"You don't have their eyes."

"Excuse me?"

"The Others have pupils in the shape of a down arrow. You can't see it right away, you have to get close to tell the difference. With contacts or tinted glasses, they can go completely unnoticed."

Kaplan shifted in his seat and kept the sour grin on his face.

"You don't believe me? Does the name Jean Vlad mean anything to you? The journalist from *L'Univers* in Paris who mysteriously disappeared? If you don't believe me, look at this."

Girodet opened his briefcase again and took out a thick file. The word *Wampus* was stamped on the cover. With trembling fingers, Kaplan took it and untied the string that protected its secrets. He rifled through the documents within. Reports on a secret invasion as well as eyewitness accounts, press cuttings and official papers on letterhead from the Department of Defense. Memos and minutes mentioning the existence of parallel worlds, Earths like ours but where evolution and history had developed differently. Among these was an alternate Earth where the wampoids were slowly replacing the human population. Kaplan paused for a while on a picture of an alternate Jean Vlad who looked exactly like the one he had met a long time ago at *L'Univers*, except for his pupils with arrows pointing down.

More and more intrigued, Kaplan grabbed another folder. They were talking about the transfer of consciousness, about energy-matter relationships, and the astronaut Ted White. The name Rita Tower came up a few times. Other names cropped up in different places, like in the *Homicron File*. Sometimes the information seemed contradictory and many details remained in the dark. Sometimes the names were false, mixed up with pseudonyms, or the places and dates were blacked out to protect the secrets, but a pattern was starting to emerge.

Kaplan felt like he was seeing the big picture, the overall scheme of things. He had to verify it. He had to know.

He examined one document after another after another. They talked about telepathy, mind-control and teleportation, expeditions to Africa searching for rare minerals in the mountains of Karunda, orchids with unsuspected psychotropic qualities, a race of metamorphs able to change into any animal and a telepath called Jaleb Jellicoe. They talked about germ warfare, electromagnetic waves, squadrons of fighter spaceships, artificial intelligence, cybernetic soldiers, photon computers, parallel dimensions and alternative Earths, myco-neural networks, cloning, genetic manipulation, nano-implants, countless armories hidden in dimensional tesseracts…

Dave Kaplan rubbed his eyes. Carried away by his reading, he had lost track of time and felt weighed down with fatigue. The early glow of dawn was creeping onto the dog-eared pages, highlighting some of the blurry, black and white photos where the details stayed obscured, shapeless in the light of the new day.

The train slowed down and finally stopped at a station. Through the window, Kaplan saw the word *Dijon* on the platform. It was almost 7:30 a.m. He had not slept. He had spent the night examining the documents full of secret information that was as unsettling as it was unverifiable. He laid his head in his hands and let out a long sigh.

"Extraordinary, isn't it, Dave?"

Kaplan had almost forgotten his old friend was still there across from him. He looked at the man whom he used to call Jean Girodet. And he got kind of dizzy. He waited a few seconds for it to pass before standing up.

"I think… I think I need a little fresh air."

Kaplan left the compartment and went up the corridor. Through the open door he felt the cool, morning air refresh him. His eyelids were heavy and he was overwhelmed.

He opened the door of the toilets, stepped in and closed it behind him. Looking at his reflection in the mirror, he saw bags under his eyes. His head was swimming. The flood of information, blurry details, unverifiable revelations, contradictory data, shifting dates, everything became clear in the bright light of the toilet: a vast web of lies; a deep, paranoid, conspiracy theory woven together with pure fantasy.

Kaplan turned on the faucet and splashed water on his face. He rubbed his neck with his wet hand and everything seemed clearer. The different lines of the grand plan of world conquest chronicled in Girodet's secret files were dancing in his memory. He could remember some details. But especially the context. And Girodet's voice echoed in his mind.

Information is power.

Even if it's unfounded, Kaplan wondered, staring at his exhausted reflection.

Being a journalist, you can't disagree with that.

Certainly not. And Kaplan finally started putting together the true information in order to compare it.

It's my job to know.

Kaplan rubbed his eyes. He was waking up from a long night's sleep.

I gather information for them.

A spy, that's what Girodet was, an informant, a snitch, a stool pigeon pointing fingers. He was just a rat taking orders.

Some of the funds come from private sources. There's never a problem finding money.

Kaplan did not even try to imagine what gadgets LION gave to a guy like Girodet. No doubt things out of the movies, remote-controlled with his fingerprint, thermal bombs hidden in his watch, but able to get in anywhere from luxury hotels to the best guarded ministries, special privileges in the circles of political power, thick envelopes for his trips and plenty for expenses.

Considerable sums are allocated. Astronomical budgets.

The image of Girodet alone in the middle of six empty seats in his compartment popped up in Kaplan's mind. The journalist thought again about his own luggage in the deserted compartment. Two compartments without passengers on a train where they had never once checked their tickets during the night.

I know where you've been. I know who you met in Rome and Milan. It was Count Saint-Germain. You met him in Paris last week. I have a file on you. It's one of the thickest.

In Girodet's briefcase, he had not seen the file marked "Kaplan". The spy must have set it aside. If he had opened it, Kaplan would certainly have found photos of himself taken with a zoom lens all over France and Italy over the past few weeks. And more.

Kaplan burst out of the toilet and ran to Girodet's compartment. The room was deserted, the six empty seats lit up by the morning sun. Beyond the window the countryside filed past to the rhythm of the train that nothing could stop before it reached the station in Paris. And Girodet had disappeared.

Kaplan jumped back into the corridor and ran to his own compartment. No one.

The journalist looked right and left. He understood, but it was too late.

Back in Girodet's compartment, Kaplan found a small, off-white card that he had not noticed before. A single word was written on it, like an instruction.

"Search."

Kaplan turned the card over and saw a few words scribbled by Girodet on the back.

"Look around you."

As he fiddled with the card, Kaplan let his eyes wander over the worn leather seats, over the seat recently occupied by the nameless man he had once called Jean Girodet.

It was coming up on 11am when Kaplan stepped off the train and walked down the platform in Paris. The sun was high in the sky and the passengers were dispersing into the big city, rushing into the metro or climbing into taxis that sped off without delay.

Kaplan watched the passenger before him carefully. When he got to the waiting area, he put down his suitcase and turned around. The other travelers passed by him to the right and left without paying him any attention. He scrutinized their faces, one by one, until the platform was deserted.

But Kaplan did not see Jean Girodet again.

The meeting with his editor lasted too long, just like all meetings at *L'Univers*. But being used to the arid frenzy of American newsrooms, Kaplan liked the Latin buzz of French journalists, the babble and interruptions. It was undiluted human life, the subject of journalism *par excellence*, and he enjoyed it every time he came to France to work. Moreover, all that lost time had made him hungry and the idea of a good meal in a restaurant in the 5th Arrondissement was cheering him up.

Kaplan stopped at a newsstand and bought a few papers; then, with the daily press under his arm, he started thumbing through the news on his way to lunch. All of a sudden, his smile was wiped off his face.

On the bottom of the society page a small article had attracted his attention. A photo, a little blurry but still recognizable, of Jean Girodet. The headline announced the death the day before, late in the afternoon, of the discreet professor who had experienced a little literary glory two years ago. The article gave a few meager facts about the death of the professor in a tragic car accident somewhere between Dijon and Paris. The rest of the text concentrated on the sorrow of the family, academic colleagues, and a few grieving writers.

Kaplan looked intently at the portrait printed on cheap paper, but the image was not clear enough to make out the eyes of the deceased. Certainly not his pupils.

Kaplan remembered the sleepless night in the Rome-Paris train just a few hours before his death. He realized that he had never had the slightest idea of Girodet's official job. He had accepted the idea that his old school buddy had become a spy, without question, as if it was the most natural thing in the world for a literature student to enter the secret world of spied. He had never met the Girodet family. He knew nothing about him, them, or even LION, that French think tank for which he was supposed to have been working.

He reread the article, not with the eyes of a friend finding out about the sudden death of an old comrade, but with those of a journalist reading between the lines. He tried to reconstruct the events, to understand what Girodet had done when he got off at Dijon. He imagined him taking a car that was parked for him at the station and heading out of town, maybe taking the highway...

He wanted to find the clues, the proof of another lie from the secret agent. He tried to distinguish the true from the false, to determine if Girodet, or whatever his real name was, had succeeded in the ultimate disappearing act, one final illusion, the last smokescreen.

He couldn't.

Kaplan folded up the paper and raised his eyes.

On the street corner stood a man dressed in a dark suit, waiting for someone or something. To his left, in the crowd, near a shop window, an individual in dark clothes was holding an open newspaper, but did not look like he was reading it. Farther on, a passerby in a charcoal suit, his eyes hidden behind sunglasses, with a felt hat pulled down low, was hurrying away.

Kaplan thought of the card Girodet had left on the seat.
"Search."

And the advice he had given. Which now seemed more like a warning.

"Look around you."

Starlock by Luciano Bernasconi

*Nick Thaler is a NASA astronaut whose body was possessed by **Starlock**, once Garlan of Styxane, a former Guardian of the Towers who was sentenced to imprisonment on Mars by his masters. This story takes place just before Starlock joined the **Strangers**; and in flashbacks, after the end of its original series, before **C.L.A.S.H.** and fellow astronaut **Max Tornado** rescued him from the evil organization S.P.I.D.E.R.*

Ghislain Morel: *Southern Patrol*

Melbourne, Present Day

It's been forever since I came to Australia, but for a few days I've been feeling physically unwell. Something is disturbing the Earth's gravitational field in a weird way, in an infinitesimal way, but I, Starlock, master of gravity, feel it in the depths of my being. And to my knowledge, nothing on this planet can create the kind of anomaly whose source I've located here in Melbourne.

Since the moment I got here, I've had the feeling that it's close. In fact, whatever *it* is, I know that it's coming for me. I made a lot of enemies in my former life, and one or more of them have traced me here.

It's the start of winter in the southern hemisphere, but the heat is still stifling. Standing on the roof of a tall building, I look out upon this city with a strange atmosphere—a new world where the influences of old Europe are mixed with those of nearby Asia. As I survey all the unusual activity above ground, despite my attention, my thoughts drift back to the past…

Somewhere in orbit, in the past

I was on my way back. The Tarantula had just brought me to S.P.I.D.E.R.'s space station, where I had met Professor

29

Mygale, a madman whose disfigured face and disproportionally long limbs made him look like a monstrous arachnid.

What made me really scared of him was his brain, both brilliant and demented, the brain of a madman with one goal in mind—vengeance. At the time, my body was shared by two entities. I was still the astronaut Nick Thaler, who had opened my prison pod on Mars and thus became the refuge for the energy being I had become. Unfortunately for him, my long captivity had unbalanced me and I only had one desire—to get off Earth and back to Styxane, my native planet. In my state of confusion, I was ready to let Earth suffer the same fate as those I had just fought, which had caused my downfall.

I had been a Guardian of the Towers, and now I was a common criminal using my cosmic powers only to get what I wanted. In my folly, I figured I could accelerate the scientific evolution of the human race by starting a third world war. It was a twisted, ludicrous idea—the kind that the Towers, my old masters, might have come up with. I had once used these vast powers to protect the Star Bridge, that extraordinary hypertunnel joining our Milky Way to its closest neighbors, the Magellanic Clouds and the Andromeda galaxy, but I had rebelled against those who had made me what I was when I had found out hoe they used the lifeforce of helpless beings to sustain their creation.

Thanks to my host, I was able to escape, and get off the desolate planet that the Earthlings call Mars, a celestial representation of the god of war in several ancient civilizations, the planet as red as blood in their iconography. The Towers had chosen my prison well. When I got to Earth, I quickly turned Nick Thaler, dedicated astronaut, into a pariah by taking over his body and committing various acts of violence that now weigh heavily on my conscience. How could I have hurt so many innocent people and almost started a worldwide war that would have left no survivors? What saved mankind was that Nick was fundamentally a decent person and I could only take over his body when the Moon, upon which rested the life-giving mystic crystal of my home planet, was in a specific astral configuration. During one of these phases, powerless, stuck in the depths of my host's subconscious, I was captured.

It wasn't the first time. After the hangar we crossed the outer ring where the gravity was equal to Earth's and got to the central part: the lair built by Professor Mygale, an evil genius far in advance of the technology of the time. He was hanging on a synthetic web that covered the ceiling and moved like the huge spider whose name he had adopted.

"Mr. Thaler, I'm happy to see you again. It seems to be a point of honor for you to ruin our plans. You are costing my organization more and more. It would be a pity to write off your wife for the price of our losses."

"Don't you realize that I can't be your accomplice? I'm not a criminal like you!"

"Now that's strange coming from a man who destroyed a whole squad of American submarines and tried to nuke Bagdad. And I will remind you that it's just business between us and I will only resort to murder in order to protect my interest. Our clients might kill each other, but remember that the weapons used to attack are also used to defend."

The professor moved upward and his hands let go of the web so that he was hanging upside down, his inverted face just inches away from mine.

"If I can't trust you, I'm sure I can convince your alter ego. But this time, I would appreciate it if you wouldn't sabotage our agreement. Otherwise, you know the fate awaiting your lovely wife. My pets need so much food…"

This man disgusted me and I was angry with myself for being under his thumb. I knew that, in the next cycle, I'd be ready to collaborate, and after that, I wouldn't be able to do anything without putting Nora's life in danger. I allowed myself the only act of courage available—I spit in the face of the merchant of death.

"Guards! Get him out of my sight! Find him a cell where he can sit and think about things for a while.

Melbourne, present day

The sun is slowly setting behind the horizon and the twilight of a very starry night seeps over the Australian sky. I take advantage of the darkness and the deserted streets to fly off the roof and check out the city. As I pass over Bourke Street going toward the ocean, I see a new building to the north of the docks where the old laboratories of the Advanced Propulsion Industry used to be. Memories come flooding back again. Only out of the corner of my eye do I get a glimpse of the shadow moving parallel to me over Lonsdale Street.

Somewhere in orbit, in the past

It's hard to talk differently about two parts of yourself without using the first person. I am Nick Thaler, at least through his memory, but I am also Starlock. Now I am the sum of these two individuals, but at that time we were two separate identities with two very different objectives. A new cycle had just begun and the evil being I had become was back in control. The cell where the astronaut was rotting away was not to my liking—time to blow out that armored door. The Tarantula was waiting for me on the other side. Before I had time to get upset and kill all her henchmen, she spoke to me as directly as possible:

"Professor Mygale has an offer that you should be very interested in."

I just nodded my agreement and followed her down the corridors to a communications room where a dozen operators were apparently in contact with agents of the criminal organization on the ground. In a rolling chair Mygale seemed to be supervising the scene, sometimes writing notes on a pad on his knees.

When I came in, he turned to face me, "You're finally back. I was afraid I'd only be able to talk to that coward Thaler. Well, come into my office."

He rolled his chair with his arms and entered a big office that had opened up behind past an automatic door. Inside I could have rid my host planet of this merchant of death for good. We were alone. But despite my bloodlust, my madness was urging me to get back to Styxane, so I listened to his offer.

"Can I offer you a refreshment?"

"What am I doing here?"

"Your alter-ego took control of things and then gave us the slip. The Tarantula managed to catch him and bring you back here. I think we got off on the wrong foot. Why not collaborate? We're both trying to sow chaos on this planet to start wars and we're also both looking for new technology. My space station is the result of my personal research and my engineers are far ahead of their time…"

"What are you getting at?"

"Work for me! With the money you make for me, I can progress in my space research and get you out of here. By the time we get to that point, I won't need you anymore anyway. You'll have the technology to return to your home planet. S.P.I.D.E.R. will control the entire solar system. Humanity will be ours, working in our factories on our planets."

"I don't trust you!"

"If you start a world war, you'll risk losing the greatest brains of mankind. You'll destroy research centers that will take years to rebuild. Despite their competitive spirit they will be years behind. Whereas with me, I'm already ahead and I plan to remain so for a long time to come."

"What exactly do you want from me?"

"Help me get hold of the technology I need. My agents will need a bit of time to connive their way into it, but you— nothing can stop you!"

"I am indeed the most powerful being on this planet. Your primitive weapons are useless against me. But why should I work for you when I can just force you to do my bidding?"

"You're forgetting about your alter-ego. Mr. Thaler won't ever let you do this, and you'll be easy to get rid of under him. But I already have him under control through his wife, who is in my power. So I can assure you that he won't interfere anymore in your operations."

I thought about it. An irresistible force was urging me to leave this planet and the way being opened before me was reasonable. But I really didn't trust Professor Mygale. However, his reasoning was sound. I decided to put him to the test.

"Prove to me that you'll work on building a spaceship that can take me home."

"I think the first mission I'll give you will prove my sincerity. Since you're already here, why not give it a shot, right?"

Melbourne, present day

At the next intersection I saw two weird-looking machines flying parallel to me over the city. Two shadows in the darkness cast by the towers in the setting sun. A reddish tint on their sides proves that they were metallic. I didn't think twice. I soared up alongside an office building and shot over the top. My pursuers noticed my trick when I didn't appear at the next corner.

Stopping abruptly between two penthouses, one of them had just enough time to get its sights on me as I dived fist forward towards one of them. It was thrown only a dozen yards before it regained control and hovered before me. I took a few seconds to get a good look. I wasn't wrong: it was a robot, a round body, even a little oval, with six tentacles coming out of it, each ending in pincers. Even though its surface was metallic it looked like it was quivering—various sensory organs and growths seemed to be running along its metal carapace. They were techno-organic constructs, a technology that few species in this space sector knew. I could guess who these monsters belonged to. I'd stopped too long, thought too much. A violent rip in my back reminded me that they were not alone.

Melbourne, in the past

I am Starlock and I don't need weak humans to help me fulfill my goal! I thought while the four S.P.I.D.E.R. shuttles came down with mine into Melbourne, Australia.

We landed at night in the Flemington Racecourse, the huge racetrack near the docks. That was the end of the road for them. They wouldn't be able to follow me despite their orders. At least not now. But if my mission was crowned with success, Mygale's men would accompany me in the air. I took off, flew over the grandstand, then went looking for the lab in the industrial zone to the west of the port.

Professor Radesh Shrankar had worked for the Indian government on the development of their future military nuclear program. The part that really interested him was the creation of missiles within the Indian space program that was primarily a cover for a nuclear arsenal capable of rivaling China's and counteracting an eventual Pakistani offensive. He had very interesting theories about new techniques of propulsion, futuristic combustibles and miniaturization processes. In Nick Thaler's memory, the engineers at NASA considered him a madman, albeit a mad genius. Nevertheless, the Indian scientist was too paranoid to share his discoveries. He finally fled to Australia, whose new space program was searching for just this kind of project leader who could lift them above their competitors.

I landed behind the building and looked for a way in. It was extremely well guarded and I could tell that every possible entrance had an alarm. So, I decided on the direct approach, which might just be the most discreet. I went to the front entrance and the two guards inside motioned that the lab was closed. I waved them over. One of them came up holding his weapon and his colleague opened the door.

"What can I do for you, sir?"

I was bundled up in a trench coat with a fedora pulled down over my eyes. The guard tried to get a good look at who was hiding behind the outfit.

"Sorry to bother you but I've come to see Professor Shrankar. I hope he's still here?"

"Yes, he's working in his office. Who should I say is asking for him?"

"Tell him Nick Thaler the astronaut is here."

The guard, an unusually large man for an Asian, seemed to recognize the name and squinted as he tried to remember where he had heard it. Finally he went back to the phone. I followed and leaned on the desk near him. His colleague, who looked like a Maori, kept a close eye on me.

He had just dialed the number when I took control of their minds. The human psyche was so simple for me and I had got them to trust me just enough to lower their mental guard. Now entirely under my control, the Asian guard announced me and then both of them led me down the corridor to Shrankar's office.

The engineer was leaning over a backlit glass table, working on finely detailed blueprints with a ruler and compass. It took him almost a minute to raise his head, focus his little brown eyes on me and try to guess who could be hiding behind my disguise. If he had recognized my name, he couldn't have been too well informed about current events. Even if the American government had kept a lid on my specific actions, an international search was ongoing and my career as an astronaut in this time of unbridled space conquest had made me a celebrity in the whole world but especially in scientific circles.

"Mr. Thaler?" he questioned, bending down and trying to see my face, "to what do I owe the honor of this visit?"

His English was perfect despite the heavy accent that made his voice sound very pleasant. I thanked my escort and sent them away. I decided to take off my hat and trench coat.

"I came for you, Professor Shrankar. I work for a secret organization called S.P.I.D.E.R. and we think your research is the next stage in the conquest of space. I came to ask you to join us, with your work and your projects."

"Ex… excuse me? But, I mean, why me?"

"Surely you know, professor. We're ready to let you try out all your theories on ionic propulsion, the nuclear energy reactors and your work on miniaturization of mechanical devices to make life easier on long-haul flights. We've got considerable resources and your lab will be beyond your wildest dreams."

Shaking his shock of curly hair, he looked deep in thought. "This is a major decision. I need more time. Even just to gather all my notes."

"In fact, professor, you don't have a choice. We're leaving tonight, willingly or not. I have no time to waste on such trivialities. If you need help, a team is ready to transport your work."

"I, er, well, if it must be so, then I have to prepare the machine I'm currently working on. Give me a few minutes."

"OK, but don't try to call for help. I am too strong for earthly weapons and your guards have no chance against my cosmic power."

I went with the professor down the corridor and into his lab. I entered with him and he started to put on a weird suit.

"I'm going to pack up my work. I'm working on a miniature reactor with certain parts replaced by very strong magnetic fields so it takes up less space and withstands incredible temperatures. But I have to work in a dust-free environment. I'm going into the vacuum chamber to pack it up so we can take it to your lab."

I was sure then that I had made the right choice. Shrankar was definitely ahead of his time and his reactors would soon be able to take me back to Styxane, the world I had no memories of, but that was drawing me towards it inevitably.

Melbourne, present day

A tentacle just slammed my back. It stung. Once I was over my surprise, I first steadied my flying so I wouldn't collide with the apartment building in front of me and smash it to pieces. I have changed. I no longer risk the lives of the people on this planet. The first thing to do was to change battlefields. At this time of the day the business district was almost empty. I didn't know what weapons these drones were armed with. Were they after me or were they just flying by, but were attracted by my ability to control gravitons?

I dropped down a few dozen yards and shot forward again, skimming the top of a bus. I headed for Spencer Street going against traffic. saw see a shape above me and sometimes the tip of a tentacle whipping over the roofs on either side of the street. So now I had at least three enemies and considering how hard the the first had hit me, this battle was not going to be a walk in the park. Moreover, they seemed to be faster than me since they were having no problem keeping up with me.

I turned a corner onto a narrow street and weaved between buildings to get to the banks of the Yarra River. A drone showed up at an intersection in front of me, hanging from a roof before launching itself at me. The shock was even harder than the first one. I went flying backwards and ended up in the metal arms of a second drone while the third came hovering over a nearby roof with its pincers clicking, ready for the bloodbath.

Melbourne, in the past

Starlock was really too sure of himself.

The noise of the hydraulic cylinder and the heavy metallic footsteps on the ground did not worry him, but I was pretty surprised at the sight of the formidable thing coming out of the lab instead of Professor Shrankar. The thing was humanoid but covered with thick metal armor. Each boot had four oval reactors. The cylinders boosted the power of its joints and gave an impression of brute force to the whole thing. The gauntlets were both shaped like ram's heads with spiral horns on each side like two small shields. The stylized snout of the rams looked like they had cannons installed. The helmet was the strangest part. Most of the face was covered by an opaque shield shaped like a truncated triangle. A ram's face in golden steel covered the top and the curved horns protected either side. An immense power emanated from the outfit despite being a little ridiculous.

Shrankar's voice, distorted by a speaker, boomed out of the armor.

"Mr. Starlock, allow me to introduce you to the result of my research for the Australian space program. This is the autonomous spacesuit AGNI Mark-1, named after the Hindu god of fire."

"I see Mygale didn't underestimate your abilities."

"Unlike you, Mr. Starlock. There is no way I'm going to collaborate with you and S.P.I.D.E.R. I left the Indian space program because my rockets will not be used to carry nuclear warheads. So, good luck trying to steal my research."

He stretched an arm out toward the walls and shot two thin jets of flame, almost blue. The temperature of the room rose immediately and I recognized the nature of atomic fire—ionized plasma. Humans had just discovered a mighty weapon, an energy matrix as hot as the core of the sun and stickier than napalm. The effects on the lab were instantaneous: the walls melted and the flames started liquefying the rooms next door.

A little taken aback, I didn't have time to react before he targeted the computers and the shelves of files that must have contained his notes. Everything was literally vaporized. The next target was the ceiling, creating a hole through which the armor slowly rose up. By the time I shook myself out my stupor Shrankar was shooting up like a rocket into the night. I went after him.

Despite my speed, I had a hard time keeping up with my adversary. The only thing keeping him from losing me for good was his lack of training and his chaotic route. I decided to cut the distance once and for all.

I drew on the gravitational field and my eyes shot out a powerful ray of gravitons at the flying man. My rays hit him like a small moon so that he must have felt like a building had collapsed on him. He did a few wicked spirals worthy of an acrobatic parachutist before starting to fall.

I dove after him to catch him before he hit the ground, which probably would have killed his mortal shell despite the armor. Unfortunately for me, he woke up before I got to him and fired at point blank range the four plasma guns at me. I tried to take cover, but I was too close and the nuclear flames covered half my body, making me scream in pain from the heat. In the final moment of lucidity I absorbed all the gravitational energy I could to lighten my body and gather the gravitons beneath my skin, transforming them into a blue steel armor that was thicker than titanium.

To an outside observer, I must have looked like a dead leaf burning and slowly drifting in a fiery cloud down to the ground. The pain was greater than I had ever felt before and brought back memories of old wounds: a solar eruption that had hit me head on; a cloud of battling micromolecular gas that I'd been caught in: a Sen'li with rock-hard claws trying to rip out my lungs. But nothing compared to what I was feeling at the moment.

I should have just fallen and I would have reached the ground faster so I could try to put out the atomic flames with the fused glass that would have quickly formed on contact with the silicon on the beach. The descent was torture. I felt like was being skinned alive even with my steel-hard skin. I tried to detach my mind from the pain so I could think and then, suddenly, I had an idea. I instantly reversed the gravitational energy I had gathered, managing to blow the flames out into an explosion of anti-gravitons.

I landed on the ground on one knee and one hand, ready to fight. I slowly raised my head. Fury blazed in my eyes.

Melbourne, present day

Four metal tentacles held me spread out around the top floor of a bank. Two other drones came up and slowly circled me. I could feel the tingle of their scanners trying to identify me. I intrigued them but they didn't know who I was. My new body wasn't in their database but they were clever and could improvise and reach conclusions. I sure didn't want them reporting my escape to the Towers.

It must have been a simple patrol. It went to check the capsule on Mars and realized it was empty. Then it probably checked the nearby planets looking for traces of unusual activity.

I had to get a hand free, just one hand, to be able to counter-attack. One of the drones saw what I was trying to do and rushed at me. Too late. I aimed a graviton beam at the tentacle wrapped around my arm and pierced the techno-organic armor, ripping through the synthetic muscles that covered the tiny ceramic vertebrae. An electronic whine that almost sounded like a scream came out of my enemy. I grabbed the tentacle holding my other arm and swung around, tangling the two others imprisoning my legs. Then I struck their metal skin with another beam of gravitons.

It was not enough to make it loose its hold but it was enough to keep it from reacting efficiently. This time I pulled myself up the tentacle all the way to its body, gathered the gravitons into my arm and punched right through its metal body.

At first, it still wasn't enough…

Melbourne, in the past

I bounded into the sky, reversing the gravitation flux to go as fast as possible. My adversary was just a tiny dot in the night sky, a sparkling blue pinhead, a slightly brighter star in the southern night. The pain only made me crazier, drowning my mind with destructive rage. How could one of these wretched humans have defeated mighty Starlock? Even though I had forgotten my origins, I knew this name had sown fear and respect in the souls of many galactic civilizations.

My enemy was till flying as erratically, but on seeing me behind him, he made a beeline for the horizon. My mind unleashed gravitational forces around me and I started catching up with the armored scientist.

I wasn't expecting his reaction. He turned around and his reactors shot enormous balls of fire when he charged me, both fists forward. Even though I was expecting more plasma fire, his move caught me by surprise and I stopped, hovered and waited. His speed and the hardness of the metal knocked me dizzy. I immediately understood the ram symbols on his armors: the animal that Agni, the Hindu god of fire, rode. The charge at supersonic speed with armored gauntlets would have destroyed anything on this planet. But I came from elsewhere.

I was, however, thrown hundreds of yards backward with the wind knocked out of me. I had had too much confidence in himself. As I started falling out of the sky, I regained control. This time, I wouldn't let him get close. I fired at him. His speed and chaotic flight saved him for a moment, but the first shot to hit him had the same effect as his had had on me. He spun out of control as if he'd been hit with a giant hammer, exaggerated by the propulsions of his ionic reactors, creating a weird fractal flower of light in the black sky.

I closed in. When he finally got back in control, I jumped on his back and wrapped an arm around his armored neck, more to control him than to strangle him.

"Go back to the lab!" I shouted with all the tension built up during this confrontation.

I heard no answer from him but he started back with me hanging on. After a few minutes, I saw the laboratory roof open. The building was still burning, surrounded by firefighters trying to contain the new type of flames that were hotter than anything they had ever seen. Water and CO_2 evaporated before even touching the fire.

My adversary surprised me once again. Instead of slowing down, he dove straight into the inferno. Instinctively, I let go as my body refused to feel the bite of plasma again. I saw the armor disappear into the flames above the stunned firefighters who couldn't take their eyes off the human form floating effortlessly in mid air over the fire.

It was no use for me to go in search of Shrankar and his technology; they had vanished without a trace. I had to find shelter fast. Nick Thaler was coming back: the effect of the Styxane Crystal on the Moon was waning and I was losing my powers. I had to land quickly before my weight would drop me like lead.

I flew over the docks and my body flopped to the ground behind an abandoned warehouse. I immediately started looking for a way to get away from the S.P.I.D.E.R. agents who must have rushed to the lab at the first fire alarm.

Melbourne, present day

With my fist crimped into the drone's techno-organic body, I was at the mercy of the two others. I balled up, planted my feet on the machine and reared back, trying to free myself. My arm started to come out a little, covered in sparks and corrosive vapor.

A sizzle. A flash. A ray's just hit my arm. It managed to cut my skin. A red gash welled up and blood slowly covered my skin. The pain came a little later, but it gave me a power surge.

With a shout I pulled my hand out of the mechanical organs. I ripped out everything in reach. It didn't do much to my enemy, but his two buddies, on the other hand, became raging mad.

I jumped into the air just when a whirlwind of tentacles flew at me. I managed to dodge most of them, but the blows made my head spin. I dropped down onto the ledge of a building between two postmodern gargoyles that stared at the glass façade of the bank across the street. I had to get back to the roofs…

On instinct, I cruised alongside the building. I should have risen up, but I didn't want to go flying into the mechanical arms of my enemy. I hadn't gone ten yards when something whipped my leg and wrapped around it. I pulled desperately at it, but to no avail.

Then the two other drones came down. I used the gravitons to change the weight of the machine grappling me and dragging me back. I couldn't really accelerate, but I got up over the" top of the tower dragging my baggage while the two other drones kept following me.

They started firing now with those weird, cold, bright rays that cut like razors. They barely missed me. I tried to bait them into hitting my captive leg, but they stopped right away. A small reprieve in a situation becoming critical. I knew I wouldn't hold out for long if they attacked again. I was going to feel the torments of imprisonment once again!

Out of the darkness of the night sky I saw a bolt of lightning drill through the drone on my right. An explosion follows, lighting up the buildings around us and launching all shapes and sizes of burning debris into the sky. Three hundred feet below, over the street, a golden, metallic, humanoid form was hovering on two blue flames.

It was now or never! I aimed at the damage inflicted on my first foe and sent a long stream of gravitons that hit him with the force of a Soyuz rocket. This time, it worked! Sparks and flames leaped out of the already injured techno-body. In a few seconds it would be totally destroyed, but the second drone didn't let me keep up the bombardment of gravitational rays. It got between us and its armor was strong enough to resist, even though it was pushed backward by the blows. The damaged drone had trouble staying in the air and hooked its antennae onto a building to shimmy up to the roof. It crawled up clumsily, but its weapons were still effective. He started scanning the area, searching for whatever had pulverized its partner.

Melbourne, in the past

As I was leaving, I saw a shape appear in the flames and rush into the ruins of the lab. Of course, it saw me and headed in my direction. In spite of my physical training as an astronaut, I was in no shape to outrun anything. When I turned down an alley, my pursuer jumped off the top of a house and landed in front of me. Although I recognized my old friend, I also knew that it was not his body, but rather a robot controlled remotely by psychic waves.

"Good evening, Nick. Well, I guess I'm not talking to Starlock right now. You shouldn't run away from me so clumsily."

"Sorry, but I can't stay here, you should let me go. I have to get away from the S.P.I.D.E.R. agents. I should never have let Starlock collaborate with criminals."

"More reason to follow me. It's time for a debriefing and for finding a way to control this monster you brought back to Earth."

"Nothing on Earth can control his cosmic power, and I can't let anyone use it for evil ends."

A burst of automatic fire echoed in the alley. The bullets clanged like gongs on the cyborg armor. The Tarantula's henchmen popped up at both ends of the alley as the shooters took up positions on the roofs.

Cybermax went into fighting mode and took out the enemy one by one with their long knives whose alloyed blades were sharpened electronically and able to cut through the armor of a tank. While the bodies were crushed against the walls and piled up on the street, the shooters tried to bring down the frenzied cyborg.

I took advantage of the confusion to try to escape, but the alley was blocked and then I felt four hands seize me and a bag was thrown over my head. As I was being dragged to one their vehicles, I was thrown to the ground by an explosion so bright I saw it through the mask.

An instant later, I was flying off toward Professor Mygale's orbiting base with the feeling that Nick Thaler might never see the Earth again.

Melbourne, present day

The dying drone straightened up on its extended appendages like an ominous gun turret dreamt up by some science fiction artist, pointing its ray guns at the new enemy. This was the opportunity I'd been waiting for. Only one drone was left for me now. These machines seemed especially designed to destroy me. I had to change tactics and not use my powers directly.

I waited for the second drone to attack me and I freefell out of the air, picking up my flight again after thirty feet or so and racing toward a tentacle that was waving around in the open air. The other pseudopods rushed toward me. I grabbed two of them along with the other and fired at the creature above who, of course, repelled it. It tried to hold me back but I moved with it, using its momentum against it and throwing it against the corner of a building, which broke off and plummeted to the ground as the metal hull split open and got embedded in the reinforced concrete.

Two of the three tentacles were left in my hands after the crash. I took the longest and whipped it around the others that were still flailing. Now that it was partially immobilized, I fired into the open wound at the drone's guts. A ray intercepted my gravitons and an eerie red light started glowing where our two rays met in mid-air. I knew it was useless to fight because it would match my power.

Keeping my eyes on the mouth of its ray gun, I concentrated on the street and reversed the gravity flux to make all the debris from the building come rushing up and smashing my enemy, which knocked its line of fire into the sky. I was still aiming at the rift in its armor and one second later it exploded and opened up half a floor of gutted offices to Melbourne's neon lights.

The time had come. The weird lights and the explosions were attracting the attention of more and more people in the streets even at this hour.

In the sky, a golden shape, which I recognized right away as that of Agni, was whirling around elegantly, dancing in the air to avoid the rays shooting aimlessly at him. I landed on the roof and ran towards the enemy. It sensed me and fired in my direction. I jumped behind a roof door.

Using this distraction, the would-be fire god who was hovering over the street engulfed the machine in a deluge of bright plasma. I grabbed the emergency exit, walls and all, and threw it with all my strength at the crippled creature. With its defenses weakened by the storm of flames, the bricks tore through its metal dome and exposed its techno-organs to the infernal heat that was already melting the roof around it. A series of explosions finished off the job as the roof collapsed into the office below.

The sirens of the police and firefighters were getting closer now. Thirty feet above me, an old foe had become a precious ally. He gave me the thumbs up as a sign of victory and soared off into the southern skies without saying a word.

I took a few more seconds to look at the roof of the ruined building. I fired a few rounds of gravitons at the fragments of the drones that could be gathered up and used by the Earthlings; then I, too, soared off into the great, cosmic expanse of space.

Will Earth still be a sanctuary for me? From now on, I would be expecting my old masters to be back. At any moment…

Bolas by Sergio Mantipo

Bolas was a daredevil acrobat, an artist working for the Kemp Circus, who performs around the world in the 1880s. This story, which takes place a hundred years later, features the grandson of the original character...

Olivier Vignot: *The Airs of a Clown*

Silence fell again after the explosion of applause. A circle of light suddenly appeared in the darkness. A clown dressed in black tails with a white face stood in the center, near the mallard duck. Giggles trilled like wild birds from the back of the semi-circle of folding bleachers under the big tent. Giggles that slipped out because the clown, who looked extraordinarily tall, pulled a huge clarinet out of the back of his collar. He put his lips to the mouthpiece and started playing a sweet, cheerful melody. A second clown, short and chubby, in a red costume but also with a white face, came up next to the first, searched in his sleeve and pulled out an Irish concertina to join his partner. Soon a voice could be heard over the familiar-sounding song. Probably from Mozart or some advertisement. The voice was a soprano, high-pitched and crystal clear. It sang in Italian. It was a third clown, lovely and lithe, dressed in yellow with a pale face dappled in gold, who stepped gingerly before the other two.

"*Voi che sapte... Che cossa è amor... Donne vedete... S'io l'ho nel cor...*"

Someone suddenly cleared his throat very loudly. The clowns paused. A second circle of light illuminated a tall flagpole to the right of the musicians. A young man, bare-chested and muscular, wearing dark, baggy pants, suspenders and a bowler hat cocked to the side, half his face painted white, was leaning casually against the pole. He waved to the clowns, who waved back, and then jumped onto the pole like a flag at half-mast.

The clowns replayed their song from the beginning. When the singing clown started in on the melody, the acrobat came to life. With youthful impudence full of charm, the young man shimmied up the pole like a monkey, then spun around it, making spectacular drops, arms and legs dancing, demonstrations of athletic prowess perfectly synchronized to the virtuoso voice of the amusing singer.

While he was twirling around with his arms stretched out before leaping into an elegant ascent to the top of the pole, the young man glanced over at the melodious mouth.

This girl's lips are enchanting. Floricia is a really extraordinary woman, he thought.

An unusual distraction for him. At the top of the Chinese pole he looked like he was taunting the public's fear, but he had eyes only for pretty Floricia with the white and gold face. As she began an elegant crescendo, she stared into the eyes of the young man, which disturbed him at once. He slipped and dropped down the pole. The audience immediately cried out, which woke up the acrobat who wrapped himself into a fetal position around the pole so that the friction would slow down his fall. When he felt he was back in control, he grabbed the bar, flexed his muscles and threw his legs out into the air. Everything seemed fine.

Floricia had not batted an eyelid. The concertina stopped playing. The clarinet as well. Silence fell over crowd again. The acrobat was frozen. A deafening explosion rang out. Hands clapped like whips lashing out shouts of "Bravo!"

"Ladies and gentlemen, Mesdames et Messieurs, another round of applause for the Lunaire Trio and the acrobatic poetry of Bolas!"

Ringmaster Stud, the master of ceremonies, with his heavy British accent, which revealed some uneasiness in his French, urged on the audience through their thundering expression of admiration.

Back on the ground, Bolas waved to the crowd with gratitude, then slipped quietly into the wings where he met the three clowns. Floricia took off her oval hat, which unveiled her short but messy blonde hair. Her hazel eyes sparkled mischievously when she looked at him.

"I didn't think you'd catch yourself, Bolas. You are, and will always be, a wonderful idiot."

Bolas smiled faintly, then walked away toward the big cats who would soon be in the spotlight.

"Someday you'll learn to be more talkative," she tossed at him.

The acrobat tripped, disturbed again, glanced back at the clownish singer, then continued on his way.

That Flo really is a pretty girl.

The animals were all back in the cages and enclosures. The children were certainly all in bed, heads full of magic and adventure. The ticket stubs were thrown away, the money counted to be put in the safe until the next stop in a city. In his trailer, Stud was delighted.

He who dreaded bringing the Kemp circus into French-speaking Belgium, he who spoke the language of Molière with as much finesse as an elephant serving tea, was finding that Wallonia was a warmer, more welcoming land than the annoying rains might lead you to believe. A few months into the new decade of the 1980s, Stud was afraid that the public would not attend a spectacle that was considered more and more outdated. But nothing of the sort! The Belgian people, even the French, came to the shows. Let's just hope they would come for eight days running, the period that the Kemp Circus, a small, American circus family-run for five generations now, had rented the sports field in the small town they had decided to stop in near the French border.

In spite of everything, however, a black cloud hovered over him. Just before this first show two local policemen came by on patrol and warned him that the area was known for drugs. Only two hours inside the border of the Netherlands and barely twenty minutes from France, small groups of dealers had squatted the area for years and never missed an opportunity to find potential clients. This was why Stud felt more tense than usual as the ringmaster. When the safe was full of the night's take and hidden behind a piece of Formica furniture, someone knocked loudly on the door. Bolas, out of his costume, popped in his ethnically mixed but pale face with his crew cut and deep green eyes. He came to tell Stud that he was bothered by some shifty-looking guy he had seen hanging around.

"That's what I like about you, kid. It's been ten years since you joined us; in the ring, you're brilliant, and outside the tent, you're remarkably discreet. You only talk when you feel you have to. I don't know if you're really the grandson of the man whose name you use, but he would have nothing to be ashamed of. Show me where this guy is."

The acrobat pointed to a man a few yards away, tall, in a light brown leather jacket, a cap pulled down low from which some blonde hair escaped.

Stud strode over to him, "Excuse me, could you tell me what you're doing here? You have no business hanging around the circus, Monsieur."

"Monsieur?" the man turned to the ringmaster. "Are you talking to me?"

"Who else?"

"Indeed," he looked around as he slipped a wad of bills inside his coat. "Your business is very interesting, M'sieur… M'sieur?"

"I only give my name to people who are polite enough to introduce themselves."

"Of course, forgive me. Van Tylbon. Enid Van Tylbon."

"Enid? Strange for a man like you…"

The person suddenly pulled off the cap and long blonde hair cascade down. Now unhidden by the cap the individual's face looked less masculine. More androgynous.

"Maybe that's because I'm not a man. But I still don't know your name," she spoke with a dreadful, guttural accent.

"Ringmaster Stud 'Studsy' Lawson, at your service."

"And your partner?"

"What's it to you? It's my name you want and I'm telling you that you have no business here. Instead of talking, I will kindly ask you to leave."

"I'll leave after my last client has paid me."

Just then, out of the shadows near the tent, a stooped figure stepped out slowly, wearing a top hat and a long, curly beard, a monocle and a forced smile. He was thin and at his feet was a huge, hairy animal with a long, narrow snout, standing guard.

Stud knew this figure only too well. On seeing him come out of the shadows he looked up into the sky. Salamaleck, a member of their troupe for more than twenty years, an admirable animal-trainer of (among others) all xenarthra mammals like ant-eaters, sloths and armadillos, was a real killjoy, just by nature, but he was so gifted in his work that the boss could never bring himself to fire him.

Salam walked solemnly up to Van Tylbon, handed her a few bills, then disappeared, leaving no trace but a few hairs of what turned out to be a giant anteater. Like a good salesperson, the statuesque blonde thanked her last client of the evening and then turned to Stud and Bolas, suddenly looking a lot less friendly.

"So that everything is clear between us, leave me and my business alone, or else you'll be hearing from me. I'm not in the habit of getting walked all over by dolts like you. I got a peek at your show. Your little pets were a big hit with the public. It'd be a pity if anything happened to them. You talk to the cops and I don't think their safety can be guaranteed, *klootzak*..."

"What do you mean? More details, please!"

Just then, they heard Flo's voice. She was singing a pop song, far from the lyrical world of her character in the ring. *"Love is so confusing, there's no peace of mind/If I fear I'm losing you..."*

Bolas looked over at her trailer. A smile lit up Van Tylbon's angular face. She raised up her hand and pretended to drop the subject for now. Then she backed away until she was out of sight. When she was gone, Stud reacted immediately. He went to the closest payphone, five minutes from the circus, and called the number given to him earlier by the two policemen. Bolas, who was right behind him, showed his disapproval by continually shaking his head. Stud ignored him. As manager of the Kemp Circus, who had been in his family for well over a century, he was not going to let some cocky young acrobat tell him what to do. So, Bolas went back and left the ringmaster to clench his teeth as tightly as his fists.

Someone knocked on the door. It was the middle of the night. From the window it looked like everybody was asleep but Floricia still opened the door cautiously. Standing in the doorway was a square-shouldered figure with long blond hair like a gorgon's head bristling with tentacles. Enid Van Tylbon's eyes sparkled on seeing the young woman. Floricia barely had time to utter, "What the...?", before she was thrown against the back wall of the trailer. A smooth but menacing voice spoke to her.

"I recognized you even without your makeup. You're the singing clown, right? You're a treasure for this two-bit circus. Such a pretty girl deserves to aim higher."

The heavy Flemish accent of the massive blonde frightened Flo a little but she still kept her cool. She replied that she would never leave this circus, that it was her family and nothing in the world would make her abandon her family legacy.

Van Tylbon's face lit up with a big smile, "You're the Kemp heir? Now things are getting interesting." She straightened up, then leaned forward and brought her face up to the girl's. "Mademoiselle heir should know that the executor of her estate won't let me do business like I want. Make him understand that if he sticks his nose in my affairs again, he will be putting more than just his little critters at risk... Such a cute little thing... It'd be a pity to punish you for it! Beauty is so fragile... your life as well."

Flo, usually so quick with comebacks and prompt to react to all kinds of aggression, was surprisingly powerless when the androgynous blonde put her hand between her breasts and bared her teeth. She could not lift a finger to push her away. And then Van Tylbon suddenly went stiff and jumped back, shrieking, which was a clear giveaway of her gender. A rodent had jumped on her back but she did not know what it was. When she finally managed to get a hold of it she saw four others of the same species clawing at her legs. Then the door of the trailer swung open.

"Excuse me, Flo, but have you seen Salam's myrmidons?" Bolas stepped in. "He asked me to watch them tonight but they got out of their cage… Ah! Madame Tylbon? What are you doing here?"

"What are these rats doing here?" the big woman shouted.

"They're not rats, silly. You're going to upset them. They're myrmidons, like little anteaters. They belong to your last client of the evening. But you didn't answer my question. What are you doing here with Mademoiselle Kemp?"

"None of your business! I don't have to explain myself to a gypsy who swings around like a monkey to entertain people!"

With this Van Tylbon shoved the young man aside and before disappearing out the door she pointed at Floricia threateningly, almost melodramatically, and sneered, "Don't forget, Kemp girl! Straighten out your manager or else…"

The young woman looked questioningly at Bolas, who said, "I heard a noise while looking for the little ones. Looks like I got here just in time. You should think about closing the hatch on the roof, it might cause you problems someday."

"You really think so," the young woman looked up at the hatch. "I rather think it'll save my life someday… if it hasn't already." She smiled at the acrobat. With the five small anteaters on his shoulders he winked at her, then left, closing the door softly behind him.

The second day on Walloon soil, Floricia awoke with a start to the roar and hysterical laughter of children. With eyes wide open and breathing fast the young woman left her humble home with a mixture of fear and curiosity. The sun had been up for hours, the grass was almost dry and the constant drizzle was surprisingly absent. She ran to the big cats and found a group of laughing kids standing around a huge, round cage set up outside like she had never seen before. Some kids from the area had come to admire the menagerie. But instead of a small zoo the children seemed to be enjoying an unusual spectacle.

To the right, a black panther whose hide shimmered with silver light, its fangs and claws exposed, was ready to pounce. To the left, Bolas in a sweater with the sleeves rolled up was howling with laughter like a madman facing death. The animal tamer had a big smile and was waving to the kids to be quiet. Flo was flabbergasted. Her arms hung limp at her sides. When the young acrobat's heavy breathing could be heard as clearly as the feline's growling, a slow dance started between the two combatants. Bolas copied the panther's steps. It was both frightening and enthralling. A moment of grace or pure madness.

The panther suddenly stopped, baring its thick, menacing teeth. That was when two more growls were heard. The tamer was about to let two other predators into the cage. His two lynxes that he normally brought out with the chilling dark one. Flo barely had time to pant "No!", almost inaudibly, before Bolas was standing before the three faces of death.

The young man's grin widened like a naughty boy please with his prank. The strange waltz between man and animals started up again and then, without warning, the panther leaped at Bolas, who dodged it and ran around on four limbs like a gorilla trying to get away but was stopped by the two lynxes. Cornered, in a way, he saw only one solution: he did a backflip and landed six feet behind the panther, who was amazed by the agility of the hairless creature… The three hunters quickly turned on Bolas and faced him again. The bars of the cage soon collided with the young man's shoulders. He looked at the children with bemused eyes. Then he glanced over at the pretty blonde and instead of a hello he gave her a hearty laugh. Floricia was starting to believe he really had gone crazy.

In a fraction of a second the three animals pounced on the acrobat who balled up by reflex. Screams suddenly surrounded the cage, soon fading to silence, then turning into laughter. Flo, who had refused to witness such a spectacle, pried open one eye to see the four combatants rolling around in the grass, playing together, pretending to bite one another. The kids clapped loudly, overjoyed. But Flo did not even try to hide her irritation or her relief. She walked up to the cage and said to Bolas, "My God, you can be really stupid sometimes! It's against the rules to be so reckless and insane! You'd make a great pinhead, Bolas!" And in a melodramatic display of phony anger she stomped back to her trailer.

After petting the three wild cats and waving to the crowd of young spectators with a big smile, Bolas left the cage and went after the young woman. Just before her door her hand was caught by the reckless acrobat. She shot him a furious look and could not hold back what she was feeling.

"You're completely crazy! What were you trying to prove, seriously? That you're the biggest idiot on Earth? That when you work in a circus you can risk your life just because it's show business? Or maybe you wanted to prove to the innocent children that you're a total moron? It's beyond me… What if just one of those kids tries to play 'the idiot of the Kemp Circus' and challenge a big dog only to die in such a stupid way… Did you even once think about the consequences of your actions? You can say something at least!"

"I just wanted to make the kids happy… and play with Drusilla and the twins. I always play with them like that. Look, I've been in the circus for more than ten years… and I've always done that. That's how I got accepted, something I could do."

"Yeah, okay… but jumping around like a monkey and playing with anteaters is cute when you're 14 years-old. Risking your life with the big cats is something else altogether…"

"It's my school! Don't criticize it..." he interrupted her, a little embarrassed but impassioned. "You had yours, far from this world. Mine I left to join this circus and it became my substitute mother, my school, my family... Don't talk down about it, please."

"I'm not criticizing it, it's my family, too. We grew up together don't forget."

Bolas looked up at the sky with a barely visible smile on his lips when he heard those last words. Flo had no idea.

"I'll never be able to do it, that's all."

Then she looked him straight in the eye, pointed out some snags in his sweater by touching them gently. With each touch Bolas blushed a little more. But she turned away, with a smile, and went into her trailer. When the door closed Bolas took a few steps back, a little disappointed, then went back to the animals. Some children were still waiting to meet the funny man who played cowboys and indians with the panthers.

That evening Ringmaster Stud had set up security watches during and after the show. Too worried by the threats of the strange woman with the awful accent, the boss preferred to imagine the worst and be ready for it instead of doing nothing. The orders were simple: don't do anything alone; if anything out of the ordinary happened, tell him so he could contact the authorities.

The evening started out pretty well. Bolas' act, like the night before, fired up the public, as much for the young man's agility as for the angelic voice of the clownish singer. Flo had stayed in the ring with her partners. For her it was a good way to stay close to the audience and make the show more coherent. But for Stud, who had heard about Van Tylbon's nocturnal visit to the Kemp heir, it was a good way to keep an eye on her and keep her out of danger.

Salamaleck had barely left the ring with his xenarthres when he was joined by Bolas and Stud. The latter immediately warned the man in the top hat that he had better straighten up this time and keep away from drugs, that he would be better for his circus career to become a little more loyal to the troop and a lot less selfish. The man in the top hat did not say a word, being so addicted to his role in the circus that he wanted to avoid Stud's wrath at all costs.

Then the boss told the young acrobat not to let the damned animal tamer out of his sight while he had to go play ringmaster until the end of the show. He meet up with them after the last spectator had left the tent. With their instructions clearly understood the two artists started off on their first patrol. Stud straightened his tie and collar, then went back inside with his thundering voice and stage smile.

Outside the tent Bolas and Salam walked side by side, looking around them and at each other. After five long minutes of heavy silence the tamer spoke up.

"Kid, we're not going to stare at the white's of our eyes every two minutes without saying a word. I'm not angry with you for the other night. You must've had a good reason for taking the myrmidons. Besides, they always come back in good shape after a night with you. You take good care of my pets. I have nothing to complain about..."

The young man said nothing.

"You're always such a chatterbox... You know that even if you don't talk, I'm still going to bug you about all kinds of things. For example, I've noticed you getting distracted more often and more easily during your act. It's weird because it usually happens when the Kemp girl is around watching you out of the corner of her eye..."

"Why'd you buy drugs from that woman?" the young man tried to change the subject when he suddenly started to blush.

"Oh Bobol, I'm not as gifted as you. I can't get inspired by just looking at my animals. I need a little escape. And I can't find it in the back of some trailer... well, it can happen... with a little help from the powder monkeys."

"That's what you call them? I call them criminals."

"Bobol, illegal things are not necessary bad things..."

"Don't talk to me like that," the acrobat was getting upset. "I'm not a child. And I know the difference between right and wrong, which is obviously not the case with everyone. And stop calling me Bobol, it sounds stupid!"

"Kid, you don't like when people use your real name and I think of you as one of my protégés... nicknames come naturally."

"Yeah, well, cut it out."

There was a brief lull. Salamaleck picked at his beard before speaking again.

"Oh, it's been so long since I've heard your voice. What a pleasure!" He smiled, showing his tobacco-stained teeth. Bolas put a friendly hand on his shoulder.

That was when they heard the noise. A few yards away a handful of men in leather jackets and ribbed wool caps were gathered around a figure that was easily recognizable as Van Tylbon. The two patrollers hid as best they could to observe the scene. The gorgon was giving each of them plastic bags and wads of cash and patting them on the backs of their necks. So, the Flemish woman was handling her dealers like a pack of dogs. And she barked out some guttural sounds. It must have been Dutch. Then the men scattered around the area.

All of a sudden music broke out, accompanied by clapping in rhythm. Salam and Bolas looked at each other for a second then ran into the tent to find Stud dripping with sweat in his shirtsleeves, smiling uncomfortably. Salam reported what they had witnessed and the boss immediately told them to get some animals on chains and follow him to go out and make the dealers understand that the smooth operation of a circus relies on the strength of its manager and the unity of the troop.

Bolas would follow closely to be more impressive. As for Salam, was sent to inform the police and ask for help. Although he agreed with the boss' decision he still took the acrobat aside before leaving. Rifling through the pockets of his long coat, which he had not had time to take off after his act, he pulled out a dark brown, fur hat.

"Bobol, I know its not cold but put this on. It's made of Sumatra otter. It'll make you look more beastly, more scary. It'll certainly make an impression on Van Tylbon. I'm giving it to you. Do what you want with it."

Bolas smiled, accepted the hat and placed it elegantly on his head, then went to fetch the animals.

The next day the whole circus was abuzz. The statuesque Flemish woman had become enflamed at Stud's reaction. She had been so angry, so loud, screaming and shouting and finally threatening so wildly that the entire troop had gathered around the harpy and got alarmed. She had repeated her threats against the animals but she also focused her wrath on the star of the show: the Kemp girl had better do something to stop her manager or else it was not just her inheritance but her life that would be in danger.

Indeed, they did everything possible to guarantee everyone's security but the atmosphere was still tense. When it came time to welcome the public that evening, they were waiting for one thing above all else—the arrival of the authorities who had promised, through Salamaleck, to patrol the outskirts so as not to disturb the spectators while at the same time keeping the riffraff at bay. This news in the morning had eased their minds but had not completely stamped out their fears. Floricia Kemp, in particular, had spent the afternoon rehearsing a new song with her throat choked by the feeling that she was too constricted in her gold and flannel costume. The memory of Van Tylbon's face with teeth bared like she was ready to tear into her skin… remembering the experience she had two nights ago troubled her, gave her goose bumps and turned her skin pale. An hour before show time Flo was having a hard time putting on her makeup. Her hands trembled so much that they couldn't trace a straight line on her porcelain face. It was only the arrival of Bolas that calmed her down a little.

"I'm no expert at makeup but I have the feeling that the harder you try, the worse it gets. Here, let me do it."

He took a clean brush; licked the tip to make a perfect point, dipped it quickly into a bottle of kohl and with a mixture of nonchalance and dexterity he drew the doe eyes on Floricia's powdered white face. When he started drawing the eyebrows, he leaned closer to her and a shiver ran down the spine of the clown.

"Why don't you ever use your real name?" she asked in a trembling voice. "Bolas isn't your name. I can't even remember the name of the first Bolas, the one who worked for my grandfather. It's kind of dumb, don't you think? A little ridiculous. Now that I think of it I'm not sure I know your real name. I think I heard it when I was a kid…"

"What would be the point?"

"I don't know. We've known each other for a long time. We've been like cousins since we were kids. It would be… more intimate is all."

The young man grabbed another brush, dipped it in the black and used it on himself to cover his lips, then he put the brush back in its holder and took Flo's egg-shaped hat to place it on her head so it covered her hair. He held her head delicately in his hands and stared into her eyes. The young woman thought her heart would stop. Bolas trembled being so brazenly close to her. Then he tenderly placed his dark lips on the corner of the clown's right eye.

"Just for tonight, could you try something different from your usual boyish outfit? A little teasing never hurt anyone… And for your information, I don't like my real name. My mother gave it to me, the same woman who abandoned me when I was knee-high. Her name doesn't just hurt my ears it pains my heart. That's why I want everyone to use my stage name. Being someone and no one at the same time is a nice way to live… Now excuse me, I have to get ready too. Don't forget we have a new act to try out. Oh, here," he took a photograph out of his pocket and gave it to her, "I read somewhere that she just died. Alone. They said it was suicide. Sad, right? That a beautiful person would decide to take her own life… I saw a movie of hers once. It's Jean Seberg. She was really pretty. She looks like you."

And while Floricia examined his creation in the mirror, comparing it to the deceased actress, the acrobat slipped out and left the clown in a state of wonder and bewilderment. In the corner of her eye, the trace left by his lips looked like tiny crows soaring off.

As the show got into full swing, Bolas was putting the final preparatory touches on his new act when they came to him. The tamer's his assistant was supposed to be there but he was late and no one was free at the moment to watch the cages. The young man made a sign to wait, which the tamer took as a green light to go look for his assistant.

When he finally got to the animals Bolas spotted, near Drusila's cage, one of the men in a leather jacket from the other night. He was armed with a long, thin-barreled rifle and was loading it with darts. Instantly, the acrobat's blood was boiling. He searched the pockets of his baggy pants for Salamaleck's big, fur hat. After pulling it down over his head, covering most of his face but leaving his eyes just clear enough to do what he had to do.

The thug pointed his loaded weapon at one of the twins. The young lynx hissed like a frightened cat. The man took a second to watch, fascinated by the muscular creature he was about to shoot. It was in that moment of hesitation, with his finger on the trigger, that he felt a heavy weight slam into his side—Bolas had used a thick rope like a Chinese pole and jumped feet first into the goon, who was knocked out. A glance at the scared twins with Drusilla growling in the corner and the young man entered the cage with a smile on his face to comfort the three animals. Finally, he took off the fur hat and got the panther to bite it so that there were holes for his eyes and mouth. Then he went to find Stud nearby.

After being informed of the plot being hatched, the ringmaster's first reflex, in his sudden panic, was to look for Floricia. Unfortunately, it was the sturdy, androgynous body of Enid Van Tylbon that he saw. She was sitting at the top of the bleachers, apparently waiting for only one thing: the entrance of the heir. Stud got scared. Time was short, the current act was about to end and the next was with the acrobat and the pretty singer. Bolas knew that he had to deal with the matter alone. The ringmaster was frozen to the spot, horrified by the future taking shape, another murder of another star, the headlines to follow, the disgrace the circus would suffer...

Without delay the first notes sang out of the instruments of the three harlequin musicians—a clarinet, a violin and the concertina that had been changed into a xylophone. The young acrobat shimmied up the center pole to the top of the tent. And a plan swiftly started forming in his mind.

The white clown, whose reputation had spread through the region over the past few days, one of the reasons why so many people were there tonight, the sparkling beauty made her entrance. At first they were astounded because they were expecting her dressed in white and gold but the clown came out all in white with a little black makeup on her face, including two birds by her eye like they were kissing her in flight. Soon her voice pierced the silence along with the bellies of the public. Like a mass hallucination, a visceral disorder. Everyone was deeply touched by the voice coming out of this unique creature. Then, slowly, a strange figure descended from the red and yellow sky. A figure part human, part animal with two long white ribbons trailing behind it. The women in the audience were captivated by the apparition. The men were in awe of the strange creature's muscularity. The children thought they were dreaming. Van Tylbon kept her eyes on the young Kemp.

"Cruda sventura m'astringe, ahimé a languir; Come il di primo da tant'anni dura; Profondo il mio soffrir."

And while Verdi sang *La Forza del destino* through the mouth of the charming little clown, the Flemish woman stood up and made her way into the back of the aisle next to the bleachers. Thus hidden from the public, she took out a big-barreled, chrome pistol from under her light brown leather coat. She checked that it was loaded, then aimed it at the body of the chanteuse. The body that she could not keep in her sights because something kept floating between her and her target. The thing was Bolas who was hanging from the two ribbons tied to the roof of the tent and dancing around the singer. A tremor of bitter anger ran through Van Tylbon's entire body as her mind focused solely on her mark. In a split second she no longer cared about getting caught, only about hitting her target.

Fixated on the singing beauty, the Flemish woman got closer to the edge of the ring. She did so discreetly so as not to attract attention. Nevertheless, Bolas was aware of her every movement. Floricia was completely absorbed in the intricacies of her melody so she saw none of this, concentrating on her next crescendo.

Van Tylbon took aim again at the young Kemp who was easier to see now among the constant twirling of the acrobat. When the young man saw the gorgon's arm stretch out, he spun out one of the silk ribbons, which was done in perfect rhythm with the song, and threw it like a lasso at the pistol. The ribbon wrapped around Van Tylbon's wrist and yanked her forward. With a flick of his wrist he sent the gun flying under the grandstands.

Stunned by her sudden fall, Enid Van Tylbon took a few seconds to pull herself together. The moment's hesitation allowed Bolas to make a few spectacular stunts to distract the audience who were completely unaware of what was happening on the ground. When the giant blonde shook herself back up on her feet, the acrobat started a weird climb that looked like he was rolling himself up to the skies, stopping just inches from where the two silk ribbons were attached, then he spun his legs around in a spellbinding dance like a gymnast on a vaulting horse.

The Flemish woman on the ground, steady on her massive legs, stepped into the darkened ring towards Flo, the enchanting voice, the pearl of the pageant, she whom the gorgon held responsible for all the stumbling blocks to her criminal commerce, this white clown whom she could not buy off or hush up—she was going to strangle the nightingale to death with her bare hands.

That was when the singer launched into her final measures. Her voice rising up into the dizzying treble heights, intoning dazzling curses, Van Tylbon was transfixed by so much beauty and strength. In the same spirit, Bolas spun down to the ground, slamming into the evil woman and flattening her at the feet of the musical goddess. The lights went out and the spectators exploded in awe and respect. When a circle of bright light shined on the ground again, it showed Bolas, with a fur mask, black lips and wearing only short, baggy pants, bowing before the beautiful singer with her sparkling, exuberant smile and the gaping musicians. At the edge of the ring, wrapped up like a baby, Enid Van Tylbon lay unconscious on the ground, her face being licked lavishly by an armadillo and Salamaleck's anteaters.

Just then, out of nowhere, the majestic, enthusiastic voice of Ringmaster Stud rang out full of emotion. "Ladies and Gentlemen, Mesdames et Messieurs, kids of all ages, give another big, well deserved round of applause to the Lunar Quarter and the great Bolas!"

Bolas teamed up with the Sparrowhawk and Roxy
Pencils by Roberto Castro

Zembla by Manuel Martin Peniche

Pierre Marais, a.k.a. **Zembla**, *the "Lord of the Lions," is the protector of the African Republic of Karunda, ruling over its jungle, big cats, apes and other wild animals. This story pays homage to the original comics of the 1960s...*

Jean-Hugues Villacampa: *Black Guards*

Karunda, 1963

"…and setting up the French embassy that we financed has raised concerns lately at the Quai d'Orsay.[1]"

"That doesn't surprise me. The only interest of Charles the Great[2] is in our contracts for priority distribution of the products of our mines."

"The ones they know about!"

"Yes, Traore, but please don't talk about that, even to me. The forest also has ears."

"But Zembla, don't forget, I'm a Dioula! My six years at Stanford didn't weaken my knack for business or for keeping secrets."

Zembla smiled. Traore raised his voice to be heard over the sound of the *djembe* drums flooding the clearing for over ten minutes now. "The elections should take place in a few months and sides are being taken. Just like you predicted, pressure groups organized by the colonists are out there lobbying. But they're not getting what they wanted. Our meetings with the tribal chiefs are panning out. So they've become a lot less active."

Zembla furrowed his brow, "They'll give up very soon."

Thirty or so natives, looking magnanimous, marched by them and headed for the center of the clearing. They were dressed in simple, cotton loincloths that showed off their

---

[1] French Ministry of Foreign Affairs.
[2] Nickname of President Charles De Gaulle.

smooth, muscular bodies. Zembla had been invited, like every year, to the initiation ceremony of the Dioula Honor Guard, an elite selection of men from all the tribes, between 19 and 25, chosen among the hardiest, strongest and... smartest. The ceremony took place in a secret location that changed every year. Only ten of the roughly one hundred men would join the elite group.

The young men's nervousness could be felt in the air. Night was falling and fires had been started, lighting up the scene with a reddish glow. The men were squatting in a circle around an as yet unlit pyre.

Zemblas's friends, Rasmus and Ye-Ye, sat near a group of huts on the edge of the clearing, watching while sticking their spoons into big, steaming, metal bowls containing a stew made of rice, black beans, okra and antelope meat, with plenty of spices.

Traore put the official papers that Zembla had just signed into his leather briefcase and gave it to one of his aides who took off right away in a Mercedes Unimog.

Young women dressed in colorful *boubous* brought smoldering clay pipes and wooden cups full of yellow liquid to each of the young men. Zembla, to whom they also offered this gift, refused both. Traore took the cup. Rasmus and Ye-Ye caught Zembla's scowl and refused the pipe, but accepted the drink.

The night was getting dark fast. The young women returned, took out some gray, metallic-looking powder from the leather satchels hanging over their shoulders and tossed it onto the fires. Thick, white smoke rose up and spread over the clearing. The strong odor shrouded the familiar scents of the forest.

Traore started pacing nervously, his muscles flexing visibly under his shirt. Zembla had an amused smile on his face. They had placed before him a huge bowl full of food that he started to eat greedily.

The young men stood up, their bodies swaying in rhythm, covered in sweat. Zembla knew that their perceptions had been heightened and were changing quickly under the effect of the drug that they had just taken. Zembla was naturally in a state of perception beyond that of most common mortals and the experience he had lived through in tasting just a little of what the women had innocently offered him a few years ago had led him beyond doors of perception that were still alien to him.

Rasmus was dancing to the beating of the drums whose rhythm was slowly speeding up. Ye-Ye was lying above him on the roof of a low hut, hugging a clay jar tightly. His mischievous smile piqued Zembla's interest. The little man was waiting for "the greatest magician of the savanna" to walk by so he could pour the oily contents of his jar on his head.

The young men were squatting again as the initiation drug was making their eyes pop out and their bodies jerk spasmodically.

All of a sudden the drums stopped beating, creating a heavy silence broken briefly by Rasmus yelling at Ye-Ye.

A few seconds later, the pyre lit up as if by magic. A figure jumped out of it, ten feet in the air, and landed agilely on the ground, squatting. The apparition frightened everyone. Rasmus stopped looking for rocks to throw in revenge. Traore stared with his mouth open but had stopped breathing. Even Zembla, despite being used to the ceremony, had dropped his amused smile...

A woman was squatting with her legs open and her back to the pyre. Her head was lowered and her long, curly hair hung down, covering part of her body that was dressed only in lacework of various jewels and precious wood that were still swaying from the jump.

Abruptly she looked up, setting off the drums again to a different, wilder rhythm. The clearing was suffused by the smoke from the pyre and the odor of musk mixed with the heady fragrance of flowers.

The female divinity shot up in a quick, serpentine motion. Her beauty could have graced the pages of high fashion magazines. The beauties of her very dark skin, perfectly oval face, fine, sharp features, superbly curved body, shapely buttocks, breasts like perky pears, flat stomach, strong, muscular shoulders and thighs, were accentuated by the oil covering her, which was not unlike the oil poured over Rasmus.

The body of the goddess started slowly, languidly moving to the rhythm of the music, then she started dancing around the fire. The reflection of the flames snaked over her oiled body and her gold jewelry. The sight would remain engraved in the memories of the men surrounding the scene, just like their whole encounter with THE woman, the beauty, the savanna, a divinity of the earth.

Two veterans of the guard struck their spears together, bringing the initiates out of their trance. They realized that they were not guests at a Broadway show and they, too, started their ritual dance. Each of them saw the shapely deity brush by them in turn, then embrace them briefly before going back near the fire, leaving them breathless. One of them tried to hold her back by grabbing her arm. Her scented, oily skin slipped easily out of his grip. The young man was thrown out of the circle by two veterans.

Despite the noxious atmosphere Zembla stood up, all his senses on alert, eyes narrowed. Traore watched him worriedly and prepared himself for action.

Rasmus was frozen still, his mouth hanging open, and had been joined by Ye-Ye, who was obviously concerned, holding a long thorn from a nearby plant in his hand, ready to "wake up" his companion.

A sinister staccato boomed over the sound of the drums.

Three young men dropped to the ground, their bodies twitching horribly, and a fourth stood staring at the bloody stump of his left hand. It did not seem to be painful because of the substances coursing through his body.

Men came surging out of the trees. They carried machine guns and bayonets.

On the opposite side from them, Zembla immediately recognized the khaki uniforms and white kepis. "The Foreign Legion!"

Traore looked at him stupefied, "What are you talking about?"

The drummers ran away screaming. The goddess had taken a giant leap, landed on the shoulders of one of the invaders and knocked him out with a couple of powerful punches. A man armed with a rifle ran at her, ready to stab her with his bayonet but one of the initiates got between them.

Before rushing into the fray, Zembla let loose a long, strangely inflected howl. A lion roared in response from the jungle. Traore ran for cover in the huts. The soldiers marched into the white smoke shooting at anything that moved.

A legionnaire tried in vain to catch Rasmus, who was still covered in oil, but he slipped away, laughing and cursing his enemy. Finally, the latter took out his combat knife when the magician slipped and fell on his back. He backed away as fast as he could from the menacing weapon of the grinning giant. Just then, Ye-Ye stuck his long thorn into the thigh of the big soldier.

Zembla had jumped into the middle of the fight looking for the goddess. Seeing her facing off with a soldier, he took hold of her, grabbing her jewelry so she would not escape and dragged her quickly to a safe place, whispering to her, "Yabuka, you MUST stay alive." Then he went back to the fight. Rasmus and Ye-Ye had disappeared and Traore was right behind Zembla armed with a brand new Colt 45 brought from the United States.

Bodies were scattered over the clearing. Mixed with the scents of the ritual was the stench of blood and sweat. The soldiers were starting to show signs of confusion due to the initiation drugs that saturated the smoke. The young men, being unarmed, were trying to escape. The legionnaires were falling back under the rain of spears cast by the veterans of the Guard, only firing sporadically when under cover. Despite their wounds. the withdrawal was perfectly organized so that Zembla's allies could not get close without becoming an open target.

Everything happened fast. They heard the sounds of engines and the sinister song of a machine gun. Zembla shimmied up a tree and moved through the forest canopy toward the noise. A roar could be heard, followed by pistol shots and a scream. Zembla dropped down next to Wombo, the lion with a snow-white mane and one paw resting on a prone legionnaire. Two soldiers coming back to look for their partner turned right around on seeing the huge lion next to the giant armed with a knife as big as a small machete and a dozen steadfast warriors coming up behind them. They ran back to their trucks followed by Zembla who barely had time to drop to the ground to avoid the machine gun fire from behind the tarps as the vehicles sped off.

Traore saw him come back while he was examining the soldier lying next to Wombo. "He's dead, his neck's broken."

The lion was busily licking his back paw, which was stained with blood. Zembla patted the beast on the back and looked at the superficial wound. "You can go now, Wombo." The lion licked Zembla's face with his big tongue and limped away.

Karantao, the village chief, had lined up the bodies in the clearing. He looked up when Zembla and the others came back with the soldier's corpse. "Four dead and ten wounded. But why did the French send their killers?"

"I don't understand either," Traore said. "They went back on their word."

"We're going to ask them but for now let's examine this body," Zembla huffed.

A square jaw, close-cropped hair, dirty blonde, around 40 years old. Traore undressed him quickly, revealing a massive body covered in scars from knives and bullets. His arms were covered in strange, abstract tattoos.

"A cult?" Traore wondered aloud.

"I don't know. The easiest thing would be to ask Colonel Matelly at Fort Flanders."

That was when Ye-Ye's alarm went off and made everyone jump. Rasmus smacked him on his head. "Leave me alone, Rasmus, you slimy eel."

Zembla gently separated the two old friends and said, "Pay homage to our dead. We leave at first light tomorrow."

In the early dawn Zembla had left the village and was now standing transfixed by the distant mountains. On the edge of the forest Traore was on top of the first vehicle along with two Dioula honor guards, Seydon and Doulogo, who had swapped their ritual ornaments for camouflage suits and firearms. The legionnaire's body was lying in the vehicle. A second truck was full of a dozen guards similarly equipped. Ye-Ye and Rasmus were on either side of Traore.

All of a sudden Zembla waved his hand and put on a thick, leather armband. A black point in the sky was quickly growing bigger and Traore raised his rifle when he saw the huge eagle plunge toward his friend but it flapped its wings vigorously and alit gently on Zembla's arm, which did not move an inch under the weight of the animal. He put his hand on the neck of the bird of prey. Two long minutes passed while the eagle rubbed its beak against the giant's hair before he made a wide sweep of his arm to set the eagle soaring into the sky. Only then did the trucks join him.

The vehicles drove through the wide open doors of the fort a few hours later and parked. The guards with white kepis had greeted the passengers with a friendly wave. At six and half feet tall, Colonel Matelly marched directly toward Zembla with a big smile on his face, holding out his hand. Zembla shook it without hesitation.

"To what do we owe the pleasure of your visit?"

Without a word Zembla led the officer behind the trucks and gestured to Doulogo to lift the canvas covering the soldier's corpse.

The colonel did not flinch, "Who is this guy?"

"That's what I came to ask you."

"I don't recognize him. Bring him into the infirmary." Turning to an orderly he said, "Raoul, go get Captain Ramone." And he answered Zembla's unspoken question, "He's my new intelligence officer."

"So, if I understand correctly, the Legion didn't attack our camp last night?"

Matelly looked astonished at Traore, who had just spoken, "We're too busy as it is with the decolonization of this country where everything's falling apart to go and make a mess of the one place where things are working. Thanks to our friend and compatriot Zembla, all's well in Karunda. Besides, half our troops have been sent away... elsewhere."

The "doctor", a short, stout man from Marseilles with a half-smoked Gauloise hanging from his lips, was examining the naked body on the metal table with a big magnifying glass.

Captain Ramone, with his steel gray eyes and short, brown hair, had glanced at the corpse. "I don't know him. We should bury him quick, he's starting to stink."

"Well, shit, the guy wasn't kidding around with that spear." The doctor said, then hovering over the arm, "Well, at least we know where the bastard came from!"

Zembla stepped closer and saw in the armpit, camouflaged under complex designs, the traces of an "A" with a "+" sign. He turned to the colonel, "There are SS in the legion?"

The officer looked troubled. "The Legion recruited some old soldiers from the Reich after the war, including the SS. The Germans are on the front lines in Indochina where we need experienced fighters. But there's no 'Devil Guard' solely composed of SS like the legend says. Maybe there are a few here in Africa, but there can't be many." After a short pause he suggested, "Let's go get a beer."

Zembla smiled, "I'm going to take a little walk and I'll catch up with you." He left the fort and put on his leather armband.

When Zembla entered the mess the colonel and Traore were talking over a beer and Ye-Ye was amazing everyone with his skill at throwing darts.

Matelly moved over for the newcomer and went on, "Anyway, attacking the honor guards, even just armed with their traditional weapons, was a blunder that I would never make."

Zembla was gazing at a map of the region hanging on the wall, "Do you still have outposts on the Sabaharan border?"

Matelly answered him, "Yes but with fewer troops. We've got three camps at most."

"Three? I see four."

Matelly smiled, "Show me!"

Zembla approached the map slowly before pointing to four points on the map. "It's hard to escape Icarus' eagle eye."

The legionnaire was astonished. Then he put a finger on the map, "But this one has been empty for six weeks."

"Icarus, however, saw a bunch of men, vehicles and weapons there."

"Raoul, go get Ramone! Double time!"

The man vanished and came back a few minutes later to report, "Captain Ramone just left the camp in a hurry, colonel. Apparently on a mission."

The two men who were still examining the map exchanged a knowing look.

Zembla spoke first, "It'll be dark in half an hour and hard to follow him." He turned to Traore, "Tell the men that we leave before dawn tomorrow." Turning back to Matelly he asked, "How well do you know Ramone?"

"Not well. He's came out of the Saint Cyr Academy while I worked my way up through the ranks. Our methods are different. I know he lived it up and has a lot of influential friends in the city but that's about it…"

"Good night and thanks for your help, colonel."

According to the map the camp was in a wooded, mountainous region. Ramone had stopped for most of the night as

77

evidenced by a makeshift camp they found abandoned. The two trucks had been driving slowly since they had left the paved road and were now in a sparse forest. Zembla gave orders to stop and then beat his chest while howling loudly. A huge, back shape came out of the shadows of the forest and lumbered toward them. Zembla walked up to the gorilla and gave him a big hug. Traore saw the muscles on Zembla's back tightened to endure the force of the colossal beast. Any other human's ribcage would have been crushed like a pile of twigs under such pressure. The man put his hand on the head of the big ape who did the same before loping back into the trees.

"It's fine! Wombo is there with some friends so the sides are more equal."

The men got out of the trucks and entered the forest, flanked by an escort of great apes.

Gunther was bored stiff hanging in his tree, perfectly camouflaged, his sniper rifle aimed at the path 25 feet below. To keep from dozing off he pictured himself strolling through the English Garden in Munich with a pretty Aryan girl tossing bread for the swans. Then with his friends feasting on white sausages and Paulaner beer on a terrace where they would end up dreaming of a grand, united, pure Europe. Okay, this was not enough to keep his mind sharp.

He thought back to those stakeouts in Moscow when he could wait for hours on end to hit a bull's eye on one of those degenerate red stars. Much better.

He thought he heard sounds in the distance so he concentrated on his task at hand. The usual rustling of the bushes did not foretell an enemy attack. But being dutiful, he took out his binoculars and saw the big ape advancing slowly. Something out of the ordinary at least. Then he leaned over on his rifle when he heard the leaves fluttering overhead. With his veteran instincts Gunther looked up while grabbing the Luger that his Nazi father had given him on his 20th birthday. Only to find himself face to face with a huge, black nose and what looked like a smile that revealed a set of very unsettling, yellowish fangs. Before his weapon was out of the holster a gigantic, almost human hand wrapped around his head and twisted it 180 degrees with a sinister crack.

The gorilla rejoined the group wearing a camouflage helmet perched ridiculously on his big head, but looking more than satisfied with the corpse under one of his arms.

"Wombo told me there were men hiding in the trees so I'm going to scout them out with him," Zembla explained.

He came back half an hour later. "All's clear. Let's go!"

The SS base set up against a rocky cliff on which could be seen a nest of machine guns. The camp itself was made up of four big, canvas, bunkers and an open space of around 50 yards where ten men were busy at their work. Next came a barricade of vehicles with some crates and metal barrels surrounding the camp, guarded by five men on duty. Outside of it were four fresh graves bearing witness to the Dioula Guards' skill in combat. There were three piles of sand with shovels and wheelbarrows proving that the soldiers were working hard.

"Okay," Traore turned to Zembla, "thirty or so men not joking around, a good two hundred yards to cover before reaching the barricade under machine gun fire… We're going to need a plan."

Zembla smiled as he stared at the camp. "Let's back up. There's no use getting spotted right away. I'll check out the cliff and take care of the machine guns. At my signal you can attack."

"What kind of signal?"

"You'll know it."

Four soldiers were in a circular hole at the top of the rocky hill. Two of them were behind the guns, the other two with binoculars were watching the space around the camp below and the gentle slope leading up to their position. Zembla recognized the notorious MG34s, a little obsolete but still reliable and terribly effective. Some dirt had been upturned in places where there were conspicuously no footprints. Mines! This was not going to be as easy as expected.

Herman spotted movement at the bottom of the slope. "Look! A lion with a white mane."

"Magnificent! That would make a nice trophy for your room in Pretoria."

The four men were watching the big cat who was following Zembla's instructions and against its will was keeping a safe distance away. The soldiers had just enough time to notice the huge shadow before they were attacked by beaks and claws under a rain of feathers. In their confusion Zembla rushed into the battle, sidestepping the mines. Icarus soared up just when Zembla leaped feet first into the chest of the only man standing. The soldier dropped to the ground, screaming and smashing a crate in his fall.

Traore looked at his companions, "That must be the signal. Let's go!"

Up above, Zembla was quickly taking care of two other enemies, knocking them out with a single punch to the head. The last one had pulled out a knife and was grinning wickedly even with one of his lips split open by Icarus' claws. Blood was still flowing from a large gash in his face, which did not seem to bother him too much. He attacked without warning and with amazing speed. But not fast enough for Zembla who grabbed his wrist and shoulder and held him on the edge the cliff where a few rocks tumbled down. Down below one of the SS who was watching the scene jumped behind an ATV and took aim at the giant dressed in a leopard skin. A bullet fired by Doulogo hit him in the shoulder and he dropped his rifle.

The man with the knife was finally tossed over the edge and fell on a stack of crates at the very moment when the Dioulas and great apes came howling out of the forest. The soldiers were stupefied for a few seconds before orders were shouted in German by Captain Ramone. They shook themselves out of it immediately, grabbed their comrades from under the fallen crates and took up combat positions. The gunfire had cooled the gorillas' enthusiasm in spite Wombo's grunts as he kept moving forward. The Dioulas had already breached the barrier of vehicles and were fiercely attacking the men who had killed their brothers in arms.

Zembla surveyed the scene from on high. The SS troops outnumbered them and were expertly organized. All of a sudden he spotted a movement in a pile of sand and saw the barrel of a rifle emerge. He let loose a few inarticulate cries as he jumped behind one of the MG34s and started raining bullets onto the pile of sand. Wombo and his fellow apes obeyed Zembla's order and made swift work of the other two piles where men were hiding.

With Icarus' help to steady his landing, Zembla jumped into the middle of the combat. After a few moments of advantage the tide was turning in favor of the numbers. The Dioulas were losing ground. Wombo was working his way through the SS ranks but he was wounded in several places. The other gorillas held back to show off their impressive demonstrations of hostility, which did not seem to be overly impressive to anyone since they were too busy fighting. Zembla despite the many blows he suffered, was still standing, surrounded by soldiers. Every time he hit an enemy, they fell to the ground. Ramone was a few feet away, fists perched on his hips and an evil grin on his face.

His smile was suddenly wiped off his face when Matelly's loud voice boomed over the sounds of fighting, "Everybody raise their hands or we'll show no mercy!"

The camp was surrounded on two sides by white kepis. The legionnaires were looking scornfully at the soldiers engaged in combat who had sullied their honor by wearing their uniforms. A half dozen SS tried to point their weapons at the newcomers and were immediately shot down. Ramone let loose a cry of rage and ran into the forest through the gunfire.

Zembla waved at the captain of the Legion and shouted, "Stop firing!"

Ramone entered the forest on the run and came back out less than a minute later without his feet touching ground, his head behind held in one of Wombo's hands as he examined him curiously, sniffing him all over before tossing him brutally to the ground at Zembla's feet. The latter yanked him up and pushed him into the hands of two bearded legionnaires.

The doctor, always with a Gauloise in his mouth, was already taking care of the wounded, starting with the Dioulas. Matelly walked over to Zembla who was sporting some whopping cuts and bruises.

"You all right?"

"Sure. Just some scratches."

"I figured you didn't want me coming with you."

"Likewise."

The two men smiled at each other.

The return to Fort Flanders went smoothly. All the participants in the battle were more or less seriously wounded, turning the fort into a field hospital.

"The old SS are going to be sent to one of our bases on Corsica to be interrogated."

The colonel, Traore, Zembla and the doctor were taking a short break in the mess while the rest of the room were watching Ye-Ye and Rasmus play darts, which was about to degenerate into using live targets.

The doctor lit another cigarette with the butt of his last, "If you want I can interrogate that bastard Ramone." He caught Zembla's disapproving look. "Oh come on, don't get your panties in a bundle! A colleague gave me a concoction that loosens tongues. Your creep will blabber like a gossiping school girl."

Ramone easily told them how much an independent Africa was wrecking the plans of powerful businessmen. Pressure on the colonizers was proving useless so the big Western companies were changing their targets, directly attacking the countries on their way to independence. Destabilizing a nation in such a situation was a lot easier in order to put a puppet in power "democratically" who would be richly rewarded for miraculously bringing peace and giving time to reap huge profits at the expense of the populace. Ramone was the head of one of the many groups of mercenaries recruited for the job. There were a lot of SS who had problems reintegrating in society.

"They gave me Karunda because everything was turning out so well there."

Zembla smiled. "This country is under my protection and I'm ready to sacrifice everything to keep things going as they are."

The Dioulas were graciously invited to spend a few days at the fort until they felt better. After saluting Matelly and the doctor, Zembla gathered up Rasmus and Ye-ye who were drinking beer in the yard and went back to the savanna. In order to keep his promise.

Ozark by Alfredo Macall

*Russell Red Horse, a.k.a. **Ozark**, is a Lakota warrior who inherited the shamanic mantle of his old master, the wise Wa-Tan-Peh. He and his magic horse, Mustang, fight supernatural creatures threatening the Earth...*

Eric Nieudan: *The Shaman's Geis*

On any normal day Las Vegas was a strange city. Without the countless megawatts that lit it up after the sun went down, it was looking more and more unbelievable. The only lights visible from the air were the headlights of the cars abandoned at the intersections and the flashes of occasional gunfire.

Ozark was grateful to the authorities for the blackout. A shaman floating over the Strip would not fail to attract the attention (and bullets) of snipers. Not that a few ounces of lead would bother him, but having to cast a protection spell on top of his necromantic search ritual would be a drain of his energy. And at 4 a.m. there was not a great deal of energy left in him.

Ozark concentrated on his astral vision. The sun would soon be rising and the zombies would be going back into the casinos where tens of thousands of tourists had taken refuge. If he did not act quickly, it would be impossible to stop the epidemic. At least, not without obliterating the gaming capital of America. As he approached the Venetian Casino, Ozark could not help spitting on the replica of Saint Mark's Square. The scent of the living dead transformed into a full sensory spectrum under the influence of the mushrooms he had ingested. Judging by the bitter taste on his tongue, he was very close to the nest. The feeling was quickly verified by his natural senses. The teeming mass down below was grunting like a herd of swine and smelling almost as bad. It was time to beat the drums.

"Majata," he spoke softly.

This word put an end to his levitation. A less gifted magician would no doubt have smashed into a car, but Ozark only lost a little altitude. He had inside him all the experience of a long lineage of Lakota shamans, and he knew that the universal laws would let him float down to the nearest peak. Nature did not like to have to explain a suicidal fall in a place where all the windows were sealed shut.

While his magic drifted him toward the top of the fake Eiffel Tower, Ozark focused on the horizon. Freed momentarily from his prison of flesh, the shaman's spirit flew over the Grand Canyon all the way to the New Mexico mountains behind which the sun was starting to rise.

"O grandfather, I need your fires," the shaman prayed. "Allow me to borrow them only for a few heartbeats."

As he landed on the top of the fake Eiffel Tower, Ozark looked down at the back of his hand. The radio he had drawn instantly came to life.

"Ozark?" the voice crackled.

"Captain Fevre," the shaman responded. "The round up's begun I hope you don't pay for your ammunition."

"Don't worry, C.L.A.S.H. has a special budget for dezombification."

Hanging onto the antenna of the Tower with one hand, Ozark watched contentedly as the sun rose to the far north of the Strip. The corpses wandering in the parking lot of Caesar's Palace grunted and growled in unison. Fat partiers, skimpily clad prostitutes and street peddlers all turned together in the opposite direction. Ozark smiled, satisfied. At the other end of the avenue, the same scene was unfolding: a second dawn was rising on the south side. The cross streets were also lit up by miniature suns, driving the thousand or so zombies toward the huge fountain in front of the Bellagio. There, entrenched behind their flying vehicles like behind the walls of a fortified castle, the three squads from C.L.A.S.H. waited for them in motorized armor.

Ozark ended his necromantic localization spell when the first automatic grenade launchers boomed between the buildings.

"Once again, World War Z will not happen," he said to himself.

Two hours later the massacre was over. Under the one true sun the C.L.A.S.H. soldiers were getting rid of the dismembered bodies with their plasma incinerators. The ashes would scatter over the desert sands leaving only a few burn marks on the Strip. Ozark found the officer in charge of the operation.

With a whoosh, Captain Fevre's helmet disappeared and he gave the shaman a triumphant smile. "Mission accomplished, Ozark! Thanks for your help."

"Fighting against this kind of threat is what I do, captain."

"Do we know what happened? Did someone go and desecrate an Indian graveyard again?"

Ozark ignored the bad joke. If he had a poker chip for every time he had heard it, he would buy the Coliseum just for the pleasure of closing down Celine Dion's show.

"I'd be looking more at Area 51," he said. "The zombies had traces of Thanatax in their tissues."

"Still? I thought we'd wiped out all remains of Oppenheimer's experiment around here."

"Twice, if I remember rightly. But as you know, there are still some labs from the Nixon era."

"One of these days someone's gotta ask the Pentagon for a list of what Cheney and his cronies dug up during the Gulf War.

"Watch out. In the underground are ancient things that are best left alone."

Ozark had put on his most convincing face of the wise shaman. The officer laughed and patted him on the shoulder before going back to check on his men. The shaman sighed. The "anglos" were not what they used to be. He stepped through the bodies lying around, already swelling up in the morning sun. All of a sudden, one of them sat up. It stretched out a bruised arm and opened its mouth. Ozark froze, ready to call for help from the spirits to strike down the living dead.

"Hi, Ozark," the dead man groaned.

It's never good to talk to the dead when you don't start the conversation, but the shaman could take the risk. Just a wave of his hand and a C.L.A.S.H. cleaner would point its turbo-incinerators at the menace.

"Do we know each other?" he asked.

As an answer the corpse let out a long sigh as if it were hard for him to articulate sounds.

"It's me, Clony."

"Clonycavan! How did you end up here so far from home?"

Clonycavan was a powerful *sidhe* spirit, one of the fairy people who watch over Ireland. Like all tutelary spirits he was bound to his country by a *geis*, a spiritual duty, and could not leave the soil.

"I came through the land of the dead to warn you. But I got here too late. You killed all the zombies. The portal is closing and I'm losing you…"

"So speak, spirit. What can I do for you?"

"There's serious shit going down in Ireland, Ozark. You gotta get your ass over double quick."

The link was broken before Ozark could learn more. Despite his fatigue, he decided to go to Dublin right away. The simple fact that a *sidhe* would call on him meant it was an emergency.

He took a deep breath of the scorched air that the desert wind had not yet blown off and put his hand over the amulet he wore around his neck. Amplified by the artifact, his silent call echoed through the dimensions and soon a loud neighing answered him.

Mustang was galloping toward him through the layers of reality. In a flash, the purebred materialized and reared up on his powerful legs to greet his ally among mortals. His golden mane reflected a myriad of lights from the morning sun. The C.L.A.S.H. agents who were finishing up their gruesome work barely looked up to see the apparition. Mustang shook his head, annoyed. The white man of this time was truly jaded, Ozark thought. He jumped on the bare back of the horse and patted his neck.

"Go! Take me to Ireland fast!"

For spirits, the shortest route was not a straight line. Magic was born of ideas and it's through ideas that it grew. Mustang flew at full gallop straight toward the replica of the Empire State Building, one of the attractions of the New York hotel. The acceleration blurred Ozark's vision. Just as they were about to hit the towering façade, it disappeared. The Nevada blue sky turned into East Coast clouds. And the thoroughbred was already making a sharp turn around the real Empire State Building. The lively commotion of New York made a welcome contrast to the dead silence that loomed over Las Vegas. With his face plastered to the horse's mane, Ozark knew the way they were going to take. Mustang sped down Fifth Avenue toward Saint Patrick's Cathedral.

Next stop: Ireland.

Ozark's arrival in the middle of Saint Patrick's Cathedral in Dublin did not go unnoticed—the place was definitely less used to flying horses than in American. Mustang flew off in no time to drop off the shaman on a quiet street. The clouds were low and dark and drizzling on his shoulders. Ozark figured that his trip had cost him four hours: it was the early evening in Europe. Riding a totem-horse felt instantaneous, but in reality, one always had to pay one's obol to the guardian of time.

The streets of Dublin were busy as always on a weekend night. However, in all the noise and excitement Ozark could feel a lingering sense of fear. Crossing the city he had to pass by a crowd of people on a corner. According to the snatches of conversation he picked up, a bus had suddenly just fallen apart. The rusted frame of the double-decker was still there, surrounded by stunned police.

The shaman needed information. From one of his pockets, he pulled out an old Pennsylvania Gazette, a very sought after object before the last technological revolution had rendered it obsolete. The yellow paper cracked when he focused his will on it. The headlines of the local press appeared in faded letters.

Ozark resumed walking along the quay while reading the articles. The elephants of the Dublin zoo had turned into giant mammoths. They had to call in the army to keep them from stampeding the presidential residence nearby. Tourists had been attacked in the prehistoric tomb of Newgrange by bloodthirsty skeletons. It had rained sushi on the small town of Moneygall. Clony had not lied: Fortean phenomena had been unleashed on Ireland.

Ozark crossed the river and took a little used alley and as he expected it was the moment when the *sidhe* chose to appear.

"Still using the old ways?" he whistled from trash bin.

"I like this old gazette."

Ozark tried to remain cool-headed when he saw Clony's appearance. From between two trash bins a mummified corpse came crawling out, its skin speckled like old leather. He was missing his lower half and had no hands. The *sidhe* straightened up as best he could on his shredded stumps and cracked his neck as he turned his head to the shaman—his head that had been flattened by the centuries spent in the bog.

"You know that nowadays any phone has more information than that?" Clony snickered in a dry voice. "And they've got videos to boot."

"No doubt but I'd have problems with the network when I travel. I travel a lot, and not just in space."

"Well, I don't have that problem. Traveling! You can't imagine how much I miss it. When I was a lad, I dreamt of seeing the big, wide world. And I did. I swam in the ocean, which was a big deal at that time. Had to cross haunted forests, fight with cannibalistic tribes, risk the anger of the gods. But now? I end up more of a country bumpkin than anyone else on this rotten island. Everyone here has already taken a plane to tan their ass in the Canary Islands. And me…"

Clonycavan stopped talking when two young women stumbled into the alley. One of them was laughing hysterically.

"Don't you want to change your appearance?" the shaman asked. "You're going to cause us problems with the tourists."

"You think I like crawling around in my old body?" the spirit spewed. "My magic is screwed like the rest of the country!"

"I see," Ozark said. "Give me a second."

"Thanks. And do something for yourself while you're here." The mummy pointed his withered chin at the two girls who had stopped to look at the shaman. Maybe, in fact, walking around bare-chested in the rain was not the best way to lead an investigation.

It was 1 a.m. when Ozark's contact finally showed up. The bar where he was supposed to meet Liam was on the edge of Chinatown, but most of the people inside were European. Young people dressed in black crowded around the bar to order pints that mostly ended in the gutters. Loud, fast music boomed out of the room at the back of the bar.

Ozark sipped his beer that had got warm during the wait while Clony, whose outward appearance had changed with the Psyche of Ozal-Ohët ritual, was knocking back whiskey after whiskey. Liam spotted Ozark as soon as he entered. With his rugby man shoulders he could have forced his way through the drunken customers, but he crossed the room with supernatural grace, slipping by the people without touching them.

"This place is getting worse every day," he commented when he sat down.

"Whas wrong widit?" Clony was clearly feeling the effects of the alcohol he had imbibed.

"There's nothing but girls dreaming of *Twilight* and long-haired boys thinking they're werewolves. Sometimes I'm ashamed of being a vampire."

"Ya jus saying that cuz ya depressed."

Ozark raised his hand to keep the sidhe quiet. The fatigue was making him nervous. He had lost enough time with this.

"You told me you have some information on what's happening, Liam. Excuse me for cutting to the chase, but the magic flux I feel here is signaling an imminent disaster."

The shaman's words brought his two companions back to the seriousness of the situation. A young girl passing by their table shot them a curious look through her dark make-up.

"Listen, Ozark, I came in honor of your old friendship with us Twilight folks, but don't go getting up on your high horse."

"Ya mean his high Mustang?" Clony giggled into his glass.

Ozark did not lose his calm. Supernatural creatures were always bickering at the drop of a hat. With one hand he encouraged Liam to talk. With the other, he made the TV bolted to the wall turn a Six Nations match, which distracted Clony for a few minutes.

"The monastery of Saint Grellan," the vampire said. "I guess that, in spite of your ancestral knowledge, the name is completely unknown to you?"

Ozark nodded. Clony was absorbed by the TV, mumbling complaints about never being able to watch foreign matches.

"Me too, until recently, I'd never heard of these monks," the vampire went on. "They live cloistered in an underground building in Tullybrack in Cavan County. Now, it appears they all took a plane last Sunday for different destinations."

"Right before these phenomena started. I see. What do you know about this order of Saint Grellan?"

"Not much, I'm afraid. The monks never see the light of day, literally."

"Do you have any idea what prompted them all to break their vows at the same time?"

"Rumors are rife in our little community, you know. It's hard to know which ones to trust."

"Let me decide that."

Liam straightened up and looked around. In the gloom the young people swayed to the sound of wailing guitars. Nobody was paying any attention to their table.

"I've heard that the monastery was in dispute with the government about the amount of their subsidies," Liam said. "We're talking millions of euros."

"Why would the government pay so much to a small monastery?"

"Fer the rituals," Clony had lost interest in the match. "The old druid towers. Saint Grellan was built on an old druid site. Dint ya know?"

"Maybe we should be asking the druids on the island?" Ozark suggested.

Clony was shaken with giggling that sounded like sandpaper. "Ya serious, Ozie? The Irish druids are puppets barely able to grow lettuce!"

"He's right," Liam added. "The last real druid was assassinated by Opus Dei in 1978. It's the Church that keeps all the old rituals now."

"And neither of you know what knowledge is being hidden at Saint Grellan?"

"No. I prefer to stay away from churches," the vampire smiled, unveiling his canines.

"Goes back to before my sacrifice," the *sidhe* said. "I was someone important at the time, but not enough to be in on the druids' secrets."

"But today you're the most powerful spirit in Ireland."

"Thanks for the compliment but I'll remind ya that a geis forbids the *sidhe* from gitin involved in mortal affairs."

Clony stared at Ozark out of his parched eye sockets. The wound that had cost him his life was clearly visible on his forehead. The moment of tension was broken by a scuffle at

93

the front of the bar. The bouncers were having trouble keeping a group from entering.

"And of course they're fighting," Liam sighed.

"I'm afraid it's worse than that," Ozark stood up.

One of the bouncers went flying across the room. His dislocated body crashed into the shelves behind the bar, bringing down an avalanche of broken bottles. Someone screamed and the pub went into panic mode. Scared youths ran farther inside, pushing the other customers before them. At the door the second bouncer was writhing on the floor. Someone had jumped on him and was eating his face.

Ozark rose up and shot a ray of energy at the assailant, singeing the top hat of one of the escapees. The creature was hit hard and fell back with its chest smoking. It waved its arms and legs like a helpless beetle on its back. Fangs the size of steak knives were jutting out of its bloody jaws.

"A *jiangshi*!" Liam said. "These stupid monsters drive me up the bloody wall."

"There are more," Clonycavan said.

A dozen creatures were lurching spasmodically through the door they had ripped open with their claws. Ozark started an incantation. It would cost him a lot of energy but he could get rid of the creatures without damaging the bar or its customers.

Before the spell could take effect Liam put a hand on his shoulder, "No worries, my friend. It's been a long time since I let off a little steam against soulless horrors. Go find those monks."

"Good idea," Clony agreed. "I'll go with ya."

"You can't leave Ireland," Ozark reminded him.

"I know but... as tutelary spirit, the least I can do is go with ya to the exit, right?"

Ozark smiled. He turned to Liam who was taking off his coat and laying it carefully on the table. "You're sure you can handle the situation?"

"Don't insult me," the vampire bared his glistening fangs.

Rio de Janeiro, Cancun, Monte Carlo, and now a private beach in Phuket, Thailand. The Saint Grellan brothers had all chosen sunny destinations and they had all met the same end. Everywhere he followed them Ozark found nothing but seals and dried blood splatter on the walls. All the victims had their hearts ripped out and probably eaten. It was the best way to make sure that their souls would not talk, even after death.

Ozark leaned on the railing of his bungalow and contemplated the twilight. The last rays of the sun were illuminating the sea and every grain of sand was sparkling like a tiny diamond. The shaman took pleasure in breathing the scented air that was rustling the palm leaves, letting his frustration melt away from his muscles that were aching from lack of sleep. He was at an impasse.

The trail stopped here, at the site of the murder of the last brother. Nowhere had the authorities found the slightest clue. No witness had come forward. The shaman suddenly stood up straight. No witness? The other attacks had taken place in closed rooms. This one, however, had happened in front of all the spirits of the beach.

Before his mind had finished making the connection his lips were reciting the Lakota chant of liberation. With his hand on the amulet of Wa-Tan-Peh, he dropped to the ground as his astral soul was set free. Rising into a universe of silvery mist he let his senses get used to the atmosphere of the higher worlds.

"Spirits, do you hear me?"

His voice spread out in brightly colored waves in the mist. Nocturnal insects, exotic flowers, a lizard sleeping under the floorboards, everything appeared distinctly to him. And yet nobody answered his call. He tried again. The spirits shied away from the colored wisps but no one spoke.

"They won't tell you anything, shaman. They're too scared."

The sound was a wave of crimson flames. Ozark spun around. In the bungalow, in the place where the monk had been dismembered, a demon was floating. His head was crowned with many horns and a long, snaky tail flicked behind him.

"By the tears of Shakti!" Ozark sputtered.

"Your invocations won't protect you," the monster growled.

"Who are you? By the pact of Al-Azhred, I command you to tell me your name!"

The demon shuddered, rattling his glistening scales. None of the inhabitants of the lower worlds liked to be reminded of the treaties that bound them to mortals.

"I am called Armârôs but you can call me the Priest Devourer."

"Who summoned you to commit these murders?"

"Your pact doesn't make me answer your question," the demon rumbled.

"That's true, but I can make you serve me and when I've had my fun, I can send you to guard an underwater ditch for a millennium or two."

Armârôs shot out his forked tongue at the shaman. The idea of sitting in the ocean with only fish and crustaceans as possible victims was not very appealing.

"I can tell you that it's someone who wants to make sure that the monks don't go back to their work," the demon hissed.

"What work are you talking about?"

"They take care of the Circle of Slumber."

"One of the ancient Circles? Crom Cruach!"

The demon laughed seeing the panic in the arabesques of his voice. The circle of Slumber was part of the most dreadful secrets in the history of humanity. All over the world, in the depths of the earth, under frozen oceans, lay entities that had to be kept asleep. The great Cthulhu, the giant Uluru, Fenrir the wolf of Ragnarok, Shivar, Queen Mauve, Kra'ach, Typho... All of them without exception had the power to put an end to mankind. Each Circle was the responsibility of a group of initiates who kept their magic active. If the order of

Saint Grellan was one of them the problem Ireland was facing would be the awakening of Crom Cruach.

This deity was so ancient that even Ozark did not know its origins. And it was so powerful that even the ancient Fomores had feared it. Its first shudders had been enough to plunge the island into an unprecedented magical chaos; freeing it would cause a cataclysm like hasn't been seen since the Great Flood.

When the shaman spoke again his anger unraveled around him like an ice storm, "Who's responsible? Talk or I'll bind you to Halley's Comet for eternity!"

"Armârôs doesn't like your threats, little mortal. You'll pay with your life for this insolence."

With these words the demon disappeared. Ozark searched the astral fog in vain. Only the shy form of a bougainvillea was still visible nearby.

"On the physical plane," the small, dewy voice of the flower spirit said, "he's going to take it out on your body."

"Ancestors!" the shaman swore.

Closing his inner eye Ozark traveled back into his mortal coil. Slowly, too slowly. Helplessly he could already see Armârôs, incarnate now, wrapping his claws around the throat of his inanimate body. He swore again. A mage was always most vulnerable during astral projection. That's why the shaman never left his body without taking precautions. At the moment he regained consciousness in his physical body, he had just enough time to glimpse a crimson flash.

When he opened his eyes, he was covered with fuming slag. Nothing and no one could resist the Espérandieu Protector, a spell specially developed to protect astral travelers.

Frustrated by the disappearance of his last lead, but thanking his ancestors for still being alive, Ozark went back into the bungalow. He snapped his fingers at the huge TV screen that lit up immediately. The images flashed by while the set searched for the subject desired by his will. He did not wait long. All the news channels were broadcasting the same aerial pictures: a gigantic worm in a dust cloud was stretching out its rings among the ruins of an Irish village. On the right half of the screen a clearly terrified reporter was commenting on the activities of the C.L.A.S.H. units. Three squads had already been destroyed without slowing down the monster at all.

"They won't get it like that," Ozark groaned.

Despite the A/C the air in the big room felt muggy. Most of the fifteen members of the Security Council had spent the night there. The President of the United States did not get there until dawn. Staring at the wall of screens that showed both the images on the news channels and various satellite views, he sighed.

"The alert was given too late," he said.

"Obviously," the Secretary-General agreed as he adjusted his glasses. "The Irish should've warned us that they'd stopped paying. The budget cuts are no justification."

"Typical of the western mind: no respect for ancestral traditions," the Chinese representative said.

"It's true that everyone doesn't drown its historical treasures to build dams," the British ambassador scoffed as he signaled for more coffee.

"I won't stand for that!" the Chinese was indignant.

The Secretary-General stood up and spoke calmly, "Gentlemen, we're all tired and it does no good to bicker. Mr. Arnaud, what do you recommend?"

The French representative had spent the last ten minutes nodding over the telephone. He let out a sigh of relief when he hung up. "The President will be here in two hours, but he told me to support the resolution."

The room started buzzing. The members of the Council had trouble accepting the fact that they were discussing the use of atomic weapons.

"It has been proven that the monster is growing exponentially," the Russian ambassador wiped his forehead. "The middle of Ireland is already decimated. Dublin will be destroyed in a few hours. If we do nothing the creature will get big enough to devour the UK tomorrow. We have to act now!"

"The Pentagon assures me that a limited attack will have very little fallout," the President shot a glance at the British representative.

The Secretary-General sat down amidst the uproar that followed. "We're going to vote on it. If each of you wants to consult your government, you can do so during breakfast," he said and nodded toward the doors.

A small man in white, escorted by two soldiers, pushed in a cart piled with sandwiches and tea. As he passed behind Nigeria, the representative leaned back and asked, "What are your vegetarian options?"

"I don't know, Madame," he answered.

The man took off his waiter's coat and seemed to grow two heads taller. With Olympian calm he walked into the middle of the Security Council with a big, golden amulet sparkling on his bare chest.

"Ozark!" the American President exclaimed.

"Where's security? Arrest him!" someone said.

"I took the liberty of asking the firearms not to let their carrier attack me," the shaman said.

The soldiers at the doors of the room had their guns in hand but looked paralyzed.

"This is unspeakable," the Russian barked. "You don't have the right!"

"If the Council would just listen to me," the intruder said. "I want to help you fight Crom Cruach. Give me a chance to stop him before voting on this resolution. I'm only asking for two hours."

The room buzzed again with questions and exclamations. Everyone had something to say. Raising his hand to demand silence the Secretary-General took the floor, "We're going to take a different vote."

The icy cold of the stratosphere did not bother Ozark. Riding on Mustang's back he could have passed through a black hole without feeling the slightest discomfort. He had asked his horse to come out at this altitude so we could get a good view of the situation. Even at 100,000 feet above ground Crom Cruach could be seen. It was dragging a scar of destruction across Ireland from west to east, from Sligo to Dublin. Driven by an ancient hunger the devouring deity was heading for the most populated part of the Island.

"Mustang," the shaman thought, "it's time to go into battle."

The mystic thoroughbred obeyed immediately. He folded in his legs like a bird of prey and dove toward the ground. The amulet of Wa-Tan-Peh quivered against Ozark's chest as he chanted protection spells. It was not every day that he confronted an antediluvian god and he did not want any nasty surprises.

Crom Cruach had now grown to around fifteen hundred feet. Its tentacles were grabbing cars by the dozen on the highway. Its mouth was swallowing houses whole. Mustang skimmed over the monster's back, his eyes shooting rays that left two long, smoking stripes on the slimy skin. Crom Cruach reared up. Its cry of pain sent out shock waves that almost knocked Ozark off his horse.

With an angry neigh Mustang regained altitude. Now that the shaman had attracted the god's attention, he was hesitating to offer to him to surrender. Did the mass of gauzy skin even have any reasoning power? Before he could make up his mind the monster let loose another cry, more of a shriek this time. Mustang disappeared under his rider's legs, banished from the physical world. Ozark fell. One magic word was enough to keep him floating but another sound wave thrust him back toward downtown. And he was in free fall again.

"By the horns of Baphomet!"

Crom Cruach's assault was interrupted by the shaman's spells. He had to cast his flying spell again to land on the roof of an old railway station. There he recited the words for Kronan's Shield. The shining sphere enveloped him in seconds and he could breathe more easily. There was no better ritual for protection against supernatural attacks. Half a mile away Crom Cruach continued its path of destruction. Ozark used his extrasensory perception and checked to see that C.L.A.S.H. had evacuated all the inhabitants as planned. Relieved, he took a long breath.

"It's just you and me," he gritted his teeth before soaring off again.

The shaman's fists were flashing with lightning but before he could unleash his power the round mouth of Crom Cruach opened wide. The wave of disruptive magic traveled at the speed of thought. Ozark was hit head on and plummeted to the ground, crashing into a tree. He was surrounded by a chaos of broken branches. Flashes of pain ran through his weary body. He slowly got control over the pain and confusion. Struggling to his feet he saw that he had dug a deep furrow in the middle of the park. The titanic polyp was still moving forward. It had already crushed the old royal hospital only a few hundred yards behind it. Ozark knew that his levitation spell had been broken again, even through Kronan's Shield.

"It's a devourer of…"

Ozark dropped to his knees, worn out. It was not life that had lured Crom Cruach to the capital but the divine part of every intelligent being. The shaman's field of vision had been reduced to a tiny window. His legs were so weak he could barely stand. He had not slept in thirty-six hours and the only thing that kept him going right now was a kind of anti-jetlag.

The devouring deity fed on magic. The rituals that protected Ozark were snacks for it. He was jolted out his thoughts. Slimy tentacles were stretching out for him. He had to get away. He staggered through the trees. The sinister snapping of branches behind him told him the hungry god was hot on his heels. The shaman almost fell down when he hit a wall. A mossy old wall but too high to climb in his condition. He huddled against it, running out of ideas. Running out of hope. The immensity of the monster blocked out grandfather Sun. Ozark put his hand on the amulet and prayed to his ancestors. The metal was still a little warm. It had not been drained of all its magic. He could still cast one last spell. He could flee.

The doubt in Ozark's mind lasted only long enough for an even more unthinkable solution to present itself. The risks were huge. But could he give up? The gigantic tentacles were on him when he cast the spell. It was a simple incantation in Lakota, just three simple words that meant: *I accept the power of the Earth.*

The last word got lost in a howl of delight. The energy of Maka, mother earth, rushed through his veins. For a fraction of eternity he knew what it was to be a god. A burning sensation in his wrist wrenched him back to his mortal condition. A tentacle was trying without success to pull his arm toward the gaping maw of Crom Cruach. Lowering his head the shaman realized that he was not far above the city. No magic, however, was making him fly. Looking down he saw the wall that had stopped him, crushed under his feet.

He was standing up, an equal match for the devouring worm. All the telluric energy of Ireland was pouring into his giant body. His skin had turned the color of peat moss; his hair was like oak leaves and water from the lochs glistened in his eyes. With a roar he pulled free of Crom Cruach's hold, depriving it of Maka's magic. The worm god shrieked in frustration with a shockwave that blew Ozark off his feet. For the brief moment that he was in the air, cut off from contact with the nourishing mother, the shaman felt the pain. The corrosive contact of the tentacles burned his entire body. He dropped into a river, causing a wave to crash into the other bank. Ozark did not have time to absorb the shock. The water gave him the power of the Earth once again. And with the power came anger. A timeless, universal rage that drown out all coherent thoughts. He was an earthquake, a storm, a force of nature.

He who was no longer called Ozark stood up, trampling a brick building underfoot. Facing him Crom Cruach was also filled with boundless fury. He curled up his tentacles ready to pounce. The shaman grabbed the top of a nearby building. It was a panoramic bar, a round, glass and metal floor that tore off easily. It hit Crom Cruach as he was launching into attack. The wave of pain would have knocked Ozark down again if he had not prepared himself. Sheltered behind the building he let it absorb the wave before he rushed at the worm who was writhing on the ground. His rock-hard fists pounded the mouth, spraying geysers of vital fluids into the air. Teeth rained down on the streets. Ozark was nothing but a vehicle of vengeance for Nature that had been mutilated by Crom Cruach's assaults. He struck again and again. Every blow caused a little earthquake that shook the city.

When the shaman regained consciousness the sun was rising. He lay on the ground, shivering, human, vulnerable. Alone. Nothing around but destruction. Not a single building was left standing. The sea had filled the rifts that slashed through Dublin. Outside the city Ireland was just a shattered island. A nation of ruins.

The images on CNN were unbelievable. The fight with Crom Cruach had been filmed from the British coast. The giants fought on the horizon, crowned by clouds. Two gods without the least consideration for the mortals at their feet. Besides just ravaging the Emerald Isle they had caused tidal waves to flood Wales and Cornwall. They were talking about more than two million dead or disappeared.

Ozark had taken shelter in his shamanic lodge to regain his strength and accept the extent of his failure. For two days the entire world had been cursing his name. He had saved the planet, but no one had the guts to defend him. Who could blame them? Even he felt no satisfaction. He was about to become public enemy number one and it would be only fair.

Squatting on his fur rug, head in his hands, he decided to give up. He had failed all his duties and he had to pay.

But something was keeping him from leaving his refuge. He shared the responsibility with someone else. The Irish government could not ignore the abandonment of the monks of Saint Grellan. The Church, in some way, should have sounded the alarm. And who had summoned the demon Armârôs? Zembla often said, *Look for the woman and if there's no woman, ask yourself who gains from the crime?* How stupid!

Who would want to destroy the world, Europe or even just Ireland? Who was capable of so much hatred for...

"The little bastard!"

Ozark stood up, all traces of despair replaced by bitter determination. He sent out a silent call for Mustang and got ready to confront the criminal.

Clonycavan was lounging on the beach in Ibiza with a cocktail in hand. Now free to use his magic he had taken on the appearance he had when alive. Bigger and better, obviously. Seeing his tanned body the girls swishing among the lounge chairs smiled at him. He was wondering which one he should spend the night with when a familiar voice made him jump.

"Free at last?" Ozark said sitting next to him.

At least his ridiculous costume wasn't too out of place on the beach. But obviously he had to answer, Clony thought.

"Yeah at last. You can't imagine how nice the 90 degree sun feels when you've spent two thousand years in Ireland."

"Well done, really," the shaman said, clenching his jaws to sound sincere.

"Thanks. I'm sorry you had to take the rap. I had no other choice, see? I needed someone who could stop old Crom."

"Don't worry about me. I'm going to disappear."

The shaman sat up on the lounge chair and put his feet on the ground. He stared at Clony with his impassive, Indian chief look, demanding something without asking. The *sidhe* gave him a bright smile.

"You want to know how I did it, right?"

"I admit that it would help me sleep at night."

Clony could not help laughing out loud. He could do him this little favor.

"It's really stupid, you'll see. When the brothers found out they weren't being paid anymore, they decided to retire. They wanted to find a sunny spot to spend their millions. I understand them completely."

"Even if leaving would mean the destruction of Ireland?"

"You got to understand that they're no different from anybody else—business is business. For the prime minister it was more complicated. I had to 'convince' him that Crom Cruach was a groundless superstition and he had no reason to be spending millions on these monks to keep them chanting over the grotto. When the Church got involved I did the same thing with a few of the Vatican robes." Clony laughed again when he saw the expression on Ozark's face. The mask had cracked. It was the funniest look of incomprehension he had ever seen.

"But... Your *geis*?" the shaman asked. "You don't have the right to interfere in human affairs."

"No right? And who's stopping me? You think the few gods we have left care a wink about old vows? Over the past twenty-three centuries I've had time to step back and take a good look at my duties. My geis is in the loo with the glory of the Celts!"

Ozark's face turned impassive again. There was a sparkle in his eyes that made Clony shiver. With a wave of his hand and without the spirit being able to do a thing about it, the scenery changed. Gone the heat, vanished the girls: the shaman and he were in a damp and muggy cave. Worse still: he was crawling on the ground, stuck in his old, mummified half-body.

"What... Where...," he stammered.

"We're in Crom Cruach's prison under Tullybrack Mountain."

"How dare you!" Clony shouted in fury.

"Be careful not to speak too loudly," Ozark warned him. "You wouldn't want the old devourer to hear you."

The shaman watched him with his arms crossed. Raging mad, Clony tried to use his magic but his gestures had no effect. His power was gone.

"It's no use. The ritual of Saint Grellan abolishes all spells."

"I... I don't get it. Saint Grellan doesn't exist anymore! And Crom Cruach—you killed him yourself!"

"Yes and no," the shaman had a smug smile on his face. "See, magic is a game like everything else. When you cheat, you change the rules for everyone. You broke your geis so I was free to ignore mine."

Clony understood at last. He was on his knees. He had disobeyed the universal laws and was going to pay the price.

"Your geis..." he muttered.

"My geis are the constants of the multiverse. The laws of causality, the flow of time. By freeing me you gave me the power to rewrite reality. The devouring worm was not freed and Ireland was not destroyed."

Clony felt a laugh rising up in his withered chest. He had exchanged one prison for another even more cramped. His laugh echoed through the depths until Crom Cruach devoured it for the first time.

Eternity was going to be long.

Ozark by Luciano Bernasconi

The Agent With No Name by Barbato

*Master of disguise, the **Agent With No Name** is a freelance spy who sometimes uses the name of "Monnet" (obviously a fake identity which he chose as an homage to the famous impressionist) and often works for a mysterious Geneva-based freelance intelligence organization headed by one Monsieur Leroy...*

Philippe Pinon: *Ninouska*

*For my wife Nathalie and my son Ethan.
For my pal Tommy for his musical inspiration.
Thanks to Thomas, Olivier, James, Julien, Cécile,
Laetitia and Yvonne for their valuable proofreading.*

I

It was a pretty nice evening.

Despite the harsh December, the weather was granting Paris a much appreciated respite. Taking deep breaths of the almost springtime air, Monnet was fully enjoying his night on the terrace of his luxurious apartment in the 19th arrondissement. From the top floor of the opulent building, he overlooked a good part of the capital and when weather permitted, he had a stunning view of the city. Like tonight. A clear sky let the starry heavens blanket Paris and, in the mild temperature, he could enjoy the view of the Eiffel Tower without shivering inside a heavy coat.

Tearing himself away from contemplating the view, which he already knew like the back of his hand, Monet crushed out his cigarette in a smooth, swift motion and grabbed a glass of gin that was sitting on the ledge. Then he went back through the French doors into the living room of his luxury penthouse.

The living room was a huge open space split into three sections. In the back of the room, across from him, was the dining room with an open-plan kitchen. To his right was a co-zy sitting area with a plush, leather couch that took up an entire wall and faced a latest generation plasma screen. Finally to his left, where he was headed, were two adjoining desks, each with two computers on it and a jumble of papers and post-its.

Monnet sat in the comfortable executive office chair in front of all the screens and put his glass down beside him. His fingers started typing fast on the keyboard and his eyes focused on the webpage he found.

A notification beeped on one of his other computers and pulled him out of his concentration. With a quick jerk of his hip he slid the chair to the left and his eyes riveted on the screen. After a few seconds a faint smile crossed his lips, abruptly replaced by a pensive furrowing of his brow. He leaned back in his chair, clasped his hands under his chin and stared at the screen. Only his eyes moved, reading and rereading the articles from the big newspapers. Anyone watching him at this moment would have thought he was analyzing a chess move in the middle of a game when the opening gambits had been played and the two adversaries were in the first "off-board" confrontation.

After a few minutes, Monnet stood up, pushing the chair far away. He took out his phone and started dialing a number.

"Hello, uncle?"

Monnet's voice was particularly cheerful when he spoke, in contrast to the grave and puzzled look on his face an instant before.

"What's that? You don't hear me? Yes, go on, put me on speaker, I'll do the same."

Monnet went back to the desk, connected his phone to the computer, hit a few keys and went over to the TV screen. His face had become serious and preoccupied again. On the huge screen a face popped up, a narrow, gentle face of a man about fifty, with graying hair and steel blue eyes. The thin glasses on his slightly balding head were so worn and mended that they looked like relics from another age. The man waved his right hand before his eyes as if to break his concentration and looked straight ahead.

"Good evening, Monnet."

"Good evening, uncle," Monnet responded.

"It's alright, the link is encrypted and secure, your IP address as well as mine are floating so you can stop calling me 'uncle'. If only you knew how weird I feel every time you say it. Me, an only child, being called uncle makes my heart break a little."

Monnet shot him a quick smile that even more quickly faded. "Sorry, Monsieur Leroy but I can't take any risks."

"I can imagine, but you've got to find something else to call me. Anyway, I guess this is no time for dillydallying. If you called me so late, I'm sure it's not to talk about the last movie you saw."

"No, it's not, monsieur."

While going back to the computers Monnet continued talking. "I'm sending you the internet links for some articles about some recent local crimes in Paris that have attracted my attention, even though I couldn't understand why at first."

In a few clicks several web pages appeared on the huge TV screen. Leroy pointed his finger and flipped through them speedily.

"They're all murders, assassinations, suspicious deaths, whatever, call them what you want, they all happened recently."

"So? Unfortunately, it's nothing new."

"I know", Monnet said, "but if you look more closely, you'll see the first is a librarian from an annex specialized in ancient books, the second an Arab bookseller who collected religious tracts, and the third, a printer specialized in restoring old works."

"Yes indeed. Léon Marcheteau... the name rings a bell."

"Of course, monsieur," Monnet replied with a smile, "he was found guilty of forgery for a work he sold a few years ago. Anyway, that's not important right now."

Monnet stepped up to the TV screen. He took out a cigarette and lit it before speaking again.

"Since the murders were bothering me, I decided to do a little investigating myself. I was thinking all these murders were likely connected because of the victims' profiles. Nothing to do with your usual, everyday crimes. I pretended I was a journalist, but I didn't get very far. Disguised as a janitor? I was denied access as well. So, I went and passed myself off as a special police investigator and then I got to see documents like the autopsy reports and crime scene photos. And it's been two days since my computers have been grinding away at it."

"And?" Leroy had suddenly become very interested in what Monnet was saying.

"What if I told you—silk fibers in the throat, a small puncture wound around the collar bone and a broken neck."

A long moment of silence followed. Leroy's face turned pale for a second before the color came rushing back. He lowered his glasses and adjusted them carefully before answering.

"Hmm, the Black Coats..."

"Exactly, monsieur. I came to the same conclusion. But what I didn't manage to find out is why this rather old-fashioned branch of CRIMEN executed these people."

"Listen, Monnet, I'll get some information and call you back in an hour." He started to get up from his chair but changed his mine. "Uh, in fact, Monnet…"

"Yes, monsieur?"

"I'm going to leave the channel open. That way, we can avoid the 'uncles' and all that nonsense."

Monnet could not help laughing. "OK, monsieur, see you later then."

"See you later, Monnet. Get a little rest in the meantime, I think you need it."

Monnet nodded and turned away from the screen. He grabbed his glass and headed for the bar to refill it. Then he went back through the French windows to the terrace and leaned on the railing to lose himself in the myriad of lights illuminating the capital.

II

The lights of the Eiffel Tower had totally hypnotized Monnet. He was lost in the ceaseless sparkling of the thousands of bulbs that lit up the glittering iron tower. His glass was empty, his fingers clamped the butt of the cigarette that had burned down without him realizing it. He was pulled out of his reverie by a voice from the living room.

After a few seconds he realized that he was alone and the voice, which was starting to sound angry, was Leroy's on the TV screen. He straightened up, walked through the doors and stood before the screen.

"So, Monnet, were you asleep?"

"No, monsieur, I was just lost in thought."

"Well, it's time to come back down to earth, my young friend. I've got some information and it's not going to bring a smile to your face."

Monnet was fully attentive now. He knew only too well the old man's tone of voice and what it meant.

Leroy fiddled with his glasses, took a deep breath and said, "I've got information on what you told me about."

"Go on," Monnet was getting anxious.

"CRIMEN is trying to get its hands on a very old book through the Black Coats."

"What book?" Monnet asked.

"The *Book of the First Men*."

"What?"

"Oh, Monnet, your youth is showing along with your ignorance of our elders."

"Hold it, monsieur," Monnet started to say.

The old man's face cracked a smile, "Does the *Necronomicon* mean anything to you?"

"No, monsieur."

"H. P. Lovecraft?"

"Er, vaguely."

"Well, young man, Lovecraft was a writer who 'invented' the *Necronomicon*. The book, supposedly written by a mad Arab called Abdul Al'Hazred, contains the secrets of eternal life as well as other revelations that would spell the ruin of mankind if it fell into the wrong hands."

"What's the connection between CRIMEN and an autistic writer in the early 20th century?"

Leroy raised an eyebrow. "How the devil did you know Lovecraft was autistic if you barely know he even existed?"

"You know, monsieur," Monnet replied with a mischievous smile, "I like to pretend to be more ignorant than I really am. In my work it's important to know how to hide your true nature."

A big smile lit up the old man's face, delighted with his young apprentice's answer. "*The Book of the First Men*, Monnet."

"But I thought it was the *Necronomicon* that Lovecraft invented," Monnet was a little lost.

"Indeed, young man, you're right, but you don't know that, as brilliant as Lovecraft was, he was inspired by real books to build his mythology. And you're surely aware that ancient literature abounds with books about eternal life, necromancers and all kinds of ways to raise the dead."

The man behind the screen pushed up his glasses as if to focus his attention on the one watching him. Then he continued, "You know, Monnet, eternal life is a dream for some, just like the Philosopher's Stone. The man or woman who could get a hold of the secret, if it exists, would become the most powerful being in our world."

Monnet twitched nervously.

The old man pretended not to notice. "*The Necronomicon*, therefore, was thought up based on reality or allegedly so. And this reality, *The Book of the First Men*, is what CRIMEN is looking for. It's totally unacceptable. Just imagine the horde of zombies they could raise up thanks to it. Imagine the destruction they could cause, the unpunishable crimes they could commit. Really, how can you kill someone who is already dead? How can you threaten a soulless being come from beyond the grave? How can you interrogate a rotting corpse that fears no pain?"

The old man let out a weary sigh and looked straight at the screen. Monnet looked him in the eyes.

"I guess that's where I come in, right?" he asked with a half-smile.

"That's right, my young friend," Leroy said. "And urgently! Given what you told me about those murders, I think there's no doubt that CRIMEN is on the right track, maybe even already there. It's absolutely imperative," he stood up and hammered the desk with his finger at every syllable, "IM-PER-A-TIVE that we get that book before them. I don't have to draw you of picture of the tragic consequences we will be facing if we're not the first ones to get our hands on that book!"

"I understand, Monsieur."

Sitting back down at his desk, Leroy started typing on the computer in front of him. He resumed the conversation without looking up. His voice was grim and determined.

"In the next few minutes, I'll be sending you all the information I've been able to gather from C.L.A.S.H. so far. I'll leave you to connect the dots and put it together with what you've got. Plus, I've informed Girodet at The Lion of your discoveries, and he's promised his help if you need it."

Monnet sighed at this last bit. "Monsieur, you know very well that I work alone. Even though I have great respect for The Lion, you know I can't—won't—take orders in what or how I decide to work."

"I know, Monnet. I know how you feel about it, and I respect that. But I have to give you the official line on the matter."

"Yeah, well," the young man replied, "you know what you can do with your official line…"

With a flick of the remote control he cut off the communication and any answer the old man might have given.

III

The alarm clock read 3:12 a.m. Monnet had not closed his eyes since his conversation with Leroy. After receiving the information sent by his mentor, he had spent part of the night comparing it and connecting it to his own notes.

It was obvious that the Black Coats were on the right track. Everyone who had been killed lately had had some kind of knowledge of the book. The information furnished by Leroy gave him a new clue: *Ninouska*. This was the name of a nightclub located near Pigalle and a known front for the Russian mob. It seemed that the owner had been in contact with someone who had offered to sell the book for a big load of cash. It sounded like a good starting point. But if Monnet knew this, it was certain that CRIMEN knew it too. He had to act quickly.

Monnet sighed deeply, wearily, took a cigarette from the bedside table next to him, lit it and sank back into bed, his vision blurring in the blades of the fan that decorated the ceiling of his bedroom.

He knew that he was getting mixed up in something that was completely different from what he was used to. There was no luxury car here, no five-star hotels in Monaco. No beautiful gowns, either, being worn by elegant women. No meals in the best restaurants. All he had was rotting corpses.

This last thought made him smile. And he closed his eyes.

IV

The stars were still shining in the Paris sky. The night was cold now. The early evening warmth had turned almost bitter cold, nipping at exposed skin. At this late hour, the few people who were still walking the streets were in a hurry to get inside where it was warm.

The alley was almost completely black. It was amazing that there were still areas in Paris that were so similar to the cutthroat districts of the 19th century. All that was missing was a blanket of fog and a prostitute dressed in a petticoat to look like Whitechapel in 1888. The pale glow of the scattered streetlights only added to the suffocating vertigo of the place. However, despite the feeling of utter desolation of the dead-end street, everything was not as calm as it seemed.

A man turned the corner and stumbled into the narrow alley. He had a lot of trouble staying on his feet and had to rest his left hand against the wall to keep from falling down. He raised his right hand to the collar of the thick, swanky coat hanging off his shoulders, but even this simple gesture threw him off balance. He looked up at the sky and took a deep breath of the cold, Parisian air as if it could inspire confidence in him, but the light, as feeble as it was, made him blink. It would have been obvious to an observer that the blood-alcohol level of this wealthy drunk was dangerously high.

The man let out a satisfied growl when he pushed off the wall and realized he could stand without falling. He dug in his pockets, took out a beautiful cigarette case, a Dupont lighter, and worked on lighting a cig. He sucked in the first puff and blew the smoke out slowly through his nose... and almost threw up. With an angry, clumsy movement, he tossed the cig-arette to the ground and stamped on it with his wobbly foot.

He was starting to turn around to go back when he heard a faint, steady rhythm coming from the back of the alley. He squinted to see as far as possible through the darkness to lo-cate its source, and he noticed a blinking sign. Trying to pull himself together, advancing unsteadily, he went to get a closer look. If he had been sober, he would have approached more warily because the place was not the most inviting. But to the foggy mind of a wasted night owl, nothing seems dangerous. He zigzagged forward, hearing the sound that got louder the further down the alley he went. His eyes got used to the dark and, thanks to the halo from the sign on the wall, he could see a massive shadow.

"What a funny idea to put a statue in an alley like this," he mumbled to himself.

The noise kept getting louder as he neared the huge statue. Now he could see a big door decorated with a heavy gold ring that was outrageously shaped like a lion's head. As for the sign, he could see it clearly and it read, *Ninouska*.

"How kitschy!" he thought out loud and continued staggering forward in his alcoholic haze.

Now there was no doubt about the sound: it was the beat of music he was hearing. Given how far he still was from the door, he figured that either the people inside were completely deaf or there was a big party going on, and what better way to end a night of drinking! He smiled at this thought and his gin-soaked face lit up. But the light went out right away.

He stopped short with a scared look on his face. The statue had just moved and was coming towards him.

V

"Who are you and what are you doing here?" asked the statue with a heavy Slavic accent, halting its movement a few feet in front of the drunk.

The man stood there in disbelief for a minute. He had just figured out that the huge bulk he had taken for a statue was, in fact, a bodyguard, or rather a bouncer, seeing that there was no body in sight to guard. The look of fright faded from his face and he could not hold back a burst of laughter. When he saw the expression on the hulk's face harden, he pulled himself together quickly.

"What's so funny? Accent too hard for puny drunk?" the hulking figure asked.

"Sorry, but I thought you were a statue from back there. Just so there's no mistake. I understand you fine," the drunk rattled off, stumbling backward a couple of steps, surprised by the seriousness in the muscleman's voice.

"*Da!* What runt want here so late in night?" the hulk softened his voice a little.

118

Slightly less tense, the man pulled a pack of cigarettes out of his pocket and lit one. *You're not gonna scare me, Mr. Muscleman,* he told himself.

"Well, friend, I heard the music as I was passing by this charming street," he tried to sound as calm and confident as possible, "and I said to myself, Hey Charles—yes, that's me, Charles de la Patellière at your service," he bowed before the former statue. "...Charles, there are people celebrating here, so why not see if a friendly party might not bring back your zest for life."

He paused, looking for a reaction from the giant, who furrowed his brow as if he did not understand a word of what the French dandy was saying.

Charles went on, "There's music back there and I want to party."

The Russian nodded, "Nightclub. If you want in, you pay. But if you too drunk, I throw you on your ass."

"Oh, I believed it was a private party with exotic appetizers and bottles of expensive champagne," the rich lush replied. "But so be it, let it never be said that Charles de la Patellière refused an invitation to a party, entrance fee or not!"

The mass of muscles looked thoughtfully at the man for a minute, then stepped aside and said, "You can go in."

The man straightened his coat, ran his hand through his blonde hair to look more presentable, and pushed open the heavy door.

VI

The door closed behind Charles with a sharp click. The music was strangely as muffled inside. He found himself in a chic corridor, the walls richly decorated with red velvet, obviously very expensive, but overdone. The wall lamps looked like old chandeliers, giving off a light that was supposed to be dim, but was brutally intensified by the bright red velvet. A young woman, tall and thin, certainly of Slavic origin too, wearing heavy makeup and a short dress, surged out of an alcove a few feet from the entrance, making Charles jump.

My God, he thought, *I thought I'd come across a classy establishment but it seems I was mistaken.*

She gave him a smile that was supposed to be charming and seductive, but despite his drunkenness, Charles could see that the only thing that interested the young lady was to get as much money off him in as little time as possible.

"Good evening," she whispered in his ear, leaning close to him lasciviously. "Here you have all you want, blonde beauty," she swept off his coat so brusquely that he almost fell backwards.

With a wave of her hand, she invited him forward. Charles looked in the direction the hostess was pointing and went down the corridor. Feeling a little less drunk now, he could walk straight ahead. The corridor veered a little to the right. He made out a curtain behind which the music and the sounds of dancing could be heard more loudly and clearly than before. Lights flashing to the rhythm of the music glared around the edges. He paused in front of it, already feeling deafened by the noises. He straightened his suit one last time, ran his hand through his hair again, cleared his throat, tilted his head left and right to crack his neck and threw open the curtain. The music drowned him along with the lights.

Charles took a deep breath and stepped into the heart of the nightclub.

VII

On the second floor, sitting in the VIP section of his own club, Dimitriev Dorchenko looked pleased as he watched the dance floor down below. Once again the *Ninouska* was full, despite the cold and late hour. He took a drag on his huge cigar and blew out a thick, white plume of smoke, which spread around him to the dismay of the young people sitting with him in leather armchairs. Which made him guffaw.

In spite of his imposing stature, he shot up from the chair and grabbed the railing overlooking the dance floor. His big hands gripping the rail showed off the huge rings on each finger, from index to pinky, on both hands. His 6'3" height was not quite enough to bear his 300-pound carcass, apparently, because drops of sweat were pearling on his forehead. Unless it was his expensive designer suit that was too warm. Whatever it was, nothing showed in his eyes because they were hidden behind small, dark sunglasses. Finally, to complete the picture, his long, gray, slightly thinning hair was neatly slicked back. Not a single hair stuck out.

Yes, Dimitriev Dorchenko did stick out—that was the least you could say about him.

VIII

It was not easy for Charles to move through the crowded club. His eyes had finally adjusted to the strobing lights. There was only the smoke machine, spitting out every thirty seconds, that still bothered him. Bumped every which way by the oblivious dancers, he did his best to get to the bar. Pretty much everywhere around him he saw young women swaying their hips and men trying to get their attention with a wave of their hand or a glass held out for them. There were small, private spaces in the corners of the club with sofas behind flimsy, white curtains. And behind them, Charles could see prurient bodies in erotic embraces. He had thought he was coming into a high-class party and here he was in a cheap nightclub.

All that's missing is a poker room, he thought. *But then, I play poker pretty well.* His face lit up with a smile at this thought and he stood up straighter to get a better look at the place and maybe find a back door somewhere.

When he got to the bar, he smirked at the bartender. "A Vesper, please," he asked.

Unfazed, the bartender opened a fridge and took out a cocktail glass, which he set down in front of him. Then he turned around to grab a shaker and the bottles of gin, vodka

121

and Lillet. He looked up at Charles and spoke as he worked, "So, three parts gin, one of vodka and half of Lillet. Shake and pour in a cold glass. Does the gentleman prefer a twist of lemon or orange?" he asked with a satisfied smile.

"Uh, lemon," Charles answered, a little baffled that a bartender in a dive like this in Paris would know what a Vesper was.

With a sweep of his hand, the bartender took a few lemon zests that he put on the rim of the glass and, pleased with himself, held the cocktail out to Charles. The latter gave him a twenty-euro bill and motioned for him to keep the change.

With glass in hand, he turned around and leaned back proudly against the bar, determined to take full advantage of the situation. He looked up and saw the huge figure of Dorchenko overseeing the club from the second floor like a king smugly watching his people.

Ah! I'm looking at the owner!

Charles finished his cocktail while staring at Dorchenko's dark glasses and put his drink on the bar behind him. He had spotted a stairway leading to the second floor. If there were a poker room here, he thought, that tubo'lard surely knew where it was.

Swerving again, Charles left the bar and stumbled into the crowd of dancers, determined to end the night risking a little cash at a poker table. He elbowed his way through the swaying bodies until he reached the stairs, which he started to climb unsteadily, feeling the effect of the Vesper.

IX

Dorchenko was watching the crowd below while his eyes tallied up the money in the till with every new customer or every drink served at the bar. The more he counted, the bigger his smile got. Another good night for "Double D," the nickname his associates had given him. Dorchenko was used to the nickname now, even though he had throttled people for using it at first. Of course, being a big shot in the Bratva (the Russian mafia), he could not let his name be ridiculed. But over time, the nickname ended up scaring people and his enemies stopped laughing. He had become proud of it. On his business card, the two Ds of Dimitriev and Dorchenko were oversized so that everyone could clearly see the importance of the "Double D."

He let out a sigh of contentment and was about to go back to his armchair when he saw a customer hand a twenty-euro bill to the bartender. Dorchenko scrutinized the server to make sure he did not pocket the money, but put it in the register, which he did. So, with a satisfied grunt Double D glanced at the generous sucker.

"Bah! Another rich Frenchman who doesn't know what to do with his money," he muttered and shrugged his shoulders dismissively.

Even if the guy looked like he was swimming in his suit coat, Dorchenko, a respected Russian dandy himself, could not help recognizing that the man had good taste in his choice of clothes; Parisian tailors were, of course, among the best in the world. He kept an eye on the guy as he forged his way through the crowded dance floor. And he raised a surprised eyebrow when he saw him stumbling up the stairs to his VIP area. Dorchenko turned around and said something in Russian to one of his bodyguards, who headed straight for the stairs.

Double D sat down calmly, curious to know what the elegant visitor wanted with him.

X

Charles struggled up the stairs holding onto the railing to keep a little composure and dignity.

My God, he thought, *that cocktail was strong. Maybe I should have stuck to something lighter, seeing it's so late. How am I going to play poker like this?*

He looked up to see how many steps were left on this staircase that felt as high as Everest. A large man was standing at the top, arms crossed over his chest, legs spread, as if to keep him from accessing the second floor.

Charles sat down, caught his breath and smiled at the man. "Hello, my young friend," he said as he climbed the final steps that separated him from the VIP section. "I'm looking for the owner of this quaint establishment and I figured he ought to be in the quietest room of the house, right?"

The man did not budge.

Charles was now standing on the last step, right below him. He continued, "When I came into your charming *discothèque*, I couldn't help noticing the second floor, and I told myself, Charles, if you're looking for the boss, he must be there."

The bodyguard had still not moved a muscle. Charles was only inches from his face. He cleared his throat, feeling less confident again. But he went on, his voice a little shaky.

"And, uh, I was… right, wasn't I?"

The man in front of him stared him straight in the eyes without blinking. Charles felt his throat tighten and he almost fell over because of the stifling heat of the club, which only added to his drunkenness. He tried to grab the railing again but he misjudged the distance and his hand clutched empty air. He felt himself falling backward and closed his eyes to hold back the scream that was building up inside himself.

My God, I'm going to break my neck!

He almost choked when he felt a hand grasp the collar of his coat. He opened his eyes and saw the bodyguard holding him in one strong hand. He let out a sigh of relief. Then a hearty laugh startled him so that he nearly slipped out of his rescuer's grip. He held firmly to the bodyguard's forearm as it pulled him up out of his compromising position.

Charles regained his composure as he shook loose of the iron grip. And he turned to the "tubo'lard" who apparently found his misfortune terribly amusing. Holding back a snide comment, Charles made up his mind that he was still wise enough not to anger the big man sitting before him if he did not want his neck broken, which he had just been saved from. Instead he gave him his friendliest smile.

"Good evening, Monsieur. Thanks for helping me out of that sticky spot," Charles made a little, very aristocratic bow.

Dorchenko swallowed a second guffaw and returned the smile of his surprised guest. "Good evening, little man. Sorry for laughing, for finding you very funny when you almost fell on the stairs."

"I'm glad I made someone laugh," Charles forced a smile that he tried not to twist too much. "I probably would've broken my neck if it weren't for your man there."

"*Da!* Very funny too! But I don't like to see blood in club. In club, we dance, we drink. Not die! Drunks die in dark alleys, not at Dorchenko's!"

"Sure, absolutely… but I really had no intention of dying, OK?"

"I hope no," Double D's tone suddenly turned more serious. "What are you doing here?"

Charles took a few seconds to think, not wanting to say the wrong thing. He looked around to gain a little time and noticed the outline of a door behind the Russian but it had no handle.

"I was wondering if your establishment might not have a room where one could, among gentlemen, barter a little money over the more or less lucky fall of the cards, if you know what I mean," Charles concluded his phrase with a wink.

The Russian froze.

Charles saw that he had asked the wrong question. Dorchenko sighed and shook his head. Even through the sunglasses, the Frenchman felt the Russian's eyes pierce him. Charles took an awkward step back. Dorchenko shot a few quick words in Russian to his bodyguard and pointed at the Frenchman with contempt.

Charles saw the man who had just saved him come over to him, but this time, he knew it was not to help.

"My apologies, Monsieur, if my question upset you," the drunk had suddenly sobered up, keeping one eye on the bodyguard walking over, "but I thought that…"

"You think wrong!" Dorchenko cut him off. "You spoiled rich French bourgeois drunk and insulting! You go right now!"

Charles knew it was hopeless and it would be better to leave before things got ugly. He started back to the stairs, which had almost taken his life a few minutes ago, but he tripped over the bodyguard's foot and fell to the floor. Double D jumped out of his armchair and loomed over the poor, fallen body.

"You pathetic! Useless bourgeois full of booze and money. Go back to your rat hole. You not worthy to talk to Dimitriev Dorchenko, or even to be in his nightclub. You disappear! For good!"

Charles was lifted to his feet by his coat collar but, this time, the bodyguard pushed him toward the stairs instead of saving him from falling down them.

"Excuse me, Monsieur, many apologies. Sorry, really," Charles stammered as he started down the steps backwards, arms stretched out as if to protect him from the Russian's anger. "I'm leaving, I'm going home to sleep it off and I won't bother you again, promise."

The hulk was stationed again at the top of the stairs. Charles was afraid for a moment that he would rush down and throw him out of the club but he just stood there doing nothing but giving Charles the evil eye. In the middle of the stairs, he tried to calm down a little and catch his breath before continuing down, now turned in the right direction so that he would not fall. His heart was beating a mile a minute. He forced himself to breathe steadily and slowly to bring his pulse down.

He looked up and saw, at the bottom of the stairs, off to the right, a door marked with a sign for the restrooms. He hurried down and headed for the door, pointing to it so that the bodyguard would understand since he was still watching. He scampered through the crowd and grabbed the door handle.

XI

Charles closed the door behind him. The noise of the nightclub faded. He walked over to the sinks, leaned both hands on one of them and looked at himself in the mirror. He smiled. His coat was in bad shape and his hair a complete mess. In short, he looked like hell, certainly not like himself.

But of course I'd rather look like a nobody than like that nitwit Charles de la Patellière.

Monnet took off his coat and laid it on the sink to his right. He unbuttoned his nice, white shirt, rolled up the sleeves and turned on the faucet. He cupped his hands and soaked his face in the cold water. Then he straightened up, looked at his dripping face and did it again.

When he stood up straight again he froze. In the reflection of the mirror was one of Dorchenko's henchmen. He turned around to face him. The restroom door opened again and a second man entered, carefully locking the door behind him. The three men stood there without moving, just looking at each other. Time stopped. It felt like hours.

XII

The punch came flying out of nowhere. Monnet ducked quickly and swung around, bending his arm and delivering a hard elbow into the chest of the first attacker who let out an "Oof" before stumbling back with his hands on his chest, then falling to his knees. Monnet stepped forward and kicked him in the face. The man's head shot back and smashed into the swinging door of one of the stalls, tearing off its hinges.

The Frenchman looked over in time to see the second attacker rushing at him with a switchblade in his hand. The man plunged forward trying to stab the fake aristocrat in the chest. Monnet moved swiftly and grabbed the thrusting arm, swung around again and threw his attacker into a sink, making sure to snatch the knife in the process. The man's back crashed into the porcelain, which caused his face to twist in pain.

A groan pulled Monnet's attention away. Glancing to his right, he saw the first goon holding onto the toilet and slowly rising to his feet inside the stall. In spite of all the blood, the fury on his face was written more clearly than the pain. With a flick of his arm, Monnet threw the knife at the Russian. The blade stuck in his skull with a thump. The man had time to raise his eyes and see the handle of the switchblade before his face froze in death.

A sharp pain in his lower back almost knocked Monnet out. He had forgotten about the other guy! The second attacker had just punched him in the back. The Frenchman dropped to his knees, gritting his teeth so as not to cry out in pain. A hard kick in his ribs threw him to the floor, making him jerk convulsively. He kept rolling, however, out of range, for the moment at least, of his adversary.

He got to his feet and turned around, instinctively protecting his face with his arms. Thus he blocked the furious punch swung at him. Quickly, he ducked around his attacker and grabbed him around the waist. The man tried to get free, pummeling the aristocrat's sides with his elbows. Monnet held fast, grimacing, then throwing his enemy against the sinks. The man hit his head against a mirror, smashing it to pieces. He roared in fury, grabbed a piece of the mirror and swung around trying to slash the Frenchman's face.

Monnet had anticipated the move and already stepped back. The Russian almost lost his footing. The Frenchman took advantage of the moment, squatted down and with a sweeping kick knocked the goon to the floor. When he fell, his neck hit the sink. A sinister crack echoed through the restroom and the giant sank motionless to the floor. His eyes were still open, staring at the painted ceiling. This would be the last thing he saw before he died.

After catching his breath, Monnet went straight to the door and listened, checking if the noise of the scuffle had attracted attention. When he was sure nobody was coming, he walked calmly to the sinks, casually stepping over the bodies. He turned on a faucet, cleaned the blood off his face, fixed his hair and put his coat back on, making sure there were no traces of the struggle. He leaned over one of the bodies, rapidly searched his pockets and headed for the exit with the key to unlock the door. He tossed the key ring behind him, grabbed a small sign hanging on the inside handle and turned out the lights before closing the door behind him. He hung the sign on the handle so that everyone could clearly read, *Out of Order*.

XIII

Before closing the door of the restrooms, Monnet glanced upstairs at the VIP lounge. He did not see Dorchenko but caught some movement at the back where he had seen the door without handles. Lowering his head, he walked quickly to the exit curtain, which he slipped through. At this late hour, there were fewer customers. He headed down the red corridor and straight for the hostess whom he recognized.

"Are you having a nice evening?" she sounded just as friendly.

"Very instructive," Monnet smiled politely. "I would love to stay all night, but I'm afraid I enjoyed too many of your excellent cocktails and my head is spinning a little. Could I have my coat, please?"

"Leaving already? Too bad. I finish in a hour. I chill with you with big glass of water in my apartment if you want," her smile widened.

"No thanks, Mademoiselle. You're gorgeous, but I really have to get to bed."

Reluctantly, she went to fetch his heavy coat, which she wrapped around his shoulders, seductively. "You really sure? You don't want a good relaxing?"

For the last time, Monnet turned to the hostess with the same charming smile on his lips. "Sincerely, no, thank you. Besides, I talked with your boss, who assured me of the spotless reputation of your club. I wouldn't want to make a liar out of him."

The young woman stepped back, surprised.

The Frenchman put a friendly hand on her shoulder. "No worries, I won't mention your 'extras,' Mademoiselle. Good night."

She smiled timidly and opened the door for him. The cold air hit Monnet as he stepped outside. He turned up the collar of his coat and left. The "statue" was still at his post. He rewarded the Frenchman with a "good night" as he passed by. Monnet nodded in return and went down the alley, leaving the *Ninouska* behind him.

XIV

At the corner of the alley, Monnet looked at his watch. It showed 5:47 a.m. He headed back to his luxurious apartment sunk deep in thought.

An hour from now, the last customers will have gone. That's when they'll clean up and get rid of the two stiffs. Got to give the Russians two or three hours more. Anyway, they won't call the cops, too risky. Just have to find out whether everyone is going to leave or not. My feeling is that Dorchenko has his apartment in the club behind that hidden door. I have to be sure. If, as I suspect, he's got the book with him, I have to get it before the Black Coats make mincemeat out of him. Seeing how easy it was for me to deal with two of his goons, there's no doubt that they could massacre his gang in minutes. And if Leroy's right, there's no way I can let the book fall into the wrong hands. The only thing I don't get in all of this is, how such a book ended up in such inept hands as the Russian mafia. Unless Double D is made of different stuff than his henchmen? I should hope so, otherwise his Ninouska *is soon going to be turned into a graveyard.*

Monnet was still lost in his thoughts when he got to his building. Instead of entering by the front door, he ducked into a dark side-alley. A few seconds later, the light in his apartment went on. The bells in a nearby church chimed six times. Dawn would come in an hour or so. He had to be ready.

XV

His watch showed 11 a.m. Monnet was back in the alley. This time, he had left his Charles de la Patellière disguise at home and was dressed appropriately for what he had to do. He had spotted no unusual activity from the street. As he had expected, there was no sign of the police. He had taken time to check the Internet, but no news site reported any murders at the night club. Which was logical. Dorchenko could not let the cops get mixed up in his business.

He took a few steps down the alley and squatted down, pretending to tie his shoes, but keeping an eye on the back of the alley. During the day, one couldn't see much more than at night, because it was so narrow and the buildings so tall. Still, there was enough light to see the other end. And it was empty, except for a few garbage bins along the walls and trash on the ground. Looking behind him, Monnet saw that there was little traffic. He took the opportunity to move further down and thus out of sight of the passers-by.

In a few seconds, sneaking from shadow to shadow, the Frenchman made it to *Ninouska*. There was no trace of the "statue," or anybody else for that matter. But something caught Monnet's attention. The heavy door was not closed tight like the night before. He went up to it and looked at the lock. It had been jimmied. He put his hand on the door and pushed slowly. It opened a few inches, then was blocked. He pushed harder, but it would not budge. He froze, listening— not a sound inside the club.

He took out a small mirror from one of his pockets, stuck it on the end of a extensible stick. He put the mirror on the ground and slipped it through the crack in the door. No light. No movements. Pushing the mirror a little farther, he froze. The reflection of a manicured hand showed up. Letting out his breath, Monnet easily recognized the pale purple nail polish of the hostess who had propositioned him last night. He put away the mirror and pushed the door just enough to squeeze through.

He entered and saw, lying on the ground, the twisted body of the young Russian. A quick check verified that her neck had been broken. Monnet bent down and closed her eyelids. He caught the smell of sulfur, but could not tell where it was coming from. He stood up straight, all senses on alert. Still no noise. The girl's body was still warm so she had not been dead for long. Monnet took out his Beretta and screwed on a silencer. Then he proceeded down the hallway cautiously. The thought passed through his mind that, even if he found the decoration a little excessive last night, it was better than finding the still warm corpse of the Russian girl.

He made it to the curtain that had muffled the clamor of the nightclub the night before. Now, there was not a sound. And almost no light, except for the little bulbs indicating the emergency exit. Monnet used the silencer to crack open the curtain. Everything seemed calm behind it. The dance floor was empty. The place had been cleaned up, the floor was spotless. He slipped into the room, letting the curtain fall back behind him. Glancing quickly to the right and left, he saw no one. The bar was neat and clean. The ashtrays had been emptied and the chairs wiped. Monnet stepped into the middle of the room looking toward the stairs that led to the second floor, to the VIP lounge and the door he had discovered last night.

Strange. How is it that there's a body at the entrance left out in the open, but nothing anywhere else? How is it that the Black Coats found the hostess all alone and no bouncers or waiters?

Monnet was pulled out of his thoughts by the sound of a door opening upstairs. He heard voices, loud, as if they were arguing, and one he recognized, even if it spoke Russian— Dorchenko. He saw a halo of light and knew exactly where it came from: the "secret" door.

It closed, but he heard footsteps approaching the stairs. When he saw a thin figure start down the steps, he ducked behind the bar. As he bent down, he knocked over a bottle that fell on the floor and broke. He cursed his clumsiness. The figure on the stairs froze. Monnet jumped up.

"Hello!"

"What the…?" the figure stammered.

"No problem, just looking for olives," Monnet said and he fired two shots at the man, who collapsed, one bullet in the chest, another in the head. Monnet came around the bar and as he stepped over the body lying on the stairs he said:

"But all I found were prunes."

He took the stairs two at a time. At the top, he could hear the voices. There was an argument going on. They were speaking in Russian and French. He knew the voice of Double D and he heard another voice speaking Russian, but in a higher pitch. A woman. As for the French, he could make out two or three different voices. He looked around and saw that he was alone in the lounge, which had also been cleaned up.

He was on his way over to the secret door when he heard a piercing scream, which was quickly choked off. He recognized the Russian woman's voice. A minute later, he heard Dorchenko start to roar in anger, then the sounds of a scuffle. From the tone of his shouting, the giant was raging mad. Even though Monnet knew no Russian, he could tell that they were not exchanging pleasantries. The door shook when something big hit it hard. Monnet guessed that Dorchenko must have grabbed one of his attackers and thrown him into the door like a toy.

"ENOUGH!" yelled a deep, firm voice on the other side of the door.

"NEVER!" Dorchenko barked in answer. "I tear you all limb by limb!"

"You're dreaming, you fat pig!" a different voice responded.

Monnet heard Dorchenko swearing in Russian, then more fighting. But not long. A gruesome crack was heard, followed by the sound of a body dropping to the floor.

After a short pause and some more scuffling, the conversation started up again.

"Just do it, you never know," the first voice said. "We might need him later."

"Are you sure?" the second voice questioned. "I don't like it."

"I'm not asking for your advice, just do as I say, got it?"

"Got it, Boss."

A few seconds passed in silence before Monnet heard chanting. He decided it was time to step in.

He backed up and kicked the door hard. It swung open and slammed into the wall. Monnet was looking into a big room, a suite. To the left of the door lay the body of the Russian woman whose voice he had heard. She had had her throat slashed and was swimming in a pool of her own blood. Double D lay on the floor a few feet away, lying on his back. A hooded man was leaning over him. He was the one chanting, apparently. To the right, a little farther back, stood a second man, also wearing a hood, standing before the body of the "statue," the huge bouncer from the entrance of the *Ninouska*. And lastly, in the very back of the suite Monnet saw a third figure, squatting in front of an open safe.

"Hey, ladies!" Monnet kept his gun pointed at the man on his right. "Mind if I join you?"

The three men turned their heads toward him in utter amazement. The man on the right went for his gun. Two muffled gunshots whispered and he fell backward with two bullets in his chest, right onto the body of the "statue," cracking the ribcage of the poor bouncer. The figure at the back of the room ducked behind a desk. As for the man on Dorchenko's bed, he stood up slowly and stared at Monnet defiantly.

"Whoever you are, you're too late," he said. "Behold the power of the Black Coats!"

Monnet turned his gun on him, unfazed. "Make a move and you'll join your pal."

"I have no need to move, I just have to speak, and say…"

He was stopped by a bullet in his forehead.

"Shut up!" Monnet told him calmly as he sank to the floor.

"*Ctuh'n Slivah Shoggoth Er'Lieth, Flang-Tragh!*"

The incantation came from behind the desk where the last foe had taken refuge. Monnet cursed his carelessness a second time and marched over to the desk.

"Get up and give up," he growled. "It's your only chance of getting out of here alive."

"*Ctuh'n Slivah Shoggoth Er'Lieth, Flang-Tragh! Ctuh'n Slivah Shoggoth Er'Lieth, Flang-Tragh!*" the voice repeated, still hiding.

Monnet went around the desk and found the last man on his knees, chanting, with his bulging eyes raised to the ceiling and an open book in front of him.

"Be quiet!"

And Monnet emptied his clip into the man's body. The victim stayed on his knees, frozen in death, his chest riddled with bullets.

A faint groan made Monnet turn his head quickly. And he stepped back. Dorchenko was standing up, facing him in the middle of the room. But his pallid eyes showed that he was no longer alive, that he had been brought back from the dead by the other ma's incantation.

Monnet rapidly ejected the old clip and slipped in a new one. With a steady hand, he unloaded its thirteen bullets into the zombie's chest. But the only effect it had was to make him look down at the holes. When he looked up again, a creepy smile crossed his face. His mouth spit out black blood. Then he came at Monnet, who understood that bullets were not the solution. Standing his ground firmly, he awaited the Russian's attack.

The giant tried to swing his fist, but death apparently slowed down his movements. Monnet had no problem ducking under the blow. While his adversary was momentarily off balance, he kicked him in the ribs. Bones cracked, but Dorchenko's only response was a little grunt. He grabbed the Frenchman's leg and swung him around.

Monnet was thrown across the room and crashed into the wall. He clenched his jaw in pain. But he immediately looked around the room until he spied the swords hanging on the wall. He went around the desk, keeping it between him and the Double D zombie, and ran over to grab the blades.

As if he understood what was happening, the zombie smashed his two fists into the desk, which cracked but did not break. He did it again, and this time the wood exploded; the desk split in two.

Monnet was *en garde* like a fencer when Dorchenko charged him, his arms stretched out, reaching for the Frenchman's throat. Monnet stepped to the left and the two swords whistled through the air. Dorchenko grunted again and looked at the floor. His two hands had been sliced clean off by the Frenchman, who took a few steps back and got in position again.

Raging mad, the Russian started bellowing when he charged again, head on, his stumps shaking in anger. His momentum carried him past Monnet who danced to the side. The blades whipped the air again. Dorchenko stopped. He turned around slowly. His eyes were lost in a fog. Then his head fell to the floor and his body collapsed.

Monnet lowered his swords. He planted one in the Russian's body and kept the other, which he slipped into his belt. He went back to the man on his knees and picked up the book with its thick, leather cover. He closed it carefully and put it into the backpack he was wearing under his coat. Without looking back he left the room.

All was quiet in the nightclub. He walked calmly down to the ground floor of the *Ninouska* and headed for the curtain, which he threw open this time. Once again, he was in the velvet corridor that exuded such bad taste. As he approached the entrance, he saw the lifeless body of the hostess. He pulled out his sword and, when he passed by herm he brought the blade down hard and severed her head from her neck.

At least your death will be undisturbed, Mademoiselle. No one will bring you back from beyond the grave to torment you or make you torment the living.

Monnet dropped the sword. He let out a weary sigh, then lit a cigarette with his Dupont. He took a few puffs and set the lighter next to the velvet wall. It caught fire right away. Calmly, slowly, Monnet left the *Ninouska*, making sure to close the door behind him. He went up the alley in no hurry and turned left on the street, letting the nightclub burn behind him.

XVI

Later that day, Monnet was preparing to send Leroy the book he had picked up from the Black Coats. He had wrapped it carefully in an airtight box to protect it. During the whole time, he could not help thinking of what would have happened if the information was false or incomplete, or if the book had not been at the *Ninouska*. In any case, he was sure of one thing: the plans of CRIMEN had been foiled, and the Black Coats had suffered a serious setback. Monnet was secretly hoping that it would stir up some chaos in the heart of the criminal organization.

As for Dorchenko, he had obviously not grasped the significance of his acquisition. Monnet was sure that, in spite of everything, the mob boss would have kept his distance if he had realized what the book could do.

Monnet read the last lines of the letter he had written to go with the package:

…and, Monsieur, remember that, even though I am your faithful servant, under no circumstances will I ever join an organization, as prestigious as it might be, like C.L.A.S.H. For years now, I have worked alone, and it's this solitude that protects me… as hard as it might be.

Hoping to hear from you soon,

Monnet, the Agent with No Name.

Monnet sealed the letter. He got up from his desk, went to get his glass from the low table before going out on the terrace. He took out a cigarette and lit it. Then he let his eyes wander over the immensity of Paris and he abandoned himself to it.

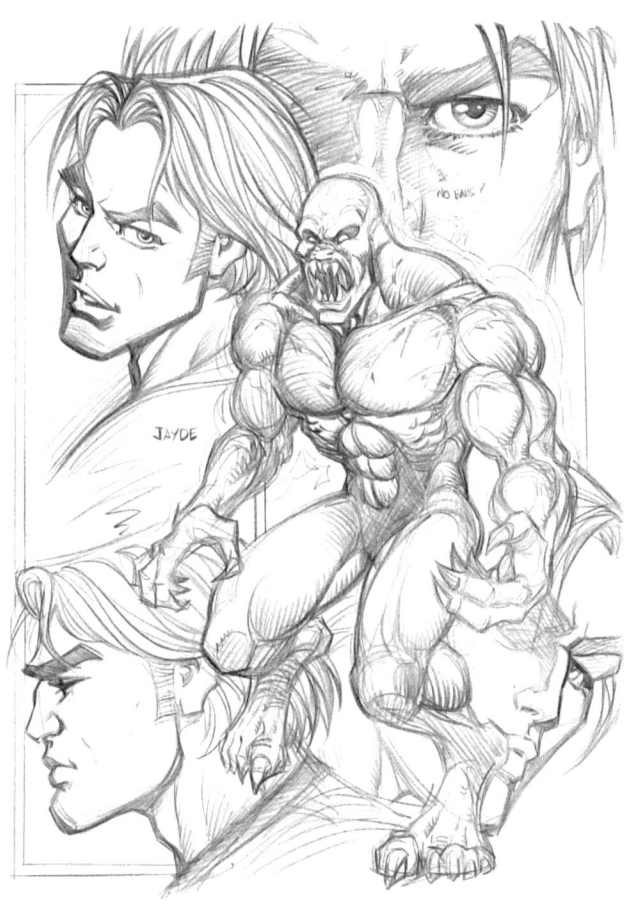

Jaydee by Alfredo Macall

X-101 by Alfredo Macall

*Stranded on Earth as a child, **Jaydee** is a Salamandrite—an artificial life form created by the mysterious Weapon-Makers of Zade. At one time manipulated by The Tarantula, a S.P.I.D.E.R. agent, he was used to serve the evil Necromancer's plans. Rescued by **Futura**, he ended up putting his metamorphic powers and superhuman strength at the service of the **Strangers**. This Parisian adventure fits between Seasons 1 and 2 of Strangers.*

Julien Heylbroeck: *A Snake in the Grass*

"Stop! This is the Empire of the Dead."
Inscription over the entrance
to the Catacombs of Paris

June 5, 02h33

Mary was there, as beautiful as ever in the little dress that outlined her delicate silhouette. Tonight, he had taken her to the movies. A romcom was playing at the theater. Jaydee did not really like sappy movies, but he knew that Mary had a good time. To celebrate the anniversary of the first time they had met, nothing was too good.

He turned up his coat collar. It was cold and drizzling. The weather was bad. Mary huddled up to him as they walked. A strong gust of wind had destroyed their umbrella. At first, Jaydee had tried to bend the ribs back, but it was no use. While he struggled with the broken umbrella, they had both gotten soaked. The useless object had ended up in the trash. Mary had suggested they continue on foot. After all, they were already wet and not too far from her home, so there was no reason to hail a cab.

On the front steps of her building, the young woman stood up on her tiptoes to kiss her sweetheart. Jaydee breathed in her intoxicating perfume and felt her wet curls brushing against his cheek. The feeling was strange… weird… rough. Icy even… Dead?

Jaydee opened his eyes and his heart skipped a beat.

Mary was there, but she was now a grinning skull. Her black eye sockets were lit up with a macabre flame. Her big smile revealed all her yellow teeth coming loose. Her hair was just a kind of muddy smear that looked like a crown of rotting algae.

Jaydee held back a scream when the grotesque skeleton approached him. The cold, sticky contact made him shudder, as if an electric shock ran through his whole body, through his nerves and muscles, paralyzing him.

The skull twisted its grin. The fragile bones shrieked like the howl of a banshee, like a high-pitched siren. Jaydee covered his ears to stop the pain that was drilling his eardrums.

Jaydee sat up abruptly. He was soaked. His clothes stuck to his skin. He was in his bed. The open window had let the spring shower pour in on him like it did on the Parisian sidewalks.

Another nightmare.

Mary Stone again.

The girl, more real than in reality, was haunting his nights. How could he think about grieving when the love of his life was nothing but a mirage created by a secret criminal organization?

They had done a good job—implanted in his memory 1001 space adventures of him saving his beloved. Jaydee still dreamed of a past life that had never been real.

His therapy was not doing much good. But what could a psychiatrist understand about the doubts and torments of a Salamandrite, a killing machine genetically created by a mighty extraterrestrial race? A creature with extraordinary strength, who had been exploited by S.P.I.D.E.R. and subjected to a virtual life in order to be enslaved?

Obviously, the young man had to watch what he said. Sometimes, feeling bratty, he would talk openly about his

worries, but the good Doctor Debornot took it all as a meta-
phor. Jaydee would smirk. These sessions usually made him
feel a little better. But it did not do much for him to mock the
psychological limits of an old shrink when the absence of a
being who maybe had never existed was tearing his soul to
pieces.

The doorbell rang. A long ring, meaning the overexcited
visitor was leaning on the button.

The door opened to reveal the shadowy figure of Agent
X-101. He came right in without waiting to be invited and
trampled the carpet with his wet shoes. He was tall with
blonde hair, and also dripping wet.

"Emerson, what's wrong with you? We agreed before
your training. Weren't you supposed to be able to control
yourself? Or did the C.L.A.S.H. scientists in Aspen botch it?"

"Agent X-101, I don't like the way you're talking to me.
Don't make me angry, it's a *very* bad idea. Can I know why
you came over here to see me in the middle of the night?"

Jaydee put on a black sweatshirt and sweatpants.

X-101 was dressed in his usual black "street wear" uniform; he started pacing. As Jaydee was temporarily staying in
a small one-bedroom apartment in the 13th arrondissement of
Paris, he soon reached the opposite wall and marched back
and forth.

"A body's been found in the metro, Arsenal Station.
DNA was lifted from the corpse. The analysis just came back.
They think their sample was contaminated by a bacteria or
something. In fact, it was perfectly fine. But the DNA isn't
human. We immediately sent the data to C.L.A.S.H. Take a
guess, kid. It was your own DNA. A pure blood drop from a
Salamandrite."

Jaydee was shocked. This was serious business. Of
course, he had not killed anyone. But what was his DNA doing at the scene of a crime?

"You know very well it wasn't me," he said. "First, I'm
monitored 24/7. Also, I'm no killer. In the past, when I wasn't

in control of myself, I did kill some C.L.A.S.H. agents on Space Station Samael and caused a lot of damage, but I'm no murderer! Anyway, I'm in control now."

"I know. But Mr. Song is not as forgiving as I am. We have 48 hours to solve this mystery, or they'll be coming for you."

X-101 turned to leave the apartment. He had said what needed to be said. Jaydee would have to investigate this by himself. The agent could not do more than he already had done. The young man let him leave without saying good-bye.

June 5, 08h46

Jaydee was ready. Newly shaved, dressed in combat pants and a hoodie, he presented his press card at the welcome desk of the Institute of Forensic Medicine. He was met by the institute's communications officer. Despite his best efforts, however, he could not get access to the corpse, only learn that the victim was an African in his early twenties, unidentified, probably an illegal immigrant because he was dressed in rags and his health was poor. He must have been living on the streets for a while.

The body had been found utterly wrecked, limbs broken, skull fractured. The work of a savage endowed with great strength. Jaydee had wheedled these last details out of a young female technician he had bumped into in the hallway.

The newspapers had covered the murders, especially the free papers handed out at bus stops and subway stations. The press was already talking about the "Metro Killer" who attacked the homeless.

June 5, 22h12

Jaydee took the metro to Bastille. Arsenal was an unused station located between Bastille and Quai de la Rapée. After a quick glance, he climbed down the few steps at the end of the platform. Soon he was in darkness, walking along the rails next to cables covered in filth. He heard a train screeching by in a nearby tunnel and the unpleasant sound echoed through the tunnels. A few rats scurried by him, oblivious of his presence. After a few minutes, he arrived at the abandoned station.

At this late hour, the police had pulled out their surveillance so there was nobody on the platform. Jaydee ducked under the tape cordoning off the crime scene and examined the ground. The body had been taken away, but the gruesome bloodstains were still there to remind him that a murder of unimaginable barbarity had taken place on this very spot a short while ago. And they were everywhere. Jaydee's flashlight could not cover them all. A chalk outline delineated the place where the human remains had been; little numbered yellow signs studded the platform.

The young man put one knee on the ground, feeling a little sick. His flashlight rolled away, lighting up the end of the deserted platform. He had no unusual memory of the night before. He remembered going to bed, falling asleep after reading a Schildiner novel and waking up to go to the gym. No nightmares, even though he dreamed almost every night of Mary. Could he have done this? Could he have ripped apart a poor innocent man for no reason, like some wild, monstrous sleepwalker? Wouldn't he have some snatches of memory, snapshots of horror, rising up out of his tampered memory like bubbles of lucidity?

Jaydee choked back a sob, almost a hiccup of sorrow, before pulling himself together. No! Even during his most frightening fits, he had never attacked a human like this. Of course, there had been people hurt. Seriously hurt and even sometimes fatally. And a lot of property damage. But even as a Salamandrite, Jaydee was not a bloodthirsty monster who tossed around human bodies like a lunatic.

While he was gathering his thoughts, making up his mind to follow through the investigation to the bitter end, he noticed a weird mark in the beam of his flashlight. The station had been left abandoned at the beginning of WWII. Except for a few adventurous souls and some homeless people, nobody set foot on it. Nobody waited for trains that had stopped coming for more than fifty years. The recent discovery had brought in a fair share of police trampling, but when one stepped back a little, there was still a layer of dust, thick and black.

Except at the entrance of a small service tunnel.

Jaydee went over to it. There were footprints, but not ordinary prints. These prints were not human. Big paws with claws had left a mark. Jaydee could not help thinking that they looked like his own feet when he was in his "natural" shape.

He went to pick up his flashlight, crouched down, and entered the small tunnel. He had to bend over because the ceiling was only four feet high. Soon, he stumbled upon a little trapdoor, like a manhole cover. He held his flashlight between his teeth and grabbed the cover with both hands. It was hard to lift. It unleashed a horde of cockroaches that scurried every which way, reflecting the light off their shiny backs before vanishing into the surrounding shadows. Then a nauseous stench filled the space, turning Jaydee's stomach.

A metal ladder descended into the darkness. It was not long. On one of the rungs, Jaydee's hand touched a sticky, dark green substance.

Salamandrite blood.

Was it possible that another creature like him existed? If he had been created by the mysterious Weapon-Makers of Zade, was he just one in a series, like a cheap car? How many others like him were there?

All these ideas bounced around inside his head as he began to dread the outcome of his investigation. Whether it was him, or a twin of his, he was going to learn more about his past. But at what price? Again he pictured the blood-stained platform of the Arsenal station.

He reached the bottom. Before him was a tunnel with walls made of brick. There was total silence, except for the disgusting sucking sound that he made with every step. The ground was, in fact, a wet, reeking layer of mud. Water from the nearby Seine was seeping in everywhere, trickling down the brick walls and leaving black streaks.

He ended up in a vast quarry. Several alcoves dug out with pickaxes told him that he was in an old limestone mine dating back to the time of Louis XIV. The huge cavity had a high ceiling supported by pillars, some man-made, others natural.

The young man also noticed big, steel barrels and silos. No doubt these quarries had been recycled into underground breweries in the 19th century. It all looked long abandoned. Jaydee ran his hand over one of the old barley silos covered with dust and his fingers left a long trail on the gigantic vat.

A little further, the traces of the creature were still visible. It had snaked its way between the metal structures, skirted around some collapsed spiral stairs that must have once led up to the surface, perhaps the cellar of a bar. The footprints ended up disappearing on the gravel covering a tangle of railway tracks. The rails crisscrossed in pairs; everything was rusted. No, not everything...

Jaydee leaned over. One series of tracks looked fresh. The top of the rails was clear of rust. The Salamandrite started following them. He went past trolley cars lying on their side, the little offices of foremen long since forgotten. Inside one of them was an old clock forever frozen at 4:45 p.m.

The railway ended up splitting away from the main line, as if it was trying to get away, to be alone, abruptly turning to the left whereas the other tracks continued on toward a garage or disappeared into dark tunnels.

Jaydee entered the huge space. The walls were concrete, much more recent than the damp bricks elsewhere. The ground was also concrete, almost new and well maintained. He saw a switch and long neon lights attached to the ceiling. Everything seemed to point to a recent installation. The corridor led to a thick, reinforced door, cracked open. The tracks ended right next to it. A few newer cars were parked there, marked with a capital F.

Jaydee squatted and put his flashlight down. He thought it might be a better idea to shift to his natural shape before exploring further. He threw off his sweatshirt and kicked off his shoes, put one knee on the ground and supported himself with his right hand. Then he started concentrating. He felt his blood beating against his temples. As if it was getting thicker, it forced its way through his veins, giving him a terrible headache. Then his muscles were affected. He knew that his blood was turning green and syrupy, spreading his Salamandrite genetic agents throughout his body, overloading his synapses with their powers. He held back a shriek of pain when his heart started beating so fast, so hard, that he thought it was going to burst open his ribcage.

A moment later, he was himself. His artificial human form had disappeared, just like the bottom of his pants, ripped off at the knees and lying on the ground. The most dangerous killing machine in the universe flexed his muscles under his dark green skin. His massive form was almost ten feet tall. His spine, bristling with pointy bones, stood out in the beam of the flashlight still lying on the ground, creating a terrifying shadow. Jaydee looked at it, but left it there. His red, glowing eyes gave him perfect night vision. He threw his shoulder against the door and crashed through. Subtlety was not his strong point. As a Salamandrite, he felt powerful. So powerful! Immortal!

The creature who was living there jumped up when the door hit a rolling cart, which fell over spilling tools and glass jars on the tiled floor. The creature turned and saw Jaydee. It was green, too, the same color as Salamandrites. Smaller than Jaydee, it was still a good seven and half feet tall. Hunchbacked and with a weird, elongated head, its oversized skull throbbed to the rhythm of its heartbeat. Its heart was located in the middle of a weird chest, an exterior ribcage like a thick exoskeleton. It growled, showing its sharp, eel-like teeth and ran towards Jaydee.

The Salamandrite did not wait for the warped creature to reach him. He had time to note that it was a long room with a white floor, equipped with four lab benches and four big cylindrical vats, almost as tall as him. One of them was broken.

He turned around and tore the door off its hinges to throw it at his adversary. It bounced off the ground two times, tearing up the tiles and leaving a deep furrow in the floor before hitting the creature who let loose a short cry of surprise.

Jaydee jumped on top of the door, giving a little more weight to the one-ton impact. With a furious roar and a sweep of its arm, the creature broke free and grabbed Jaydee's ankle. It spun around, trying to toss its enemy against the wall, but he managed to kick free.

Then Jaydee grabbed the creature by the throat and lifted it up. It tried to bite him with its mouth, foaming with rage. Its small, crimson eyes glowed with unimaginable spite. It brought its legs up and kicked both its feet into Jaydee's chest, sending him flying back against the wall and allowing itself to jump away. Jaydee sunk almost a foot deep into the cement and plaster that exploded on impact.

The hunchback was already picking up one of the huge, glass vats. Tearing it off the ground with a geyser of sparks, it threw it at Jaydee who was still catching his breath. But the young man managed to get out of the way. The glass shattered against the wall and sent shards flying everywhere. The Salamandrite took a good look at the deformed creature. It was panting, its muscles quivering in anticipation of the battle. Of the slaughter of its enemy.

Jaydee ran at his adversary, dealing it a series of blows that threw it off balance and knocked it to the ground. He kept at it, driving the creature into the tile and concrete. The hunchbacked monster jumped up and bit Jaydee's upper arm. The jaws broke through the flesh and green blood started seeping out of the wound. But Jaydee paid it no attention. He grabbed a radiator, ripped it off the wall, and smashed it over the hunchback's head.

The creature was stunned for a moment, allowing the Salamandrite to grab it, lift it up and let its spine drop on his knee. There was a loud crack followed by a painful groan

149

from Jaydee because one of the bony spikes of the monster had stuck him in the thigh, tearing his muscle. A little blood was trickling out of the creature's mouth as it lay face down.

Jaydee stood up slowly and painfully, and used all the energy he could muster to get back into human form so he could fashion himself a tourniquet.

June 6, 11h17

X-101 watched him with a strained smile. Jaydee limped up to the counter and ordered a coffee with cream. The waiter, holding his ever-present dishtowel, nodded and started making it. The spluttering coffee machine echoed through the café.

"I have something for you," Jaydee told him.

When he sat on the stool he grimaced in pain. His right arm was bandaged from shoulder to elbow.

"Me too," the agent replied sipping his sparkling water. "Believe it or not, we found another victim. In another metro station. Not the same one. Porte d'Orléans on line 4, last night or early this morning. Probably around 1 or 2 a.m. according to the coroner. Some poor guy waiting for the last train. And guess what, in the forensic lab, they found another Salamandrite DNA sample. Mr. Song has been informed. He can tolerate one alert, but not two. I expected them to, er, contact you very soon."

Jaydee said nothing for a minute, then, lowering his voice and leaning closer to X-101, he said:

"Last night, I was at the Arsenal station. And I found something very interesting too," "I fought with a Salamandrite, but one that was all deformed and less powerful than me. SI killed it, but I didn't come out unscathed. The thing is, what you said means that there is at least another one like it in Paris."

"Hold on! Are you trying to tell me that there are other Salamandrites with the same genetic code as you running around the Paris metro? Do you have many psychopathic twins that you haven't told me about?"

Jaydee did not smile at the agent's dark humor.

"Believe it or not, it was no walk in the park. Spare me your twisted sense of humor! *My* Salamandrite was hiding out in a weird lab inside an old, abandoned brewery. I found huge empty vats and a whole set-up for research, but everything was clean as a whistle…"

Then he took a manila envelope out of his pocket and slid it over. It contained two small test tubes.

"I brought you this. It's a little sample taken off the body and some drops that I picked up off the bottom of one of the vats. Could you get it analyzed for me?"

X-101 slipped it inside his black coat.

"Of course! But I must tell you, I'm worried, Jaydee. I got a glimpse of your power when I tried to stop you before. For Christ's sake, you almost destroyed an entire block that day! Knowing there's another you haunting the metro and killing people is no comfort. My bosses in Brussels aren't going to be happy. C.L.A.S.H. is going to go bonkers. I'll have to bring in the Guardian of the Republic, The Lion, Black Lys, the Ace Brigade, and who knows what else… Not to mention that we know nothing about these 'clones' of yours. Where do they come from? How many are there? Who made them? What the hell was that one doing in an abandoned underground lab?"

"I think it escaped. I saw four big vats. One of them was broken. What if the twisted Salamandrite got out and the scientists who made it evacuated the place in a hurry?"

"That's possible. And if another of these monsters is still at large, we have to capture it and learn more about these creatures asap. I'll contact you as soon as I get the results of your samples. Don't take any unnecessary risks, but work fast. I think Paris is going to get very busy very soon."

June 6, 14h31

Jaydee took out a fake police ID he had bought from a street vendor in Barbès. It fooled people for a few seconds. In

151

fact, its success depended on his poise, and on his ability to exude authority and pass for a young detective. The young man with slanted eyes and a shaved head nodded.

"I'll play it for you, Inspector."

"Not Inspector but Lieutenant, but thanks."

The Metro employee fiddled with the controls while the screens lit up with life in reverse on the south platform of Porte d'Orléans station. The shapes were busy walking backward like ants in a panic while the trains sped by, one after the other, in reverse. The people bustled around, scurrying on and off the trains.

While he was looking for the exact time the young Asian said, "But I already showed this to one of your colleagues. A Lieutenant Bouchard. Are you working with him?"

"He's in a different squad, but yes, we are working together."

The young man slowed down the recording. "We're pretty close now. Look at the time. 00:37. Almost the last train. You know, I also showed this to another guy, a big man, not too friendly, barely fit in his suit. He didn't want to tell me his name, but he showed me a government ID. Interpol, I think. He said he belonged to the Ace Brigade."

Jaydee felt his blood freeze. Everyone was already on the trail—ahead of him even. He was going to have to be very careful.

"That guy, when was he here?"

"Barely an hour ago. Probably be better if you just made a copy of this. You'd have to see my boss, though, because you know, me, I'm supposed to be watching the seven other screens." He made a vague gesture toward the other monitors in the room. "Looking for suspicious packages, terrorists, pickpockets or potential suicides, you know. I've got better things to do than play this same video over and over again for you guys. Anyway, like the others you're going to be disappointed. There's not much to see."

"Don't worry, I think I'm the last."

"Here it is. Watch carefully, it happens fast. I'll go in slow motion if you want."

Jaydee focused. Life on the screen was back to normal but more slowly. The platform was almost empty. You could guess a train was passing by on the other side because some litter was lifted off the ground by a gust of wind and blown a few feet away. You could see a bum sitting on a pile of cardboard. He was nodding his head as if listening to music.

On the other end of the platform, near the little stairs leading down onto the track, a lanky young man dressed in jeans and a shirt was listening to music through headphones. The train arrived. As it sped by, Jaydee saw a huge arm reach out and grab the poor guy's ankle. He fell to the ground. A huge shadow loomed over him, then quickly vanished with its victim into the darkness while the train slowed down. The back doors opened up and a young woman stepped out almost tripping over the young man's cap, which had been left behind after the abduction. There was no other trace of its owner. He had disappeared from the platform and from the screens in a flash.

"Maintenance workers found him… or what was left of him at 5 a.m. Seems he was all in pieces. What do you think? A lunatic? Did you see that arm? Huge muscles and a weird color."

"It's the cheap monitor, it distorts the light spectrum. Thanks for your help, Mr. Wu."

Coming out of the closet that served as an office for the Metro agent, Jaydee had a moment's hesitation. His spine was tingling; he had a bad feeling about this. Even in human form, he still had his Salamandrite instincts.

Behind a small group of Japanese tourists, a man was watching him strangely. It took Jaydee only a second to identify him and two others as Ace Brigade agents. They were waiting for him. Two agents were on his side, and one on the other platform. That one was just opening a sports bag and taking out a large gun. The passengers next to him panicked and started running away.

In the mad scramble a young lady let go of the hand of her little boy. The child was knocked over by a fat man who was pushing and shoving his way toward the exit. The boy fell onto the tracks. A train was arriving and heading straight for the body lying on the rails, starting to brake, but obviously too late. It was going to run over the child in a matter of seconds.

Jaydee did not hesitate. He jumped down onto the tracks and bent over to shield the boy with his body. He had only ten seconds to transform. It was not enough time and the train was going to crush them both.

He closed his eyes, ready to suffer the fatal impact.

The train hit him head on with a noise like thunder, surrounding him with tons of steel and other metals. The shock bore into his back shooting pain through every nerve in his body. An excruciating pain, like someone had broken his back. But he held fast. He had transformed. He had never done it so quickly before!

Behind him, the cars were piling up, smashing into each other like dominoes in a shower of sparks and cries of horror. The weight on Jaydee's shoulders also piled up as the cars = squeezed together.

Jaydee howled in pain and rage. He sprang up, creating an opening in the metal wreckage like a blossoming flower. Grabbing a huge piece of metal debris, he swung it around to clear out a space, then threw it as hard as he could at the agent responsible for the panic that had almost killed an innocent child. The man vanished behind the hunk of metal and sunk a foot deep into the wall, which sent white tiles flying all over. He did not even have time to scream.

The child had fainted. Jaydee picked him up gently and laid him on the platform. On seeing her son in the arms of the giant Salamandrite with drooling fangs, his mother fainted.

That was when one of the Ace Brigade agents decided to take his shot. It was a stun grenade. Jaydee caught it a split second before it hit him. He crushed it in his fist, tore it in half with his fangs, and swallowed it before throwing the other half on the ground with a savage grin on his face.

He leaped at the agent. His feet dug size-30 furrows in the platform when he landed. The guy had damn good reflexes, as was to be expected from one of Commissioner Pax's men. He elbowed the creature hard and spun to the side to be next to him. He threw a punch boosted by some sort of electric brass knuckles. The shock ran through the Salamandrite's body as he roared in pain. Jaydee tried to grab the agent but again the man spun away.

In the meantime, his partner had come over and was targeting the bloodied back of the Salamandrite with his tranquilizer gun. Jaydee's almost supernatural instinct worked again and he dropped to the ground. The syringe pierced the throat of the agent who had just hit him. He fell down foaming at the mouth and, after a couple of spasms, stopped moving for good.

Jaydee turned around, which made a few drops of green blood go flying off his wounded back. The agent wasted no time. He pulled out his big pistol equipped with a laser scope. This one was not loaded with syringes but with ammunition specially designed to bore a devastating hole through the flesh of giant monsters.

Jaydee ripped off a train door and used it as a shield to rush at the agent as he fired. Every bullet left a huge dent in the metal, some almost drilling through, but the door held fast.

When he got close to the agent, he threw his improvised shield straight at him. He dodged the door, which crashed into the screens at the front of the platform used by the drivers to see that everyone had boarded, but lost his weapon in the process. He put on his electric brass knuckles and took an agile stance that allowed him to dodge the massive attacks of the monster who got angry, growling and foaming, trying to swat the quick little mosquito who refused to let himself get caught. His fists left their marks of destruction in the ground, shattered the walls, gouged the bent metal of the wrecked train. The man stayed just out of Jaydee's reach while shooting electric arcs that sizzled and burned the Salamandrite's shin. When one of the discharges hit his back, scorching the exposed flesh,

Jaydee let loose a howl of rage that shattered the few windows that were still intact on the train. He jumped onto the tracks and tore out a rail about ten feet-long. He swung his weapon right and left like a huge sword of twisted metal. The agent was not prepared for this and thrown off balance. On the third charge he went down, hit on the right side and folding up like a ragdoll. He went sliding down the platform unconscious until he crashed into a bench that broke to pieces. Jaydee wasted no time. He waved back the passengers still stuck in the train and tore off the blocked doors so they could leave. Being cautious, if not terrorized, most of them did not budge. The Salamandrite smiled, grunted and then fled down a tunnel.

June 6, 23h18

In the bathroom of a hotel in the 14th arrondissement Jaydee, now back in human form, saw to his wounds. His back was covered in a huge bruise and the swelling was just starting to go down. He could barely turn without a shooting pain torturing his ribs. His knuckles also hurt. But he knew that he would recover unnaturally fast. His metabolism would heal his bruised flesh during his sleep so he closed the curtains to get a few hours of restful slumber. He would make sure to contact X-101 from a phone booth since he had thrown away his cell phone. The TV attached to the wall across from the bed was reeling off the news. Jaydee perked up when he heard his name.

"*...don't know where the fugitive being sought by the police is at present. I repeat, his name is John Douglas Emerson, an American citizen in his early twenties. Suspected of a double murder in the metro, he is also involved in the tragic accident that took place at Porte d'Orléans. That accident claimed three victims, including a conductor. The suspect is extremely dangerous so it is strongly advised not to approach him...*"

Jaydee saw a sketch of himself in the upper right hand corner of the screen with a phone number to contact.

"*...And now on to sports. The PSG lost again yesterday in their match against...*"

Jaydee turned off the TV by slamming his finger on the remote control. He thought he would have trouble getting to sleep but he still lay down and closed his eyes. To distract his mind and avoid dreaming he put on his headphones and fell asleep to the disembodied voice of Gary Numan wailing and begging that we listen to him:

You are not the plan
And you're beginning to annoy
You are just a game and It has won
You will never see
The places promised by your faith
You will never know eternal peace. »

Jayde was fast asleep before the end of the first song.

June 7, 06h47

It was raining again. Big drops hit his face as if they were trying to get into his mouth and nose and eyes. In fact, it was the strong wind that was driving the rain into his face like fistfuls of sand. Jaydee looked around. He was on a railway track in a kind of ravine, but a ravine dug out by man. He looked up and saw the trees and bushes whose foliage stuck out of the big ditch he was in. It must have been sixty or seventy feet deep. A voice came from behind him.

"Well, you foul monster, are you coming or do you want to feel the bite of my electric whip again?"

It was a woman's voice, very authoritative and self-confident. He was much bigger than her because he was in his natural form, but nevertheless, he felt he scared. Jaydee saw only her shadow in the half-light. She moved her arm and a stinging pain lashed his chest. He screamed.

Jaydee opened his eyes when someone banged against his door. He heard a woman giggle and footsteps faded away toward the elevator. He was still in the hotel. That dream was really strange. Like it wasn't his. It was as if he was there in someone else's body. Could there be a link between him and the creatures whose DNA he shared? A common mind, like in a hive? It had never happened to him before.

He got dressed quickly. Black jeans, sneakers, a shirt and a leather jacket. He had stolen someone's suitcase when he was running out of the metro. With the money he had found inside, he had bought a cap and a phone card.

Outside, he found a phone booth and dialed the number X-101 had given him. The Agent picked up on the first ring like he had been waiting for the call.

"It's me, Jaydee. I had big problems in the metro. I... I'm sorry, I didn't mean to kill those humans. They... They... made me. This little boy fell onto the tracks..."

The agent cut him off, "I saw the video. They followed none of our procedures and put all the passengers in danger. They deserved what they got and, as much as I respect my colleagues, they died because they acted like complete idiots. You saved that child."

"Three people died."

"Could you have let that kid get run over without doing anything? I think not. Don't feel so guilty about it. But do what you can to stop these murders and clear your name as soon as possible. I have the results of your samples. The creature has exactly the same DNA as you. It's your clone, Jaydee. No doubt about it now. The DNA matches that of the sample taken Porte d'Orléans. As for the liquid in the test tube, it's a nutrient bath for accelerated growth. They're using it to make living organisms grow more quickly. It's a derivative of what we give farmed fish or chickens, but concentrated in unbelievably strong doses and adapted to the physiology and metabolism of Salamandrites."

"I have one more question. After that, I'll hang up, just to be careful. A train track in a kind of ravine around sixty or seventy feet deep with trees up above. Does that mean anything to you?"

"Let me think. *La Petite Ceinture?* It's an old track that ran around the outside of Paris. It was opened in the second half of the 19th century and carried passengers until the 1930s. What you described could be the section that goes through Parc Montsouris in the 14th. But I can't guarantee it. I haven't been there for a while."

"Thanks. When this is all over, I'll buy you drink. I'll never forget your help."

"It's nothing, Jaydee. I know you're not a bloodthirsty brute. But work fast. Your wanted poster is plastered all over the place and your sketch is running constantly on the news."

June 7, 18h54

Jaydee walked down the path along the big pond where the ducks were swimming. The visitors had almost all left the park by now except for a few joggers who went panting by him with their headphones on and an IPhone or water bottle in their hand. The sunny day had given way to the cool evening.

The young man found the trench in no time. It cut through the park very stealthily, camouflaged by bushes. Down below were the rusty train tracks with some graffiti on the walls. Weeds and wild grass had sprouted from the rocky ground.

The metamorph found a small ladder protected by a kind of circular cage. He made sure that no one was watching, climbed over the fence, and hurried down to the tracks.

It was just like in his dream.

He moved by instinct trying to locate the exact spot where he had seen the woman's shadow whipping him. He noticed a door leading to a tunnel with a big F spray painted on it. Jaydee made the connection to the carts in the abandoned lab. They were marked with the same letter. The door was locked. He took the lock picks out of his pocket. Not that he was used to breaking and entering, but as a journalist he often had to get into forbidden places.

The lock did not resist.

The door opened onto pitch black darkness. Jaydee turned on his flashlight. A corridor stretched out away from the tracks and further under the park.

He entered and closed the door behind him out of habit. Then he started to get undressed. He folded his clothes neatly and left them at the entrance, wearing only his pants, which were much too big for him and had to be held up by a belt—which he took off. He got down on one knee, bent over, his right hand against the wall, and concentrated. The pain shot through his head and a moment later his bulging muscles had tripled in size. He was free once again to move in his natural form.

Well, natural... He knew that he was a genetically created monster. He still did not know for what purpose, for which war he had been designed to fight. Probably not to stroll around the Paris underground looking for his twisted duplicates.

Jaydee had a wicked little smile on his face, which let his thumb-sized canines peek out. He growled deeply like a dog about to get his bone stolen, slowly being filled with rage. Remembering Miss Kiss' lessons in Aspen, he tried to clear his mind, to replace the rage with a red screen, smooth and blank, on which he could picture his targets. It was the only way to control the beast within.

He dropped the flashlight and followed the corridor as silently as a prowling cat. His huge body in the darkness sometimes scraped against the walls because the space was narrowing. Then he came to a stairwell. The wall was covered with an art deco mosaic. It was colder. The Salamandrite went up the stairs as quietly as his big feet allowed. He came out in a big room the size of the nave of Notre-Dame, but all lengthwise. He felt like he had entered the hold of a giant ocean liner.

Two huge tanks stretched out, covered with pipes and red and yellow spigots with pressure gauges. Jaydee had no idea what kind of place he was in.

Seeing a poster on the wall, he went over to read it. It was an evacuation map of the Montsouris Reservoir. A reservoir that contained drinking water for the Parisians of the left bank.

There was no one around. Just a few drops of water falling on the floor, disturbed the silence that enshrouded the Salamandrite like a cloak.

Jaydee was exploring again when he heard footsteps. An experienced undercover agent would have hidden himself to see who it was. But not Jaydee. He roared fiercely and ran toward the noise. He headed down a corridor where he glimpsed a shape disappearing around a corner. A huge, green shape. His clone!

He ran as fast as possible to catch it. He had to avoid seven human bodies lying twisted on the ground. Probably the unfortunate personnel of the reservoir. The creature was running unbelievably fast, but Jayde was keeping up. It apparently wanted to go beneath the reservoir into the deep underground.

Once down there, Jaydee spotted a kind of metal girder. He jumped, grabbed it and swung with all his might to launch himself at the creature. He landed hard on his enemy and knocked its breath out. The two of them rolled on the ground into a small forklift which the combined weight of their bodies smashed to pieces. Jaydee jumped to his feet, tore off one of the loose forks and abruptly impaled the clone's chest, pinning it to the ground. The deformed creature spit out a little green blood before curling up around its wound, dead.

Jaydee heard a laugh. A woman's laugh. Like in his dream. It came from a very beautiful woman in her thirties with long, blonde hair. She was perched on a big, metal balcony with a massive shadow behind her.

"There you are at last, Jaydee! You took your time. But what's this, I see? You killed your brother?"

Jaydee growled in a deep voice, "That was not my brother. Who are you and what do you want?"

"Why, of course, where are my manners? I am… Let's just say, you can call me Alpha. I lead Phantom, an organization specialized in genetic engineering and its practical applications."

"What do you want with me? How did you manage to create these creatures?"

The pretty woman had a crystal-clear laugh. "So many questions! They're not monsters, they're your brothers. Your genetic brothers. They've got exactly the same genome as you, or almost. Because my samples were rather poor. That was the Necromancer's fault. When he disappeared, his HQ was evacuated, but I managed to get a hold of what I needed from the Tarantula's lab…"

Jaydee took a step forward, baring his fangs and growling. Rage ran through his blood, filling up every cell, infusing it with his energy.

"Yes, The Tarantula. She who manipulated you for S.P.I.D.E.R. She had taken several blood samples from you. Samples that I cultivated to birth to your brothers. But some of the genetic codes had been partially lost. Look at them, the poor things, all twisted. Morons. So weak. Much weaker than you. I created four of them. One died right away, a little green runt. Another escaped, and you ran into him. Another obeyed me well, but you just killed him too, pinned there like some butterfly. As for the last, I grew it myself, trying to improve it in some way…"

She snapped her fingers.

And a huge, bright red creature stepped forth. It was almost a Salamandrite, but more like a caricature of one. Where the others had embodied power, speed and endurance, this one embodied brute force, just brute force and nothing else. Its arms were the size of Jaydee's thighs and lined with swollen veins. A device wrapped around his chest and shoulders injected doses of neon green liquid at regular intervals. The monster's head was disproportionately large, like its brain was swollen, pushing out of the skull, which was reinforced with steel straps. Like a gorilla, its arms were longer than its legs and stood hunched over on all four. Every other drooling fang was replaced by steel spikes. Pain and suffering could be seen in its mismatched eyes, one red, the other green. Pain and suffering, and terrible hatred. Towards everyone or almost. Towards the world. Towards its own existence. Jaydee felt that only the fear of excruciating pain kept it from attacking the woman and devouring her in seconds.

Alpha seemed to be reading Jaydee's thoughts, "Yes, you can read his mind, can't you? A kind of link between you has been created, but I don't know how. I have, however, used it to my advantage. I brought you here, implanted that stupid dream in the memory of this idiot," she sneered at the huge monster. "You're the ingredient I lack. The missing piece of the genetic puzzle that will allow me, firstly, to finish my genome of a perfect clone. Then, with a little spice added to my little recipe, I'll pour it into Paris' water supply. A kind of viral strain of my personal vintage that will contaminate the inhabitants, making them half-human, half-Salamandrite. Thus I will have the most beautiful and the most powerful army in the world. The governments of men will be swept away and Phantom will at last rule the world!"

Jaydee understood now that the trap he had fallen into was closing in around him. He had to find a way out without wiping Paris off the map. He tried to strike first by attacking the woman. From his standing position, he jumped at the balcony. Alpha shrieked in surprise, but did not lose control of herself. She let go of the monster's bridle and ordered it to attack.

The red creature raised its arms and roared, full of as much pain and fear as of fury. Its fists, like rocks, slammed into Jaydee and sent him straight back to the ground where he sank more than a foot deep. A moment later, the mutant was in the air over him. Jaydee rolled away and was up trying to kick the legs out from under the creature. Then he rammed into it with his shoulder, trying to knock it off balance, which worked. The creature dropped like a felled oak tree.

The impact of the fall shook the foundations of the room. The Salamandrite immediately jumped on the aberration and delivered a flurry of punches, breaking off a few pieces of the harness. He grabbed some injectors and tossed them aside. He was hoping that it would weaken the monster. But it did not stop it from knocking Jaydee off with the back of his hand. He crashed into a tank, leaving the imprint of his body in the metal. The monster tried to crush his skull with its powerful fist, but Jaydee ducked just in time. The fist went right through the tank and a gush of boiling water poured out of the opening. The monster's arm was stuck.

Jaydee picked up the remains of the forklift and ran at the monster, aiming for its belly. Like a charging knight with a makeshift lance, he skewered the creature. The fork went through the body and stuck in the tank. With its free hand, the monster wrapped its fingers around Jaydee's skull and squeezed. The Salamandrite struggled to break free, straining his muscles to loosen the grip of the freak show attraction. It finally pulled its arm out of the metal and, without letting go of Jaydee, pulled the giant skewer out of its belly. At the same time, it brought its grotesque face up to Jaydee's and roared loudly, which dazed his intended victim for a split second.

The pressure on Jaydee's head was unbearable. He felt like his skull was cracking and would burst like an egg any second now. Which would happen if he did not do something quickly. In a surge of anger, he pulled himself closer to the monster. Taken by surprise, before it could bend its arm, the grip loosened. Jaydee threw his shoulder into the monster's chest and got free. He then grabbed the creature, lifted it up and threw it at the next tank.

The monster crashed through like it was made of rice paper. Water came rushing out of it and almost swept Jaydee off his feet. It rose quickly up the level of his knees and was getting higher. He looked up. Alpha had vanished.

She must be watching the battle from a secure position, ready to get her sample or to flee depending on the outcome, Jaydee thought.

The creature came out of the tank. Its harness was completely destroyed, hanging off of it by broken straps and twisted metal rods. Its massive chest pulsed in rhythm with its erratic and irregular breathing. It howled out its suffering once again. And Jaydee understood. His deformed brother was yearning for death. He nodded and ran at him. The monster let him grab its throat. Jaydee pulled it close and sunk his fangs in. His mouth was filled with thick, acidic blood, which he spit out. The creature dropped to its knees. It was the same height now as the metamorph. They looked into each other's eyes and the Salamandrite saw in those already dying eyes a glimmer of thanks. Then the monster fell face down into the water.

June 8, 15h48

Alpha had not stuck around for the final results. The Ace Brigade had cordoned off the area and stopped the leak, which had flooded a lot of basements and even the ground floors of surrounding buildings. X-101 was there, too. Jaydee told him everything. Obviously the authorities were ending their pursuit of Jaydee, but he would have to explain the confrontation at the Porte d'Orléans station. X-101 assured him that it would be fine and that Commissioner Pax was already aware of why Jaydee had caused the accident and fought his agents.

Later, sitting at a round table in a bistrot with two glasses of beer Jaydee and X-101 were enjoying the early summer sun.

"If you hadn't destroyed that train, the platform and two reservoir tanks, I'd say you did a great job." X-101 said, giving him a big smile.

"I want to remain a journalist, if they'll let me. This kind of investigation is not really for me. I'd rather stick to interviewing politicians."

"At any rate, given the amount of damage, I think that C.L.A.S.H. will have to increase its insurance premiums!"

He laughed loudly but Jaydee kept looking gravely at him.

"That weird woman disappeared. I don't know who she was, but her plan was really scary."

"Don't worry, if she ever resurfaces, we'll be there. And in spite of everything, if you agree, I'll still call on you in the future."

"After seeing what she did to my 'brothers,' you can rest assured that I'll answer that call."

Jaydee shook X-101's hand. He was determined to avenge the pain and suffering that he had seen in the eyes of those poor creatures. The ground trembled a little. A metro train had passed right under the café.

X-101 by Franco Paludetti

Homicron I by J.-J. Dzialowski

An energy being from far off planet Alpha, an advanced civili-
*zation of space explorers, **Homicron** fused with the body of*
astronaut Ted White, transforming him into a superhero with
incredible energy powers, Homicron protected the Earth from
the invading Kyrosians, Alpha's warlike foes, who eventually
succeeded in killing him. His successor, who is none other
than Rita Tower, a NASA physicist and Ted's fiancée, eventu-
*ally became a member of the **Strangers**. This adventure takes*
place between the classic 1970s series and the return of char-
acter in 2001.

Romain d'Huissier: *The Aborted Sun*

It was a pleasant, early spring evening at Cape Kennedy.

A car was parked not far from the small house, cloaked
in darkness at the end of the alley. A man got out, dressed casually, tall and walking like a member of the military. It was
astronaut Ted White, one of the best men at NASA. He headed
for the house and went through the gate on which a nameplate
identified the occupant: Professor Herman Jurewitz. Once in
the yard, White's gait turned stealthier, not trying to hide, but
approaching the door in a slower, more cautious pace. He saw
that the lock had been broken. Or rather melted, the target of
extreme, localized heat. Swearing to himself, White burst in
and was not surprised to find the inside a total mess.

Professor Herman Jurewitz was the kind of eccentric scientist who sometimes attended conferences at various univer-
sities. An expert in astrophysics, he regularly collaborated
with Rita Tower, Ted's beautiful fiancée, one of his fervent
disciples. She was the one who had told the astronaut of the
Professor's unusual silence over the past two days—
uncharacteristic of his usual hyperactive nature. General
Heartland, the Cape's commanding officer, would soon worry
about Jurewitz, so Ted had taken it upon himself to do a little
investigating, spurred on by a sense of dark foreboding.

Once again, his instinct was proven right. He quickly explored the scientist's modest dwelling and found the same chaos in every room. It looked as if a hasty but meticulous search had been conducted, concentrating on the professor's office: papers were scattered everywhere, file drawers had been emptied and the computer taken apart, its hard drive missing. Closing his eyes, the astronaut concentrated for a few seconds. When he opened them again, they had changed; they were now haloed by a faint aura of bluish energy.

For a few weeks now, Ted White has no longer been Ted White. The human astronaut had died after a massive heart attack and an extraterrestrial energy being has taken possession of his body. This resultant fusion of a human and an Alphan was called Homicron, had vast powers, and now protected Earth from Alpha's ancient enemies, the Kyrosians, in this new identity.

Ted—we shall continue calling him by his human name—could change into Homicron thanks to a matter-to-energy converter perfected by Rita. But even in human form, he was able to use certain gifts: like seeing a broad spectrum of energy normally invisible to Earthlings.

So it was with Alphan eyes that Ted now examined the Professor's office. It didn't take him long to spot a residue of alien energy. Alien weapons had been used: first, a plasma drill to melt the lock, then a paralyzing ray to incapacitate the occupant, and finally an ionic scanner. Analyzing the energies, the astronaut was able to identify the Kyrosian origin of the devices. No doubt his ancient enemies had kidnapped the professor and taken the fruit of his labors. Maybe the Professor had made a discovery that the Kyrosians thought might give them a decisive advantage in their fight against Alpha? Whatever the case, Ted had to free the scientist—if he was still alive—and foil their plans.

Rushing out of the house, the astronaut went to his car and opened the trunk. Inside was Rita's converter. He placed both hands on it and right away, there was a silent explosion of light. When it had faded, Ted White has been replaced by Homicron!

Wearing a blue and yellow uniform with the letter H proudly displayed on his chest, the Alphan could now use his powers at full capacity—the tremendous ability to control energy in all its forms. His perception extended throughout the electromagnetic spectrum and since thought was energy, he could even penetrate the minds around him. He focused his concentration on the wavelength used by the Kyrosians. The conniving reptilians most likely used one of their gliders camouflaged as a common automobile to take the professor to a hideout somewhere. In a split second, Homicron identified and isolated the trace energies left behind by their engine. He rose into the air by gathering a layer gravitons and shot off as fast as lightning in the direction of his ancestral foes.

As was often the case, the Kyrosians had chosen a simple, rundown warehouse as the headquarters of their sinister plan. Homicron reached it in a few minutes and hovered for a moment in the sky, out of sight, to analyze the situation. His heightened perception told him that four, well-armed Kyrosians and one human were there. So, the professor was still alive, but it looked as if it would be a hard fight to free him. Homicron landed near the building and sneaked up to a window with a broken pane to see what was happening.

His senses on alert swept over the area and allowed him to avoid the beams of the crude alarm system, obviously installed in a hurry. In a huge, bare room full of dust the professor was tied to a chair, his head raised and his eyes empty. He was talking out loud in a monotone voice, but Homicron was too far to hear what he was saying. Across from him a Kyrosian was also sitting in a chair, motionless, staring at the scientist. One of the reptilians seemed to be repeating what the professor was saying in its sibilant language into a communication device, while the two others were on the lookout, ray guns at the ready.

In a single glance Homicron understood the situation. The motionless Kyrosian was using his mind-swapping ability

171

to take possession of Professor Jurewitz and gain access to his memory. Thus he dictated his knowledge, which was transmitted directly to the reptilians' HQ—wherever it was.

In order to interrupt the session, Homicron opted for the hard way: creating a pulsing energy ball in his hands, he let it fly and explode an entire wall panel. The blast kicked up a cloud of dust that the Alphan used to get inside the warehouse before the guards could react. Aiming his fist at the closest Kyrosian, he shot a ray of lethal radiation and the reptilian collapsed, dead before he could even raise his weapon. The second guard, more alert, jumped behind a crate and avoided another burst before shooting back. Homicron hastily threw up a force field, but the impact of the Kyrosian ray still sent him back into a pile of junk.

Out of the corner of his eye, he saw the Kyrosian, after using his communicator, grab a serpent-blade and head straight for him. The sizzling sword made of green energy was whistling like the ophidian it was named after, while Homicron was struggling in his daze to get up. Rolling to his side, he dodged the first strike and threw a kinetic vector at his attacker who flew across the room and landed in a small pile of the professor's notes and files, before standing up again without any apparent damage. Now Homicron stood too, surrounded by a glowing aura whose wavelength was the exact opposite of the ray shooting out of the Kyrosian's gun.

Every shot was deflected, merely sliding off the Alphan's body. Gathering an ionized pulsar in his eyes, Homicron vaporized his enemy with one blinding optic shot before turning quickly to block another serpent-sword striking him from behind. He caught the blade in his hands, which were protected by a repelling field, and started fighting the reptilian with brute force.

The two aliens stood face-to-face, an ancestral hatred radiating from their confrontation with palpable tension. The reptilian face of the Kyrosian was warped by his hostility and effort whereas Homicron stayed focused. Waves of vibrating energy flew into his fingers, silently weakening the blade.

With a sudden snap of his wrists, the Alphan finally broke the sword of his adversary, who was caught by surprise and thrown off balance—that's all Homicron needed to pulverize him with one shot of ionizing energy.

Turning his attention to the last Kyrosian, still sitting in his chair, Homicron struck him with a shower of sparks flowing out of his fingers. The reptilian died, his mind evaporated, howling, and Professor Jurewitz was freed from his control.

The professor grumbled as he slowly came around.

Homicron kneeled next to him and started untying him from the chair. "It's OK, professor. You're free now."

"Homicron? You really exist?" the scientist stuttered in his daze.

The Alphan smiled. "Yes, it's really me. Your kidnappers were Kyrosians, my sworn enemies. But rest assured, they can't hurt you anymore."

"No!" the professor shouted, panicking. "You don't understand. The knowledge they extracted from my mind was communicated to their brethren... I could read the thoughts of the one possessing me... Their plan is terrible! They want to destroy the entire Earth!"

"Calm down, professor. You can give me the details while I'm taking you to the hospital."

And Homicron flew into the night sky, with the fragile form of the professor in his arms.

It was rare for an Alphan to think of his own death. Able to change into living energy, they possessed a kind of immortality. Of course, death was not unknown to them: the long war against Kyros had already taken a heavy toll on their people. Paradoxically, in order to explore inhabited planets by mingling with the population, it was often necessary for them to fuse their energy matrix with a recently deceased body—to have access to its memory and knowledge.

And yet, in this uncertain dawn, Homicron seriously pictured his own end. The revelations of Professor Jurewitz had frozen his very being, tempered as it had been in the fires of the brightest stars. The Kyrosians' plan was, indeed, so twist-ed that it could very well succeed—devastating the entire solar system and destroying Earth in the process.

Herman Jurewitz, a doctor in astrophysics, had for years studied the formation of stars: how an inert star, a simple heap of cosmic dust, could turn into a giant thermonuclear reactor. His favorite object of study was the planet Jupiter, which was really a little sun that had never fired up. After analyzing it from every angle, the scientist had gathered enough infor-mation to calculate precisely the quantity and kind of energy needed to start the process that would turn the gas giant into a red dwarf. The formula he theorized had just been a hobby for him, a break from his more serious work—but it had obvious-ly attracted the attention of the Kyrosians.

In fact, according to the scientist, who had shared the thoughts of the reptilian during his brief psychic captivity, the Kyrosians had figured out how to trigger Jupiter. The energy unleashed by such transformation would power their factories for centuries and help them create more weapons and more warships at an even faster pace. Under the heat of this new red sun, the human population of Earth would die and be replaced by Kyrosians, thus ridding them of the bothersome humanity and enabling them to concentrate its efforts on wining their eons-old war on Alpha.

If Professor Jurewitz had correctly interpreted the Kyrosian's thoughts, a small fleet was already en route to-wards Jupiter at this very moment, small enough to escape the notice of the Alphans. With the scientist's theory in their pos-session, the reptilians were now ready to put their sinister plan into action.

Therefore, Homicron knew that he had little time to stop them, but he also realized that he didn't have enough power to do so. At least, not yet. That is why he stood there, in a remote cove, while the sun—the real sun—was barely peeking over the horizon. Homicron had summoned his fellow Alphans al-ready wandering about the Solar System back to Earth, as re-inforcements. By absorbing the energy matrix of at least two of them, he would have enough power to go up against a Kyrosian fleet, though he was still not guaranteed to get out of that fight alive.

The arrival of his brothers snapped him out of his dark thoughts. At first, they were nothing more than points of light upon the horizon, which slowly grew bigger as they approached. Several halos of energy surrounded him before taking human form—they were Alphans sent to Earth to help Homicron against the Kyrosians.

Taking a deep breath, Homicron spoke first:

"My brothers, thank you for coming. I called you because this is a crucial moment, and we're going to need all our power to solve the current crisis."

The Alphans look worriedly at each other. One of them asked:

"What do you mean, Homicron? What crisis are you talking about?"

Homicron then told them everything, from the kidnapping of Professor Jurewitz to the genocidal plan of the Kyrosians. As the story unfolded, the Alphans became more grim-faced; some of them even showed fear in their eyes. When Homicron stopped talking, a heavy silence loomed over the cover. Each of them was now aware of the utmost gravity of the situation.

Finally, one of the Alphans took a step forward.

"Brother, my decision is made, absorb my matrix. You alone are experienced enough to defeat this menace, and if my energy can help you, it is with pleasure that I gift it to you."

Two other Alphans nodded.

"We agree. With our combined powers, you will be mighty in battle."

"Thank you, brothers," replied Homicron, stepping into the middle of the circle. "I shall surrender your personal matrices when I return to Alpha. Meanwhile, they will join mine and turn me into a formidable weapon against the Kyrosians! Together, we shall win in this battle, I promise you!"

The being who had once been Ted White turned to his other companions.

"The rest of you, stay here on Earth. Protect this planet and its inhabitants while I am gone—however long that might be."

"Don't worry," they replied. "We are ready to give our lives for this cause."

The three Alphans who volunteered to give their matrices to Homicron stood in front of him. Their bodies started shimmering under the effect of the concentration, transforming into an energy almost as powerful as that of a star. Then when Homicron had before him three shining spheres, he spread his arms in a embracing gesture and accepted the precious gift, absorbing all the power being offered to him. His body was suddenly flooded with boundless energy—like superovas exploding inside him, releasing their cosmic power through his veins. It was almost too much and he had to focus his mind in order not to retreat from this gift that was threatening to escape his control. At last, the oppressive torrent quieted down and the Alphan regained control.

His eyes shone with a light as pure as what once sprang forth from the Big Bang. Homicron nodded and smiled at his remaining brothers. Gathering a thick cloud of anti-gravitons around him, he created a field of pure force and shot up into the sky, pulling away effortlessly from Earth's gravitational field.

He had gone off to do battle, perhaps his last fight, but likely his most glorious.

Rocketing like a comet through space, Homicron took time to cast one final glance back at Earth—its blue clarity shrouded by cottony clouds and the dark brown masses of continents. Not far away, the Moon seemed to watch over it like a sentinel, faithfully guarding it throughout the ages. The Alphan flew so fast that soon the two celestial bodies were nothing more than points of light. Indeed, Homicron was traveling at close to the speed of light. At the upper limit of his perception, space-time slowly contorted, unveiling quantum events that had not yet happened. He had to tear himself away from the fascination that these temporal revelations were arousing in him, and concentrate on his trajectory.

The curvature of the universe intensified his speed. Soon, he spied Mars, the red planet that, long ago, had been the home of the proud Fomores, but was now asleep, disturbed only by the probes that humans kept sending there.

Then there was the asteroid belt. The rocks floating lazily in the cosmos were all that remained of Mû, the once glorious planet of gold.

Finally, Homicron saw before him the dark immensity of Jupiter, which hid the the planets farthest from the sun.

Using gravitational forces, the Alphan slowed down and wrapped himself in a cloud of ionized particles to hide from his foes. His trip had barely cost him any energy and had only taken a few minutes in real time. He radiated power, but moved cautiously. He progressed from one space rock to another without losing sight of the gaseous giant and taking care not to get spotted.

The huge planet now filled the whole horizon, cyclopean and calm. It almost looked alive. A titanic red spot spread over one side like a big open eye scrutinizing space. Its various moons encircled it, ridiculously tiny compared to it, even though some of them were as big as planets themselves. As used to the marvels of the universe as he was, Homicron couldn't help paying respectful tribute to Jupiter, asking it mentally to bear witness to his bravery.

The Alphan finally caught sight of the Kyrosian forces. Hope was reborn in his heart: their fleet was, in fact, composed of only three ships. There was a mighty warship with its big cannons whose ammunition can destroy cities with a single shot. Right next to it was a science vessel cruising toward Jupiter, identifiable by its cylindrical containers able to absorb the immense energy that would be released after he planet's transformation. Lastly, there was a transport ship for the space troopers patrolling around the other two ships, lighter than a cruiser, with ten fighter ships ready for combat inside it.

The three ships were dark, riddled with sharp, pointy, metal structures. Being of no functional utility, these decorations make them look more sinister and had one purpose only: to strike terror when the Kyrosians appeared, giving them a foretaste of the cruelty of these merciless reptilians.

Homicron knew these vessels only too well, having fought them before, and so often witnessed the destruction of which they were capable. His fists clench as the power flew through him. Three Kyrosian ships, but only two prepared to fight. The Alphan thought he can vanquish them. It was not as hopeless a battle as he had feared when he had left Earth.

Galvanized by this boost in confidence, Homicron summoned the united power of his three brothers and rushed into battle.

The sudden burst of power that the Alphan manifested did not go undetected by the Kyrosians. The warship aimed its heavy cannon at him while the transport ship opened its hatches to send out its fighters into space.

Homicron spread out his perception. His force field would not be enough to protect him from the Kyrosian rays and he had to be able to gauge the line of fire in order to avoid them. Since offense is the best type of defense, the Alphan rocketed toward the reptilian ships, his body crackling with energy. The first wave of fighters were coming to meet him—streamlined ships with sharp lines.

They fired a few bursts of red beams that Homicron avoided easily. He targeted his enemies and shot devastating pulses of energy. A lethal dance was being played out, dodging, attacking, side-skirting. Asteroids exploded, hit by stray beams. Homicron's force field held up and, despite some jolts, he survived his enemies' lasers. His own blasts hit right on target: fighters exploded in geysers of debris without a sound.

Zigzagging between rubble, Homicron tried to lose the three fighters still chasing him. Their attacks were jarring him enough to make him wince in pain. A risky move got him out of their line of fire and suddenly, he was in control again. Fists out front, he fired off a few cosmic busts that pulverized the enemy fighters. Using his ability to sense and analyze energy, the Alphan flushed out the last ships and destroyed them one after the other.

Then he turned his attention to the rest of the Kyrosian fleet: the science vessel was closing in on Jupiter while the warship was coming up slowly to face him. The transport ship, farther back, was sending out another wave of heavy fighters, bigger and badder…

Homicron felt a mass of ionic energy being gathered by the warship. They were preparing for a massive shot. He could feel the waves radiating towards him. The thick, destructive ray sprang out like a snake uncoiling to bite its prey. Despite this warning, the Alphan barely got out of the way, being dazed by such an amount of power. By the time his mind had cleared, the fighters were after him. He was being bombarded with painful shockwaves. This second attack seemed better coordinated, more precise… They were attacking with a plan, each vessel in formation… The Alphan couldn't afford the slightest mistake. So, he decided to fall back, to put some distance between him and the deadly swarm, dodging their fire and fighting back only when he had to—but to no avail. The horde didn't let up, each pilot maneuvering skillfully to counter his own attacks.

All of a sudden, Homicron understood the Kyrosians' strategy. A quick exchange of fire enabled him see in the cockpit of the enemy ship an old foe: Kress, a Kyrosian warrior whom he had met many times before. The reptilian's right eye, blind and slashed by a long scar with a white groove, was a bitter reminder of one of their past encounters. Kress was an enemy not to be underestimated, fully aware of all his tactics and, therefore, able to counter them.

This brief instant of astonishment paralyzed Homicron long enough for his formidable foe to deliver a clever, and almost fatal blow. All the Kyrosian fighters shot pulse bombs

179

around the Alphan. He realized the danger only too late. The silent explosions let loose a shockwave strong enough to shatter a moon. Homicron was hit head on, swept away like cosmic dust. Ted White's human body suffered serious damage and blood trickled from his mouth, forming red bubbles that crystallized immediately in the cold immensity of space.

The explosions annihilated a few planetoids whose debris hid the Alphan for a while, so that he could prevent the Kyrosians from unleashing their final, deadly blow. After catching his breath, Homicron focused his energy on the regenerative functions of his host body, forcing the human's fragile biology to speed up its healing. The effort left him panting and he knew that he had overestimated his own strength and misjudged that of his enemies. Pure power was not enough. He had to use strategy.

Confusing the enemy was the key. He had to keep their fighters from moving around in planned coordination, and its warship from using its firepower, biding its time, covering the science vessel.

When he felt better, Homicron left his hiding place and was spotted right away. He used this momentary instant of surprise to soar into range of the warship—a move that looked suicidal and would baffle his foes. The Alphan had no trouble dodging the badly-aimed laser blasts and got close enough to prevent the ship from using its heavy cannons. He only had to worry about short-range weapons while the squad led by Kress could no longer use their pulse bombs for fear of damaging their own ship.

Skimming by the cruiser, Homicron bombarded it, causing damage to the hull. His rays changed wavelength every millisecond to keep the enemy shields from adjusting properly. A few stray shots from the fighters even helped him before Kress brought his men back under control. Homicron smiled through the pain he still felt. The first phase of his plan had worked out beautifully. Now he just had to move on to the next...

Aligning his mind on the Kyrosians' radio frequencies, the Alphan made a quick survey in order to find the one used by the enemy pilots to communicate with each other. He found it rapidly and first contemplated sending an interference wave, but realized that such a basic move would be foreseen by Kress. So instead, he sent a few contradictory orders. The confusion that it caused broke up the squad's coordination just enough time for Homicron to get the upper hand.

Creating a plasma ball, he threw throws it at two of the fighters and they vaporized instantly, a split second before Kress got his troops in order again. But it was too late for the Kyrosian: their attack formation had been broken.

Under cover of the warship's aggressive architecture, the Alphan exchanged fire with the fighters and destroyed more of them, sustaining only a few wounds himself in order to make quick work of them. His higher mobility was a key factor in letting him make moves that no ship could follow, and giving him unexpected angles of attack.

The rest of the skirmish was brief: Homicron finished off the remaining fighters despite the warship's support.

Only Kress was left. Homicron could see his face twisted by hatred—this would be their final duel. Like two furious fireflies, they chased each other in turn, the prey becoming the predator, as their rays ripped through the black veil of space. Even the warship didn't dare interfere in this battle of honor; its guns remained silent.

The Alphan had to acknowledge his nemesis' skills. He was a bold pilot and his fury for victory abolished any fear of death. Homicron knew that he had to survive this confrontation—a glance at the science vessel showed him that it was getting closer—too close—to Jupiter…

Kress fired continually at him, heating up his guns too much, but forcing the Alphan to remain on the defensive. Spinning through the metal wreckage, Homicron decided to use his enemy's tactic against him: his eyes shot a thin ray of invisible microwaves aimed at the overused cannons. It heated them up fast, turning them red-hot. Filled as he was with blind rage, Kress didn't notice anything. All he saw was his sworn enemy who had taken away one of his eyes fleeing before him. He gloated. And then, his guns exploded all at the same time, destroying parts of his ship. Pieces of the hull were torn aside, and flames spread through the small ship. But Kress had had time to eject.

The entire front of the fighter detached from the carcass in a cloud of steam and literally changed shape. The metal parts adjusted their position as Homicron watched arms and legs take form, while the cockpit straightened up. What had been the fighter ship was now a humanoid construct—a Kyrosian, mechanized, battle armor. So the fight went on.

Even with most of his body burned, Kress refused to give up. He rushed at Homicron and punched him hard enough to shatter a mountain. Homicron was caught off guard and did not fully dodge the blow. He was thrown back and crashed into the warship. He was stunned and Kress attacked again. Catching the enemy in his powerful pincers, the Kyrosian dragged him along the hull of the spaceship, leaving a trail of destruction.

Ted White's body was mangled by the spikes and sharp edges; his uniform was shredded, and blood oozed out of multiple wounds. Homicron appeared to suffer this without doing much. He tried to loosen the robotic grip, but lacked the strength for it.

He decided to emit a white light, as bright as a nova, to engulf his foe. Kress became blinded, had to turn his eyes away, and, for an instant, lost his concentration, enabling the Alphan to break free and jump back. Channeling his power once again to heal himself, Homicron knew that had to finish his enemy off—or lose the battle. He clenched his fists and wrapped them in a pulsing aura.

Kress brought his machine guns into play, but the bullets melted on contact with Homicron's energy shield. The Kyrosian was blinded by hatred as he rushed at his enemy again. With a quick thrust of his arms, the Alphan let loose his power and another ray struck his adversary. Kress burned up inside his armor, but his malice allowed him one final move: he started his autodestruct system. Homicron hadn't expected this. He watched the Kyrosian explode, blowing him away like a wisp of straw.

When the Alphan opened his eyes after a brief moment of unconsciousness, pain flooded through him. He felt as if he had pushed his body too far this time. He saw the warship get into position. No longer worried about hitting its own men, it was ready for battle. Nearby, the transport ship was also arming its cannons. Even though its weapons were lighter, it was still an enemy able to damage a weakened Homicron. The two ships were positioned to cover as wide a zone as possible in case the Alphan tried to escape—or more likely, go after the science vessel. All their weapons were pointed at the tiny figure, ready to fire and vaporize their enemy.

Homicron made a quick survey of his own remaining force: unfortunately, he had just spent the last bits of the power given to him by his brothers… he had barely enough left to get back to Earth, which was not an option if he didn't foil the Kyrosians' plot. He smiled bitterly—his initial instinct had been right: this battle was going to be his ultimate sacrifice… but defeat was unthinkable. He had to win this fight at all costs.

Completing their final maneuvers, the two ships armed their weapons. Homicron felt the surge of concentrated energy flowing through their arsenal. Then, upon seeing their positions, he had an idea. They were close to each other, almost forming a right angle, a formation that certainly allowed them to sweep over a broad zone, but that considerably hindered their mobility.

The Alphan decided to go for broke. He called up one of the four elementary forces of the universe: electromagnetism. Spasms of pain made his muscles twitch while he focused his mind on controlling that elemental power. At last, he stretched out his arms, pointing at each of the ships, and released the two magnetic waves, a positive one from his right hand, a negative one from his left. The warship and the transport vessel were now charged with opposite polarities and, like magnets, became attracted to each other.

Homicron felt the panic that spread in their respective bridges by tuning in on their radio frequencies. He clenched his jaws and amplified the energy. The ships were too heavy and too slow to react in time, or escape this fatal attraction. They crashed into each other in a silent wreck, their hulls gutted by their spikes and pointy barbs. They fired at random, but their shots became lost in space. It looked like two giants trying to fuse together, hurting each other in a parody of mechanical mating. Explosions broke out everywhere. They were slowly dismantled and their fragments continued piling together, forming a bizarre, artificial planetoid that no longer posed a threat.

Homicron stopped channeling the draining flux of primal energy and closed his eyes to gather his remaining strength.

It was time to end this once and for all. The science vessel was too close to Jupiter to waste another precious second. Homicron felt the forces at work, and recognized Professor Jurewitz' equations being used.

Mustering all the power he had left, the Alphan went on the attack with a furious bombardment. He hit his target, damaging the spaceship that could only defend itself weakly. It was sheer will-power that kept Homicron going; every ray cost him a groan of pain, but he couldn't hold back now. His keen eyes spotted the fuel tanks—not far from the huge engines—and he intensified his attack, making them his target.

The Kyrosian ship started to explode all over, ravaged by the Alphan's fury. All of a sudden, a plasma sphere shot out of its hold—a concentration of power that could, on a small scale, reproduce the original Big Bang explosion.

Homicron screamed in desperation, a useless gesture in the cold, cosmic void. As the last Kyrosian vessel drifted off into empty space, the ball of blue fire reached the surface of Jupiter and slowly sank to its core.

Homicron knew that he had failed. He felt the first atomic transformations taking place in the core of the giant planet, a chain of nuclear reactions that would eventually turn it into a deadly star.

In spite of everything he tried to think of a solution: using an opposing energy, destroying the planet before it could fully transform, extinguishing the molecular fire... But he was an explorer, the closest thing Alpha had to a warrior, but not a scientist. Even though his knowledge of science was far greater than that of the humans, he didn't have the expertise needed to stop the transformation happening before his eyes in real time...

Refusing to give up, even when everything looked lost, Homicron saw a face appear in his mind: eyes sparkling with intelligence, a delightfully ironic smile, and long brown hair... Rita Tower, Ted's fiancée, a renowned physicist... She would know what to do... Channeling his will towards Earth, he tuned his mind to the frequency of the human brain to enter into telepathic contact with the scientist. Within seconds, his consciousness had connected to Rita, whose intelligence shone like a Centaurian crystal.

"Rita, Homicron here! Don't be scared, this is only a mental connection."

"Homicron! Where are you? What's going on?"

The Alphan figured out that the beautiful physician was in her lab, probably busy with some experiment. All the better. Her mind was in the right frame.

"It'd take too long to tell you everything. I'm going to send you some information hard and fast, and it might be a little painful..."

Homicron did indeed perceive the first signs of a migraine in Rita's head while he sent the images, sensations and emotions in bulk. Fortunately, her methodical, rigorous mind sorted them out quickly and she understood the problem.

"My God! Jupiter is going to transform into a star that might destroy mankind and change the entire solar system. So, what do you want from me?"

"You're a scientist, Rita. You've worked with Jurewitz. Help me stop this!"

The Alphan felt Rita's brain working at full speed. The young woman's acute intelligence was stupefying. He had trouble following her sequence of thoughts. She analyzed several hypotheses at the same time, pushed them boldly to their limits, and finally rejected them before coming up with others—and all this without letting panic overtake her or fear paralyze her thoughts. Homicron smiled when he thought that this Earthling would make a great Alphan!

"Hurry, Rita, there's very little time…"

All of a sudden, a bright light started glowing in the physician's mind.

"Time! Of course! It's totally crazy, but that's why it just might work. Homicron, can you 'download' into your mind the thoughts on which I'm going to concentrate?"

"Of course! Simply focus your mind and I'll have no trouble assimilating them."

Rita Tower forced herself to remember everything she knew about a time theory that was still cause for debate: the idea that the tachyon was the time particle. Never having been seen, the tachyon was an theoretical construct, but many scientists had modeled it using various calculations. Homicron ran through the equations and knew he could create a flux of it if needed without fully understanding where Rita was going with this.

"The tachyons are time particles, Homicron, at least if the current theories are correct, and for each particle we know, there exists an anti-particle carrying a charge—and thus, the quantum effects—that is its opposite. Therefore…"

"…If I create enough anti-tachyons around Jupiter could can invert the course of time around it… and bring the planet back to its natural state!"

"That's right. It's risky but on such short notice, it's the only solution I can think of."

Homicron felt hopeful again, galvanized by the intelligence and courage of the young woman.

"I'll try it, Rita. I hope you're right. You'll know soon enough, anyway. In case things don't work out, I'm glad to have known you."

"Good luck, Homicron."

His consciousness returned to his body and the Alphan started gathering all his strength. This time, he would reach down to his last spark of life in order to leave nothing to chance. Materializing the tachyon equation, he reversed the polarity and created an anti-tachyon, which flashed for less than a nanosecond on the edge of his perception before disappearing back in time. So, it was possible!

Homicron mustered all his energy and transformed it into anti-tachyons. Then he started spreading them around the giant planet whose core was fusing. The scope of his task made him hesitate for an instant, but he cast aside all doubts—it was out of the question that he should fail! He thought of the Earthlings with whom he had fraternized during his brief stay there: the beautiful Rita Tower of course, but also Domingo Lopez, his young protégé, and General Heartland at NASA, the windbag with a heart of gold. It was for them that he had to succeed.

His body was in agony, beyond healing. Homicron cried out in rage against the universe whose total silence swallowed his foolish defiance. Invisible tentacles of temporal antiparticles slowly enveloped Jupiter, covering its surface and sparkling as time began to go in reverse.

The gaseous planet started to turn slowly in the opposite direction, its orbit also reversing. The atoms in its core separated, the fusion stopped and the molecules went back to where they had been before. The thermonuclear explosions on the surface were reabsorbed into the gas giant. It was like a film played backwards.

Homicron did not relent, even though he felt his physical body breaking up. He kept producing anti-tachyons, ceaselessly, throwing them at Jupiter so that it would return to its original state, before the Kyrosian sphere had hit it.

At last, the Alphan felt the energy dissipating as if cast away by the planet and finally vanish into nothingness. The huge gas giant looked like it did before, majestic and serene.

Homicron gave it one last smile. He closed his eyes, completely drained. He had succeeded against all odds. He had saved the Earth—and his friends. His body started to float in orbit around Jupiter. He did not even have enough strength to keep the stasis field that kept him from feeling the effects of deep space and the lack of oxygen. The vital functions of Ted White's body shut down and Homicron's mind faded to black.

Death, at last.

No, not yet. Not totally.

In the gray zone that separated existence from what comes after, Homicron heard a voice. It was soft and gentle and strong at the same time. It was calling him.

"Homicron, son of Alpha. Wake up."

Homicron struggled to open his eyes. A silvery shape, huge and translucent, stood before him. He could see the cosmic blackness studded with points of light through it. The being was so big that it filled his whole field of vision. Was this… God? The being was smiling.

"No, Homicron. I am not God. I am called Silver Shadow. I am from seven billion years in the future, from a time when people like me watch over different parts of the fractal ocean that time has turned into."

The Alphan wondered whether this vision came from his death throes. The figure calling itself Silver Shadow cupped him gently into his huge hands. He felt swaddled in extreme peacefulness.

And suddenly, there was pain.

Homicron opened his mouth in a silent scream. Life and all its pageant of suffering rushed back into him. Once again, he remembered what a body felt like. The bones of Ted White mended, the wounds healed, the blood started pumping again and the heart started beating. Homicron's energy matrix weaved together and the power core from his Alphan brothers were whole again, just on the edge of his consciousness. In the space of an instant, Homicron was alive again—even his blue and yellow uniform looked brand new. He turned to Silver Shadow.

"Why?"

"I was pulled into your temporal segment by a major chronal singularity. It turned out to be the flux of anti-tachyons you used to save Jupiter. Our archives mentioned the 'Battle of the Aborted Sun' without giving any more details. I know now who the hero who carried the day was: Homicron of Alpha. And since it was not written that you died here, I took the liberty of correcting the anomaly."

"So it's over? I won? The Earth is out of danger?"

"The Earth will never be out of danger. But at least, this time, it was saved. Other battles await you, Homicron of Alpha. As for me, I will return to my time. Farewell, cosmic warrior."

The silhouette of Silver Shadow slowly faded away and Homicron could gaze upon Jupiter again, the planet that he had just stopped from turning into a new sun. He smiled, letting the exhilarating thought of victory wash over him. The Earth was waiting for him, as well as Rita and all his friends, including his Alphan brothers.

Leaving a golden trail behind in the shadowy vault of the cosmos, Homicron returned to Earth—the world that was, from now on, his second homeland.

Bathy-09 by Alfonso Ruis

Bathy-09 *is an elite intervention unit of the U.N.-sponsored International Oceanic Force, created to keep peace underwater. As for the* ***Cave Patrol****, it is a private group of adventurers who explore the underground and confront strange threats there. In this story, the two teams join forces to stop a menace of global proportions...*

Cédric Burgaud: *A Ristretto To Die For*

All fell silent when the radar detected an echo. In the *Shark-99*, which was floating in midwater, ensign Mike Ehmadou, the so-called "golden ear of the bathyscaph," closed his eyes and focused his attention on the signals that the sonar was transmitting.

"Diesel engine, shallow draft. Without a doubt, that's it," he reported.

"Perfect!" Lieutenant Lisa Sturm exclaimed. She was the leader of the small team of three submariners which made up Bathy-09. "Everyone buckle up. We're going to surface right in front of it. Sharkie, engine at 15 knots, south-south-east, climbing slowly. I want them to freak out when we come out of the water."

Sharkie, the AI that was ran the bathyscaph christened *Shark-99*, calculated the maneuver.

"You know, Mike, technology has evolved. You don't have to sit there with the headphones on. Sharkie can manage very well."

"Listen up, Frenchy, before being stuck with you two, I was the greatest 'golden ear' in the US Navy. No supercomputer in this sardine can is going to make me give up this gift that nature—thanks be to it—and my parents, god bless them, gave me."

Ensign Marc Pujo, a Frenchman, often teased his brother-in-arms Mike Ehmadou, who came from Western Africa, with his typically French humor that so often annoyed others but sometimes charmed women.

Sharkie's masculine voice echoed through the small control room:

"Video message from headquarters. Top priority."

The face of a man around fifty appeared on the huge console facing the three team members.

"Hello, Bathy-09."

"Hello Admiral Yale," Sturm said. "We've just spotted our target and we…"

"Abort mission, Lieutenant. Send the coordinates to C.L.A.S.H., they'll take care of the hostage-takers."

"As you want, Sir."

Sharkie paused the machines for a brief moment, then calculated a new course without anyone bothering to question the order.

"Bathy-06 just sent information about the incident on the gas rig in the North Sea six months ago. It was sabotage," said the Admiral.

"S.P.I.D.E.R.?" Sturm suggested.

"Likely. It looks the same as the sabotage of last April on one of the oil rigs in the Gulf of Mexico—that's almost three years ago now."

Pujo swore. "It has S.P.I.D.E.R. written all over it. Attacking economic interests while polluting nature."

"Indeed. But we're thinking these attacks are mere diversions. Doctor Kalamazoo will explain it better than I."

The screen split vertically. Admiral Yale stayed on the left and a new person appeared on the right—Doctor Kalamazoo, a man with graying hair wearing half-moon glasses.

"Good day to you all," he began. "You're probably not aware of it, but since the late 90s, there's been a system of international surveillance put in place after the ratification of TANT—the Treaty Against Nuclear Testing. Hydroacoustic, seismic, infrasound and radionuclide stations have been set up everywhere on the planet to detect and measure chemical and nuclear explosions, as well as earthquakes, volcanic eruptions and tsunamis. Over the past three years, the station in the middle of the Atlantic has had some random failures, two of which coincided, strangely enough, with the attacks on the oil and gas rigs that Admiral Yale just mentioned. The International Center of TANT in Vienna sent us all their information on the days immediately preceding and following the incidents. Our scientists made a chilling discovery: during these two blackouts, a spike in seismic activity was recorded. Someone is playing with our planet by unleashing underwater earthquakes on the Atlantic ridge. Thanks to our satellite images and GPS coordinates, we've been able to locate the target zone within a ten-mile radius. We've asked the IOF to survey of the area."

"Did you get that, Bathy-09?" added Yale. "You've got to get to that location and find out what's going on. Good luck."

All remained silent in *Shark-99* after the communication was cut off. Sharkie had already set course for the zone identified by C.L.A.S.H.

"Imagine if it's true," Ehmadou blurted out. "If someone really could start earthquakes. That'd be…"

"…a disastrous threat," Sturm cut in. "Nations would be held hostage."

"How could S.P.I.D.E.R. have developed such a technology? And so quickly?"

"That's for us to find out, gentlemen. Sharkie, you get us there and tell us when we're within two miles of the target zone. Meanwhile, everyone get some rest."

While the AI was executing its orders, Lieutenant Sturm watched the little green dot get farther and farther away on the radar screen. The minnow had just wriggled free, for a little while at least; Bathy-09 was now off to hunt bigger fish.

Jean Girodet, the top agent of The Lion, a private European security agency, was following the news on the wall-screen TV in his office on the Champs-Elysées while reading a report that his secretary had just brought in. He looked up when they started talking about the European crisis.

"...in a speech before the Brussels commission the French diplomat has reaffirmed the commitment of France in the current crisis of states planning to leave the Euro Zone."

"*It is urgent that we find common ground to reach a compromise that could save the economy of Greece or Spain and now Italy too from collapse. We don't accept what some ill-intentioned speculators are trying to do and, believe me, France and the French government won't be guided by the financial markets.*"

"The Minister of Foreign Affairs added that the next summit meeting of the ECB in Naples will be, I quote, *an historic meeting not to be missed*, urging his European colleagues in charge of finances to *speak with one unified European voice*."

Girodet knew that C.L.A.S.H. was teaming up with the X-Organization run out of Brussels to supervise the security of the summit meeting, unlike the previous ones that had all been run by the security services of their respective countries. Why the change? Because serious threats had been discovered by various agents in the field.

Girodet turned back to the report. He skimmed over the technical sections and the complex diagrams to concentrate on the interim findings and the notes that one of his assistants had added. He wrote a few words in the margin, then called his secretary.

"Clemence, will you call C.L.A.S.H. for me?"

"Right away, Monsieur Girodet."

Girodet waited while pondering the conclusions of the report until the light flashed on his phone indicating an incoming call.

"I have Doctor Kalamazoo for you on line 1, Monsieur."

Girodet heard the line click over.

"Hello, Jean."

"Hello, doctor. I just saw a report on some volcanic activity in the Bay of Naples. Have you seen it?"

"Hold on a second while I find it."

Girodet heard papers rustling and the doctor swearing under his breath as he searched.

"Here it is! I've got it. Yes, yes, yes… That's it, yes. Hmm. Interesting. Very interesting."

"What do you think?"

"The spike in activity is a bad sign, but it's not alarming even though there is a risk of eruption. We'll have to watch the gas escaping at Pozzuoli and take some readings on the ground to see if the numbers have changed since the last incident in 1984."

"What are the risks?"

"You know about Pompeii, of course? The same thing could happen. The lava is still bubbling in Solfatara and only needs a little extra pressure to gush out. If that happens, the Pozzuolis will be wiped off the map. Maybe Bagnoli on the coast, too. It all depends on the wind. Either Cumae or Naples. The ash and toxic vapors could bury one or the other in less than an hour."

"How could we prevent it?"

"We can't. The best we can do, as I said, is control the escaping gas and keep the crater floor from rising too much. After that, it's impossible to know if the eruption may happen tomorrow, next month or in ten years… If it's the loss of human life that's concerns you, the only option is to evacuate."

"Hmm. Evacuating thousands of people—not something you can do in a matter of hours, and the Italian authorities will probably argue about it."

Girodet looked at his notes, then leaned back in his chair and crossed his hands.

"Thanks for the info, doc."

"If you want, we could send a team over there."

"Yeah?"

"Two geologists and their assistants. They're freelancers, but they've subcontracted from us in the past and they're in Paris for a conference right now."

"Go ahead, contact them. Just keep me in the loop about what they find."

Girodet hung up, made a couple of final notes on the report and then picked up another classified document.

The Museum of Natural History in Paris was holding a conference that had brought together two groups of people who rarely had the opportunity to meet, despite their complementary specialties: geologists and spelunkers. In the full auditorium, two Americans, Terry Bronx and Sandy Crown, both around thirty, were listening carefully to a lecture by Professor Lakhoto on the origin of the karst landscape of the underwater grotto on Moyade in the Riou Islands, south of Marseille, when two men in black suits slipped into the row of seats just behind them.

"Doctor Crown, Professor Bronx," one of the men in black said politely, "would you be so kind as to follow us outside, please?"

"Why?" Sandy Brown asked point blank after turning around to examine the men more closely.

The man showed her a C.L.A.S.H. ID card.

"Oh! If you've come to get us, it must be important."

When they were in the entrance hall, the Agent handed Bronx a cell phone. Sandy tried to listen in on the conversation. The two Agents just stood back in that typical, security guard stance that never fails to attract attention.

"Got it," Terry concluded. "When we've got the exact data, we'll send them to you. Good-bye, Doctor."

"Well? Was that who I think it was?"

Her colleague tried unsuccessfully to contain his excitement.

"Yes, Sandy, that was Kalamazoo himself. Have you ever been in a helicopter?"

"Pardon?"

"There's one waiting for us at Satory. We're going to Naples!"

"But what about the conference? Our equipment? And our colleagues?"

The Agent cut in, "Your personal effects have been taken to Satory, and your two colleagues are already on site."

"I see C.L.A.S.H. has left nothing to chance," Terry observed. "Gentlemen, the Cave Patrol is ready to serve!"

Sitting at a café in Naples on the Piazza Municipio, Tobie Drugg, a 6- ½ foot-tall African-American, and John Poldus, a Native American of the Seminole tribe, were trying out the Italian coffee—the famous *Ristretto*. Surprised and a little shocked by their first sip, they drowned the rest in the water that the waiter had brought them.

"How can they drink this stuff?" Tobie grimaced.

"I hope the rest isn't like this," Poldus agreed and he forced himself to empty the cup of unusually strong coffee.

After a little while, Sandy Crown and Terry Bronx came smiling out of a black sedan with tinted windows. After saying hello and exchanging some small talk, they got down to business.

"Why are we here?" asked Poldus. "The two C.L.A.S.H. agents who ferried us here were not very talkative."

"I guess it's not for tourism either," Tobie Drugg added. "They've brought all our equipment."

The tall man pointed to the four bags full of all that was necessary for underground exploration: helmets, lights, harnesses, ropes and hooks, but also food and instruments to analyze topographical, thermal, magnetic and chemical samples.

"We've been asked to investigate the vicinity of Naples," said Sandy. "If you're not familiar with Mount Etna and the Phlegraean Fields, then you're in for an education. But right now, let's celebrate this impromptu reunion with some of this famous Italian coffee."

Drugg and Poldus looked at each other before politely declining.

A week after their arrival in Italy and an expedition on the slopes of Mount Etna, the Cave Patrol started their exploration of the Phlegraean Fields that rose out of the earth bordered by a golf course to the west of Naples and inhabited since Roman times.

"Lake Avernus used to be thought to be the entrance to Hades," Poldus read from a guidebook he had bought at the train station. "Its name comes from the Greek *a-ornos*, meaning birdless because it emits toxic vapors."

"Sulfur fumes come from the magma chamber," Tobie added.

"No worries, gentlemen! The lake was cleaned up years ago. For now, we're concentrating our study on the emanations in Bagnoli. Then we'll head for Pozzuoli and go down into the Solfatara. After that, we'll take a look at..."

Terry Bronx went on listing the sites they we're going to visit over the next few days.

After days of navigation, Bathy-09 reached the target zone. Near the ocean ridge, the abyss could reach staggering depths.

Lieutenant Sturm gave her orders right away.

"Sharkie, I want you to make a sweep with the probes as wide as possible to get a precise map of the ridge. Mike, use your 'golden ears' and listen carefully to the seabed—I don't want even a shrimp to escape our notice. Marc, you looked at the data C.L.A.S.H. sent us. When Sharkie's done, compare it with our geographic data. Let's get going."

The quiet hours that followed were dedicated to study and observation. Finally, Marc Pujo spoke up:

"I've got something. Coordinates 52° 73N, 34° 45O. Sharkie's findings and the C.L.A.S.H. data don't match. It could be a construct of about 1500 square feet."

"At this depth?" Mike Ehmadou was stunned. "52° 73N, 34° 45O you say? Let's have a listen."

With his ear glued to the headphones, Mike scrutinized the different sounds coming to him.

"Sounds like engines, like fan blades. There must be an awful lot of them for me to hear them at this distance."

"Sharkie, any sign of activity?" Sturm asked.

"My sensors are picking up no heat in or around the complex," the AI replied.

"Hmm. Surprising. Why build something here just to abandon it?"

"Maybe their tests failed?" Marc Pujo said.

"Or they were a total success?" Mike suggested.

"Whatever the case, we need to get a closer look," said Lisa Sturm. "Gentlemen, go and check it out"

Like a shadow lengthening as the sun goes down, the *Shark-99* approached the strange complex that had been built at the bottom of the ocean.

In the airlock, the two submariners, Pujo and Ehmadou, wore motorized, self-regulating diving suits that allowed them to explore great depths. They stared at the monitor showing a big, oval building topped by a glass dome.

At the controls, Lisa Sturm studied a 3D image of the area that Sharkie was creating as they got closer to their target. An interior pool would allow their craft to emerge directly inside the building, but the lieutenant preferred using the access door near the glass dome.

"Behind the service entrance are stairs that lead to the control room," she spoke into the microphone.

"Got it," said Marc.

Lit by the *Shark-99*'s powerful headlights, the two divers spun the wheel, opened the door and entered the small airlock that automatically emptied when the door closed behind them. They were on alert and decided to keep their suits on as they were equipped with automatic weapons.

Beyond the second door of the airlock the stairs took them down a circular passageway around the dome that overlooked the control room with its black screens and computers, all was empty and silent.

"We found a ladder to go down, lieutenant," radioed Mike. "There's nothing here. Everything's been wiped clean.

The computers are off and their circuits fried. There's nothing to study. It's like they left the place only after purging the whole thing… oh, hold on!"

Sitting in the *Shark-99*, Lisa Sturm was following the two men through their helmet cameras. She saw Ehmadou bend over and examine a CPU whose light was still blinking. He pressed a button. Suddenly, there was light and a woman's voice rang out at the same time as a 3D image materialized like a ghost in the middle of the dome.

"Welcome, friends! Welcome. Please excuse me for not being physically present here, but my thoughts are with you. Let's start with the introductions: my name is Rosetta and I'm in charge of this private complex. And you, dear visitors?"

The light flashed momentarily in the room, then the faces of the two men appeared on a giant screen.

"Marc Pujo, Mike Ehmadou, welcome. Delighted to meet you. Really delighted. I love having visitors, especially when they're new people. Unfortunately, we can't get to know each other better because, as I just told you, this is a private complex and you have therefore intruded into a space that you are not authorized to visit. I am forced to activate our security protocol. I'm terribly sorry about all this. Truly sorry. Good-bye."

After the face vanished, the lights went out, and explosive charges blew up the framework of the glass dome. Without support, it collapsed under the pressure of the water. Suppressing their fear in the face of this new danger, the two divers ran for a side passage and closed the door just in time. Within seconds, the seawater was thudding against the door. Trickles of water leaked through the cracks, but it held firm.

"Lieutenant! Lieutenant!" Mike shouted. "How do we get out of here? Lieutenant!"

Nothing. Marc tried next. Silence. They were alone, dazed and breathless. The Frenchman turned on his flashlight. The bright ray cut through the oppressive darkness surrounding them. The beam swept over the door withstanding the weight of the Ocean, then over to Mike who was studying the small screen on the left arm of his suit, and finally down the corridor that ran straight ahead of them.

"Well, Mike," his partner said, "tell me the good news."

"Pressure OK. Oxygen levels OK. Air temperature 5°C. You can release your helmet. Better to save our oxygen."

Feeling a little more at ease, the two divers went down the corridor inspecting the sparsely furnished rooms one by one without finding a single document. At the end of the corridor, they were faced with the choice of going right or left.

"What if we split up?" Marc suggested.

"Very funny."

Pujo was about to reply when the sound of a hydraulic system came from the left. Cautiously, he raised his flashlight. A few dozen yards away, a machine gun was rising up out of the floor and targeting them.

"Oh, boy," the IOF agent exclaimed.

They turned around and ran in the opposite direction where they found an alcove.

When the bullets started riddling the metal walls, Mike dove back into the corridor but could not stay there for long because he heard the sound of another trapdoor opening.

"This can't be happening!"

He spun around and rushed into one of the rooms they had just examined.

Meanwhile, at the controls of the *Shark-99*, Lieutenant Sturm was doing all she could to get back in contact with her men.

"Sharkie, try to connect to their mainframe."

"Negative, Lieutenant. There is an air gap. Or would that be a water gap in this case?"

"Then, plot a course for us to surface inside their pool."

"Negative, Lieutenant. The pool is now closed up."

Lisa Sturm swore.

"What *can* you do, then?"

The computer stayed silent. It was not programmed to give advice. All of a sudden Lisa had an idea.

201

"Sharkie, can our torpedoes breach the walls?"

"Affirmative, Lieutenant. According to density analysis there are seven weak spots in that structure that will be easy to breach."

Sturm looked at the seven points that Sharkie highlighted on the 3D image of the complex before making a quick decision on the one she deemed the least dangerous.

"Mike? Still there?" Marc Pujo asked after hearing the automatic weapons rattle away.

"Yeah, yeah. Another damn machine gun almost drilled me in the back. And you?"

"I'm stuck in a space the size of a closet. If I move, I'll have worse than blackheads on my schnozz. Any idea how to get out of this?"

"I've used this kind of weapon before. Without knowing the frequency to cancel their firing sequence, we'll have to short-circuit their targeting systems."

"And how do you figure on getting close enough to do that?"

Mike Ehmadou turned around to shine his flashlight on the room. He stopped at the ventilation grill.

"Through the ceiling. From above, I can shoot the circuits."

The submariner moved the heavy, metal desk in the room, climbed up on it and tried to unscrew the grill when a little green light started blinking inside the duct.

"Oh, no!" he shouted.

He jumped off the desk, rolling on the ground outside the room, forgetting all about the machine gun for an instant.

A split second later, the duct exploded, blowing the grill across the room. The shock wave sent the desk and the chair smashing into the wall, creating a hole the size of a basketball.

Salt water came rushing through the hole, quickly filling up the rooms and corridors, all the way to the ceiling. Thanks to their diving suits, the two submariners could endure the sudden pressure, which was not the case for the automatic weapons whose circuit boards were fried.

Pujo had lowered his helmet just in time. He whistled in admiration.

"Well, well, Mike, you make quite an impression, surprisingly enough. You OK?"

"Yeah, but it was a close shave. Any closer and I'd be polluting the Ocean."

"What happened?"

"The duct was booby-trapped. I think this building really wants our hides."

"Remember what that woman said: 'I am forced to activated our security protocol.' She wasn't joking!"

The "golden ear" of *Shark-99* was no longer listening to his friend because he had just heard a rhythmic banging. He went back into the room and put his helmet against the wall to feel the vibrations.

"It's Morse Code. It says 'Go north cor. Last room. Keep suit.' And it repeats."

"It's the boss! She found a way to get us out of here. Answer her and then, let's get moving on the double."

Sitting in a small, one-seater vehicle, Lisa Sturm was maneuvering its left pincer to hit the metal structure, hoping that her message would get through to her men. When she got a positive response, she went slowly back to *Shark-99*.

"Sharkie, show me the thermal view," she instructed, once back at the controls.

She watched the two red bipeds floating towards the back of the installation.

"Let's go, Sharkie!"

From the port-side tube, a torpedo shot out in a swarm of bubbles, leaving a horizontal wake and moving straight toward the underwater complex.

A few seconds later, two shadows came out of the breach and swam toward the bathyscaph. Lieutenant Sturm ran to the airlock to greet the two divers.

"You know, Lieutenant," Marc told her, "you wasted your pretty fireworks. Mike had already smashed through the other side of that shack. It was a rookie move."

"Always got to rub it in, eh, Frenchy? So what did you find in there?"

Marc pulled out a notebook,

"Well, in that last room we visited, we found four dead scientists, asphyxiated. Mike took pictures. We also found this notebook, all scribbled in. It was already wet when I picked it up. I did the best I could to protect it from the seawater."

Lisa took it and leafed through it. The more she turned the wet pages covered with notes and diagrams, ever so carefully, the more her face changed.

"What is it, Lieutenant?"

"It's all in there. Plans, explanations… They did it. They can create earthquakes at will."

Lieutenant Sturm was frantically turning the pages when she suddenly asked what location matched the coordinates 39° 51N, 12° 35E.

"Off the top of my head, I'd say the underwater volcano Vavilov, located in the Tyrrhenian Sea, southwest of Naples," answered Mike

Lisa Strum ran toward the controls.

"Let's call HQ! And C.L.A.S.H., too Maximum priority!"

Mister Song, C.L.A.S.H.'s #1 Agent, was having dinner in a chic Aspen restaurant with some friends when his emergency cell phone started vibrating.

"Yes?" he said, getting up to have some privacy.

"Jean Girodet here, from The Lion. I've got some puzzling news," he started without asking if he was disturbing his colleague. "Professors Pascale Turquin-Lemaître and Luca Van Genechten have both been dead for six months, yet they seem to be conducting some archeological work around the Roman ruins east of Solfatara near Naples. According to our investigator, these two impostors look very much like two

CRIMEN agents last seen in Tbilisi three years ago after that missile incident."

"CRIMEN?" Song blurted. "The EBC meeting starts in four days. I can't have CRIMEN agents running around there."

"Also, we thought S.P.I.D.E.R. was involved! You don't think they could be working together?"

"We're certainly going to look into it."

"Also, you should tell the Cave Patrol to get out of there asap. These guys are no altar boys—you've got plenty of widows to testify to that."

"The problem is... I can't reach them anymore," said Song. "They're already underground."

"What!? Then you have to strike now!"

"No! I'll give them a little more time." Song made a mental calculation. "24 hours. Not a minute more. Thank you, Girodet. We owe you one."

He hung up, worried.

Squatting behind some wooden crates, Sandy Crown tried to stay calm but alert. On the other side of the crates, in a large underground cave, an old magma chamber of a secondary conduit of Solfatara, the most active volcano of the caldera located to the west of Naples, ten men and women had set up a military camp.

The spotlights—the hum of the generators could be heard by the young woman even through the acoustic protection surrounding the area—were lighting the place up as bright as day. Having used this kind of equipment many times, the speleologist was fully aware of its power. The amount of electricity being generated here was far more than necessary for lights and ventilators to pump air, but from her position she could not see what else it was being used for. Whatever it was, the arsenal set up here was impressive.

The night before, the Cave Patrol had met the two archeologists, Pascale Turquin-Lemaître and Luca Van Genechten, who were making some digs around the Roman ruins east of Solfatara.

"We're looking for the Entrance to Hades," they had joked.

And they had explained that the Greeks and Romans thought that, at the bottom of the lake covering the crater, there was a tunnel leading to the banks of the Styx.

Tobie Drugg had told them they sounded like tour books writers. Everyone had had a good laugh. But Sandy Crown had felt a little uneasy, something she would have ignored if she hadn't seen the same two characters the following night, as she was looking admiringly at the skyline from the window of her hotel room. Their behavior had been strange and had piqued her curiosity.

She had hesitated about what to do next. Her friends were out on a quick errand and would return in ten minutes or so, but the strange couple was leaving and thus she'd had no choice. She had rushed out and followed them to the dig site and found the entrance that led to this secret place.

She had to tell her friends who could then warn C.L.A.S.H. She took out her cell phone to call Terry. Nothing. She looked at the screen. *Emergency calls only.*

Footsteps sounded nearby. She craned her neck and saw the female archeologist leaving their camp, passing close by. She huddled down deeper in the shadows.

The so-called "Pascale Turquin-Lemaître," in reality Emma Courdimanche of CRIMEN, was coming back from a rather awful evening when her satellite phone started vibrating.

"Courdimanche here. Good evening, Sir... No... No, I haven't heard from S.P.I.D.E.R. We should set an exact time... Vavilov, yes... No, I don't know... Tomorrow maybe...? Yes... The Cave Patrol? Elijah is taking care of them. It'll look like a gas leak... Yes, very well... Good-bye."

206

She hung up, furious. She did not like these conversations in which she was accused of incompetence. She was teetering on the edge of a cliff... without a parachute.

"They're getting on my nerves," she grumbled. "I hope the others have good news because otherwise I'm going to hit someone."

The information she received from her engineers put a smile back on her face because everything was ready for the big show. She cut short her visit to return to her cot in the makeshift camp that covered up their criminal activities. On the way, she caught some snatches of a conversation drifting in the natural echo of the grotto.

"No. It's about the hotel... I'm telling you, there's going to be an attack. Everyone must be evacuated..."

Behind the big wooden crates the woman talking into her telephone was getting upset trying to make herself understood. She had her back turned when Emma recognized her and stood frozen in surprise.

Sandy Crown heard only every other word through the bad connection. It frustrated her and she spoke more loudly. Too loudly. Far too loudly. She figured this out when she heard footsteps behind her. It was the fake archeologist leaving their camp.

Sandy reacted first. She tossed her phone at the CRIMEN agent for distraction, then grabbed the woman's collar and threw her over her shoulder like she had been taught in judo class. She followed up with a hold that choked her until she felt the woman's weight under her.

The cave was quiet again, disturbed only by the rhythmic hum of the ventilators and the growling generators. No one had heard the scuffle. Despite her burning desire to leave the place, Sandy still wanted to find out the purpose of this set up. She left her unconscious victim and snuck up toward the bigger tent. After minutes that seemed like hours, she slipped inside.

Two military-looking men were busy around a missile whose nose was open. Holding diagrams and wrenches, they were careful not to step on any of the computer equipment, circuit boards and toolboxes scattered on the ground. Lying in the shadows, Sandy saw one of them open a big black briefcase, delicately remove a small cylinder and deposit it inside the missile.

When the nose was closed again, the two men congratulated each other and left the tent laughing. Sandy waited to make sure she was alone before sneaking over to the missile, still not understanding why these men would be arming such a weapon.... Unless... No. That would be the craziest, stupidest idea.... And yet...

She studied the computer connected to the missile: a 24-hour countdown was waiting to start. The explosion was being planned here. But why? It would be too weak to cause much damage on the surface. Unless it was a nuke...

Sandy looked at the black briefcase. No doubt about it. The yellow and black warning label was there—it was a tactical nuclear bomb.

"My God!" she panted. "They want to wake up the volcano. They want to cause an eruption."

In a panic, she tried to use the computer to send a message to C.L.A.S.H. following the security protocol in case of an emergency. No network. Then she tried to tamper with the missile. No use. Finally, she decided to disconnect the whole thing by ripping out the cables. Suddenly, the bluetooth started blinking... the countdown began.

"Oh no! What have I done?"

She was panicking even more. The seconds were ticking off on the screen.

Bells started ringing. It took Sandy a minute to realize where it was coming from—the satellite phone she had completely forgotten about. She grabbed it, turned off the sound and then dialed the only number she knew by heart.

"Pick up, daddy, please pick up."

"Yes," a sleepy voice answered on the fourth ring.

Tears ran down her face.

The rest was very emotional. Anxiety, growing as the time passed on. Surprise, when the rattle of bullets echoed in the grotto. Fear, on hearing footsteps pounding and seeing the entrance of the tent moving. Relief when she saw Mister Song's face smiling at her, and finally, joy on feeling the arms of her friends hugging her after she was back on the surface.

When everyone had calmed down, Sandy explained how she had ended up there.

"Careless," Terry Bronx scolded her.

The geologist had also noticed the strange behavior of the couple of archeologists and, as a precaution, had sent a coded message to C.L.A.S.H. before doing anything. He was still waiting for an answer when they had to evacuate the hotel, leaving all their equipment behind.

When they could not find their friend or reach her on the phone, they had waited on pins and needles, afraid that something dire had happened to her. Luckily, everything had turned out for the best.

To wrap things up, Professor Bronx offered everyone a Ristretto.

In the control room of *Shark-99*, Lieutenant Lisa Sturm gathered her team to listen to Admiral Yale.

"Congratulations, Bathy-09. Thanks to your work here, C.L.A.S.H. was able to stop S.P.I.D.E.R. from setting off a tidal wave that would have destroyed the Bay of Naples. The action taken the day before yesterday led to the arrests of a lot of their agents and the confiscation of many documents that Doctor Kalamazoo and his team will be working on for many months to come."

"And the bodies we found?" Marc Pujo asked.

"Scientists sacrificed by S.P.I.D.E.R. Their disappearance was totally unknown to us. We shall inform their families."

Marc Pujo cursed up a storm.

"That will be all, Bathy-09. And again, congratulations."

The screen went black. Marc turned toward Mike Ehmadou.

"What bullshit! Stopping an underwater earthquake and a giant tidal wave should be worth more than mere congratulations!"

"Calm down, Marc. I'm sure there'll be a reward waiting for us back at the base."

"Yeah right. Three days R&R—that's all we'll get."

"Gentlemen," Lisa Sturm was back in her role as captain. "We have a new mission. Everyone to your post. On the double!"

All fell silent in *Shark-99* and ensign Mike Ehmadou, the "golden ear of the bathyscaph," put on the headphones, closed his eyes and focused his attention on the sounds he heard.

The Cave Patrol by J.-J. Dzialowski

Starlock by Alfonso Ruis

Starlock is a former Guardian of the Star Bridge, sentenced to life imprisonment by the Towers. He was eventually able to escape, taking over the body of NASA astronaut Nick Thaler; later, he joined the Strangers. This adventure takes place in his past.

Jean-Marc Lofficier: *Nomenclature 560*

The green planet bore no name.

Its star was too distant to be detected by Earth's telescopes, and it was listed in the Towers' nomenclature only as a seventeen-digit plus nine-character code.

For the sake of this story, we shall call it 560.

The inhabitants of 560 had concluded a treaty with the Tours two centuries earlier. But over the years, the trade with 560 had become scarce – until it finally stopped. It took the Towers another century to question the reason for this silence and dispatch one of their Guardians to investigate.

They chose Starlock for this mission, which they classified as routine.

The population of 560 had never been particularly large; its inhabitants, highly intelligent and peaceful humanoids— albeit xenophobic—were concentrated on the larger of its two continents.

Upon his arrival, Starlock set out to make a quick recon of the planet. He had already been intrigued by the fact that he had not been contacted by the natives when approaching their world, despite using the agreed upon signal from the Towers.

He soon discovered the explanation for this phenomenon: 560 had become a dead world.

Its cities were deserted, empty of any population, abandoned for at least half a century, if not more. The skeletons dotting the ground left no doubt as to what had happened. All the inhabitants of 560 had perished, but the reason for their mass extinction remained a mystery.

Was this a devastating virus? A cosmic phenomenon? Or a sudden attack by another as yet unknown race?

The Towers would no doubt send a team of scholars to study the situation and solve this riddle. Out of a sense of duty, Starlock decided to carry out a final tour of the capital, before setting out to report to his masters.

It was through the fronds of the trees in a large park that he first spotted the thing.

It was, without a doubt, a Salamandrite.

No Guardian could claim to be able to identify all the races inhabiting the three galaxies, but none since the legendary Battle of Toronn would have failed to recognize a Salamandrite. They were powerful living weapons manufactured by the Weapon Makers of Zade, and were rightly considered by all to be the most lethal lifeform in the known universe.

It was believed that all the Salamandrites had been destroyed at Toronn, but no one knew for sure whether this was indeed the case, or whether some had escaped, survived, or even if the Weapon Makers had not left a few more elsewhere.

Whether this Salamandrite was responsible for the deaths of the inhabitants of 560 had to be ascertained. So Starlock alighted and prepared to talk to it

"I'm Starlock, Guardian of the Towers."

"I am A-bel, protector of Zarkash," said the Salamandrite.

(*So that was 560's name*, Starlock thought.)

"What happened here? All the inhabitants are dead."

"A neutron star two parsecs from here collapsed. The radiation killed everyone on Zarkash."

"It is sad."

"Yes."

A long silence followed. Starlock had found the solution to the mystery and could have left, but his curiosity prompted him to continue the conversation.

"What are you going to do now?"

"I do not understand your question."

"All the Zarkashians are dead. You are free to go wherever you want now."

"My programming forbids this. I am the protector of Zarkash. I must continue my mission."

"But your mission has become irrelevant; there is nothing more to protect here."

"I am Zarkash's protector."

"That does not make sense."

"If the Towers were to disappear, would you stop being a Guardian?"

" It's not the same thing. We protect the Star Bridge. We..."

"I protect Zarkash."

There was another silence. Deep down, Starlock had to admit that A-bel had scored a point. Did his blind obedience to the Towers compare to the inflexible programming of the Salamandrite? Was he, too, a kind of living robot forever obeying the orders of entities that were inaccessible and incomprehensible to him?

Was A-bel condemned to guard a dead world forever?

Although this fate seemed odious to Starlock, there was little the Guardian could do to change it. Having solved the mystery of the Zarkashians' disappearance, all he had to do was go back and report to his masters.

It was then that the Eleemosynarics arrived.

The Eleemosynarics were the gypsies of the Milky Way; their many clans traveled endlessly, going from one planet to another, living on commerce and various exchanges. They were credited with strange powers – but isn't that always the case with gypsies, wherever they come from?

Three Eelemosynaric ships had landed not far from the capital, no doubt attracted by its proximity. It was doubtful that their navigators had had time to realize, let alone understand, the extent of the disaster that had struck the green planet. But that world had seemed hospitable to them, in a corner of the galaxy where such planets were rare indeed, and so, they had decided to land there.

Starlock's keen senses immediately detected their arrival and he quickly identified them by their engines. He didn't draw any other conclusions.

It was only when he saw A-Bel transform before his eyes to assume his most murderous, devastating form, that he understood the problem.

"Invaders," said the Salamandrite. "I must destroy them."

"No, they're harmless travelers who come in peace."

"They are not Zarkashians, so they are invaders. I am the protector of Zarkash. My task is to destroy them."

"I'm not Zarkashian yet you didn't attack me."

"You are a Guardian of the Towers. The Towers are allies of Zarkash. My memories contain a list of twenty-five species allies of Zarkash: Achernauts, Arenians..."

"Add to your memories to include these visitors. I assure you they are harmless."

"I hear what you say, but only a master can alter my memories."

"A master?"

"A member of the Supreme Council of Zarkash."

The Salamandrite turned and began to march heavily towards the vessels. Starlock put his hand on its shoulder.

"I can't let you destroy innocent people," he said softly.

A-bel struck first.

Starlock was forced to fight and, ultimately, destroy A-bel in order to save the lives of the Eleemosynarics.

Despite its programming, which included all of the ordinary self-preservation instructions, it became clear that the

216

Salamandrite had let Starlock win the battle – for it hoped to find in death the freedom which was now denied to it.

Breathing his last, A-bel said to Starlock:

"Do not mourn me, Guardian. It is better this way. Unlike humans, I do not have what they call a soul."

"Your sacrifice proves otherwise," Starlock replied.

And he closed its eyes.

Galaor by Franco Oneta

*This is a crossover between two of the best swashbucklers of the Hexagon Universe: **Galaor** (long before his departure for Mû), and Musketeer **Antonin**.*

Travis Hiltz: *Swords in the Night*

The night was warm and clear; torches and candles lit the streets of Paris. Amongst the multitude of revealers, guards, drunkards, whores and beggars, two members of His Majesty's musketeers made their way through the streets. One, a dark-haired man, his uniform stylish and dashing, talked enthusiastically, gesturing to emphasize his points or to smooth his trim mustache, pausing only to smile at attractive, female passersby. His companion, taller, younger and blonde, was hatless and his own uniform was plain and functional. His contribution to the conversation was the occasional nod or disapproving look.

"I tell you, Galaor, she is a vision!" the dark-haired musketeer exclaimed. "A woman to make the muses weep with jealousy!"

"She is a *married* vision, Antonin," his companion replied. "I advise caution and discretion."

"Always, my friend. But sometimes a bit of boldness is needed. A touch of adventure."

"I have had my share of adventures," Galaor said. "And none required a dalliance with another man's wife."

"I am too parched to continue this debate," Antonin announced. "Buy me a jar of wine and I'll happily discuss the morality of my actions."

"Why am I buying?" Galaor asked.

"It's your turn."

"It is always my turn."

"Don't be petty. Come, we'll cut down this alley. Should bring us to a tavern." Antonin said, moving across the street

219

and entering the alley. It was L-shaped and they came in on the shorter end. It was crowded with refuse, forcing the two men to walk single file.

As they reached the corner, Antonin exclaimed in surprise, grabbed his sword and leapt forward. Galaor struggled to catch up and, when he did, drew his own sword. A fellow musketeer was on the muddy ground, surrounded by three men in hooded robes. Crowded shoulder to shoulder, the two musketeers rushed forward, their swords flashing and driving back the trio. The fighting was fierce, but short-lived. Once the hooded men had fled, Galaor knelt by the fallen musketeer, while Antonin stood guard. The wounded man was pale, his uniform soaked with blood. He grabbed at Galaor's tunic, his mouth opening and closing as he struggled to both draw breath and speak. He gave a gurgling moan and collapsed.

"How fares he?" Antonin asked.

"Dead." Galaor replied, quietly.

"Do you recognize him?"

"No. He is no one I know…"

"What of his attackers?" Antonin asked.

"They looked like monks."

"Bit violent for men of the cloth," Antonin said.

"A man is dead!" Galaor protested.

"A man unknown to us, at the hands of attackers also unknown to us. Let some member of the city watch deal with this," Antonin said, sheathing his sword. "If they wish statements, I speak better with my tongue less parched."

Their duty done, the two musketeers retreated to the nearby tavern and were soon settled at a corner table with the best wine their few coins could buy. Antonin drank deep, smacked his lips and gave his friend a pat on the shoulder. "Cease your moping. 'Tis not the first dead man you've seen in the king's service and I predict it won't be the last."

"It is not that, Antonin," Galaor replied, not looking up from his barely touched mug. "Something about it…" He looked up at his friend. "Did it not seem strange to you?"

"Monks attacking a musketeer?" Antonin said, refilling his mug. "Yes, that would qualify as strange."

"I wonder if they were what they seemed. I swore I caught a glimpse of uniforms under one of their robes…"

"They were disguised as monks?" Antonin mused. "Perhaps they were enemies of the musketeer, members of the Cardinal's guard and wanted to keep their identities hidden?"

"I am not sure the dead man was a musketeer," Galaor said. "He, too, had another garment beneath his tunic…"

"A group of men disguised as monks attacking a man disguised as a musketeer?" Antonin asked. "You, my friend, have either had too much to drink, or too little."

"No, this all seems…wrong." Galaor said. "Not just the death, but there seems to be a mystery behind it. It can be no mere robbery or vendetta… the disguise… it makes no sense…?"

"I share your suspicions about the attackers, but they fled, like cowards. I have no love for the Cardinal's guard, but they would have stood and fought like men." Antonin shrugged, and dabbed at his mustache with a gloved hand. "Ah! That vinegar the landlord sold us has soaked my mustache. Loan me your handkerchief."

"I do not have one."

"I can see it, protruding from your sash," Antonin said, pointing. "Do not be petty just because it was your turn to pay."

"It is always 'my turn,'" Galaor protested. "And I tell you, I have no… where did this come from?"

"You are a poor actor, my friend," Antonin said, snatching the handkerchief from his friend's sash.

"It is not mine!"

Once free of the sash, an object fell out of the bit of silk, landing with a metallic clink.

"Keeping coin from me, as well?" Antonin frowned.

"Neither are mine," Galaor muttered, as he picked up the coin. "Odd… it looks foreign."

The coin was large and dark brown with writing on it, in no language he could recognize. "It feels light, for its size," he said, weighing it in his palm.

Antonin shrugged and dabbed at his mustache with the handkerchief. "Well, whoever he was, I commend his taste. This is quality silk... something else here...?"

Tucked into the seam was a tiny scrap of paper.

"There is writing on it," Galaor said.

Antonin turned the paper over and read: "*House of pages...?*"

"What does that mean?" Galaor asked.

"I don't know. *Pages* could refer to royal pages... We may have stumbled into some bit of palace intrigue," Antonin frowned. "All I wanted was a drink!"

"I do not like this," Galaor said. "Should we go to the palace?"

"What? No," Antonin said, shaking his head and helping himself to his comrade's neglected wine mug. "You keep running towards royal intrigue, whereas most smart men run away from it. You are going to cross paths with powerful men, catch their attention, and it will not be the joyful thing you imagine it to be."

"What do you expect me to do?"

"Follow the advice you are giving me daily—stop and think." Antonin replied. "And order another jug of wine... no...? Then, just stop and think—what do we know?"

"A man was killed. He was a musketeer, or at least dressed in the uniform of one," Galaor said, quietly. "His attackers were also in disguise, and seemed to be after either this odd coin, the scrap of paper, or both..."

"So, instead of worrying about court intrigue, we should be finding the meanings of the coin and the note," Antonin said, toasting his friend with his mug. "The handkerchief is good silk and that coin looks foreign. Maybe he was a merchant?"

"I have never seen a coin such as this," Galaor mused. "Seems almost like a medallion... and the monks' robes... Perhaps it is some secret sect?"

"You do have a love for complicating matters," Antonin mused, absently. "Or it could have been cutpurses in disguise, robbing a coin collector."

"But, what of this reference to the *House of pages*?" Galaor protested. "That seems to point to the palace."

"It could mean anything!"

"It sounds like a place name. What else could it be but...?"

"Are you all right?" Antonin asked, peering thoughtfully over the rim of his mug. "You went odd for a second there."

"A place name!" Galaor muttered, staring off into the distance. He blinked and looked at his comrade. "I think I know what it is!"

"Then tell me."

"A year or so back, I met a young maiden... stop smirking... and her father did not approve of destitute musketeers courting his daughter, so I would wait upon the bench of a nearby tavern, until she could arrange to run some errand for her father..."

"While I do appreciate a tale of romance, Galaor, how does this relate to the events of this evening?" Antonin asked.

"I spent a great deal of time with nothing to do but peruse my surroundings and across the street from the tavern was a bookseller called..."

"*The House of pages!*" Antonin gleefully interrupted, while slamming his palm down upon the table. "Well, lead on, my friend!"

They threw a few coins on the table, gathered their things and set out, yet again, across the darkened city. Moving quickly through a mix of narrow streets and alleys, emerging onto a wider and better-lit boulevard, Galaor paused to regain his bearings. He scratched his hairless chin as he peered up and down the street.

"Well?" Antonin asked.

"Give me a moment," the younger man said. "I have not been down this way in awhile… ah, there!"

The two musketeers made their way down the street and towards a three-story building. Galaor peered up it for several moments, a slight smile fighting valiantly to raise a corner of his mouth.

"Reminisce over her… charms later," Antonin said, nudging his comrade. "The bookseller first."

Galaor frowned at his friend and then pointed down the street. "The tavern is down that way." He led the way and soon, the two musketeers were standing in front of the *House of Pages*. It was a small, nondescript building, grey and weathered, its sign almost too small and plain to serve any practical purpose.

"I expected something a bit more…?" Antonin said, with a vague gesture. "How should we play this? I'm all for a straightforward attack, but this seems to require a defter hand. Since you are considered to be the more diplomatic of the two of us…"

Antonin made an *after you* gesture. Galaor shrugged and walked up to the equally grey and narrow door and entered, ducking to avoid bumping his head.

The building was narrow, but stretched back farther than either man had expected, giving it the appearance of being bigger on the inside than outside. There were numerous bookcases, all stretching farther back and loaded heavily with an impressive array of volumes. The room was brightly lit compared to other places the duo had been this evening. A variety of lamps and candles were scattered about. Antonin looked around, a mixture of amazement and suspicion playing across his features. Galaor stepped into the nearest row and ran his fingers down the spines of the books, as he read the titles on the spines.

"Can I help you, citizens… uh… gentlemen?" a voice said from across the room.

The two musketeers followed it past several rows. After the third row, there was a small oasis and there was a desk, loaded down with papers, inkwells and even more books. Perched on a stool, behind it was a man. He was thin, his shoulders hunched. His clothes were plain, but clean—a waistcoat, breeches and a cream-colored shirt. He looked at the two musketeers expectantly.

Galaor's forehead wrinkled in thought and then he reached into his sash and held out the coin. The thin man peered at it for several moments, then nodded and held out his hand to accept it.

"You will have to forgive my caution," he said, with a dry smile. He had a faint accent that neither musketeer could place. "I was sent word that Rodrik had operatives in the city and was unsure when, or even if, a courier would arrive. Come with me."

He stood up and shuffled off, down the nearest row with the two confused swordsmen trailing along behind. The farther back in the bookseller's that they went, the odder and dustier the books became. The hunched shouldered man drew a thick volume off a high shelf, brushed off a healthy layer of dust and opened the book. The interior had been hollowed out and inside rested a much thinner book with a white, slightly shiny cover. The man nodded to himself, replaced the bigger book and turned to Galaor and Antonin.

"I will wrap this up for you. It's best if it isn't seen," he said, returning to his desk. He searched for a place to set down the book. Having no luck, he handed it to Galaor, while he went to search for wrappings. The musketeer turned it over and studied it intently.

"Seems a trifling object to be worth a man's life," Antonin remarked, under his breath.

Galaor nodded, and ran his fingers over the book's cover. The binding and material were smooth. He frowned in puzzlement, as he opened it. Instead of writing, the pages were threaded with what looked like silver wire. The bookseller reached up and snatched the book from Galaor and bundled it up in rough, brown paper. He tied it with twine and handed it back.

"Your pardon," Antonin said, leaning past Galaor. "But, are we to convey the book to the same destination, or has that been changed due to all the, er, turmoil in the city?"

"What?" the thin man asked. "No, of course, I should have realized. You can't go to the house on the Rue Morgue. You must go to the river. The entire Hand has been instructed to converge at the boat."

Antonin nodded knowingly.

"We will be on our way," Galaor said, tucking the book into his sash.

"Did you understand any of that?" he asked, once they were back on the street.

"Not a word," Antonin shrugged. "This is why I so dislike intrigue. To the river?"

"I suppose we must. Events seem to be rushing about us."

"If we walk towards the Seine, we will pass quite a good wine shop that I know, on the way..." Antonin suggested.

"I would like to see this done before dawn," his friend said, walking faster.

Cutting through an alley, the duo suddenly found their path blocked by a quartet of Cardinal's guards.

"Ah, finally, something straightforward," Antonin said, placing a hand on his sword.

"Hold," Galaor muttered, as the other swordsmen advanced. The young musketeer caught a glimpse of fabric, poking out from beneath the lead guard's sleeve. "I do not think things are as straightforward as you hoped. Evening, my good fellow."

"It is the two from the alley," one of the guards muttered.

"I have no time for pleasantries or denial," the leader snapped. "Hand it over or we shall take it from your corpses!"

"Charming," Antonin said, with a grin. "Are you sure they aren't Cardinal's guards? Every bit as diplomatic."

"We have been charged with a task," Galaor said, grimly. "We are not the sort of men to shirk our duty because of threats."

"So be it."

All four men drew their swords. Smiling, Antonin drew his own sword, as well as a dagger from beneath his cloak and lunged past his friend. Galaor shrugged and drew his sword.

The alley was soon filled with moving bodies and rushing blades, as all six combatants struggled in its confines. Galaor placed his back to one wall, forcing his attackers to come to him, while Antonin was content to rush into the fray, lunging, dodging and swinging like a madman, partly, to protect Galaor and the book, but mostly due to his personal temperament.

He was slashed across the shoulder and fell to one knee. When his attacker moved in for the kill, Antonin swung around, burying his dagger in the fake guard's side. He swung his sword back and forth, wildly, to keep the others at bay. While Galaor had no fear of attack from behind, his two attackers were giving him no opportunity to get free or aid Antonin. A scratch across the back of his hand caused him to nearly drop his sword, and it was only his razor-sharp reflexes that allowed him to dodge a thrust, which tore through his cloak rather than his side.

He turned his body, but was too slow to avoid a sword thrust aimed at his hip. The guard's sword plunged into the paper-wrapped book tucked into Galaor's sash, and with a sound like a bell chiming underwater, all the combatants stumbled, as if the entire alley had tilted.

When Galaor recovered his equilibrium, he saw that the world around him had frozen. Antonin and the four guards had transformed from vicious fighters into statues. Gently, he pulled the sword from the book and stepped away from his attackers. Touching them, they seemed as hard as stone. He quickly moved to his friend's side, but no amount of shaking or calling his name could rouse him from his state.

"What has happened…?" he muttered. "What caused this?"

"I did," a voice replied.

Galaor spun around. Approaching him from the other end of the alley was a man. He was tall, with short blond hair and clothed in a most astounding suit of clothing. It was a one-piece orange body suit and it shone like sunlight on steel. The man's hands rested on his wide belt.

"Galaor de Montbars, Warlord of Mu, I greet you."

"What?" Galaor replied.

The other man peered at Galaor thoughtfully, and then frowned. "My apologies. That hasn't happened yet. You haven't even been to Tortuga... uh... again, sorry, I am babbling... getting old, though, I'll be younger when next we meet..."

"What sort of madman are you?" Galaor breathed, holding his sword out, to keep the new arrival at bay. "What is happening?"

"It's difficult to explain," the other man said, raising his hands, in a peaceful gesture. "My name is Jason Spell and I have come to retrieve the book!"

Galaor's sword moved forward till it was inches away from Spell's breastbone.

"I am not with them." he continued, nodded towards the guards. "Like you, I am a soldier, dedicated to a higher... ruler, of sorts. Sometimes, my tasks are straightforward, and others, like yours tonight, are enmeshed in a web of intrigue. I do not have time, ironically enough, to explain. All I can say is that I need the book, and that you will be doing me a great service, which I can swear to you, I will repay in the future."

"And if I do not?"

"Then you and your friend are in great danger—as is History as you know it," Spell said, in a quiet tone. "I do not threaten. I do understand that these events are beyond your comprehension, but you must trust me. If you keep the book, Rodrik's men will find you and they will kill you, years before your time."

"And you can make grand promises for our safety?" Galaor asked, skeptically.

"Without the book, Rodrik will be much too busy to concern himself with you two and you can both go on to live long, glory-filled lives."

"You will explain this to me at this next meeting of ours, I suppose?"

"I promise, and I will even buy the drinks," Spell replied, with a smile.

Galaor nodded to himself, lowered his sword and retrieved the book from his sash. He handed it to Spell who received it gratefully. "I understand it can be daunting to be a single soldier, unable to see the entirety of the bigger war around you, so, I will just thank you for your trust."

He gave a slight bow and offered his hand to the musketeer. When Galaor clasped the hand, there was a shock, like a fire racing up his arm. He cried out in surprise, as there was no true pain.

When he pulled his hand free, he found that only he and Antonin were in the alley. He had barely had a chance to be baffled by that when time restarted itself. Antonin, who had been in mid-lunge, leaped forward, only to find his opponent gone. He stumbled and fell.

"What in God's name?" he sputtered. "I've had opponents run away from my sword before, but never that quickly. What happened?"

"I... uh... I'm not entirely sure," Galaor muttered. "It was like witchcraft... I believe we ensured the book was delivered to its proper owners."

"Ah, well, that's good, I suppose," Antonin shrugged, as Galaor helped him to his feet.

"Tell me, Antonin," Galaor asked, absently. "What do you know about Tortuga?"

"An island, isn't it?" his friend replied, brushing himself off. "Off the Spanish main, I think? We have troops there, I believe."

"What about Mu?"

"Never heard of it. Why do you ask?"

"Something someone said to me recently… just curious."
The young musketeer sighed. "I need a drink."

"It is your turn to buy," Antonin informed him, tearing a strip of cloth off his cloak and wrapping his wounded shoulder.

"Of course, it is."

About the Authors

Brought up reading the adventures of Phileas Fogg and Captain Nemo (his father was a Jules Verne fan), it was quite natural for **Cédric Burgaud** to enjoy reading, then writing, fantasy fiction, first for himself, then for his family and friends. He has had several stories published in Rivière Blanche's thematic anthologies, including those devoted to the Hexagon Comics universe.

Julien Heylbroeck comes from the world of role-playing games, having worked on many successful products, including *La Brigade Chimérique*. He loves pulp heroes, super-heroes, and more particularly *luchadores* from Mexico. His stories have appeared in anthologies published by Malpertuis, Le Carnoplaste and Rivière Blanche. He collaborated with Romain d'Huissier on this volume.

Travis Hiltz started making up stories at a young age. In high school, he discovered that some writers actually got paid and decided to give it a try. He has since gathered a modest collection of rejection letters and had a one-act play produced. Travis lives in the wilds of New Hampshire with his very loving and tolerant wife, two above-average children and a staggering amount of comic books and *Doctor Who* novels.

Romain d'Huissier also comes from the world of role-playing games, having worked on *La Brigade Chimérique*, and designed and written an RPG based on the Hexagon Comics Universe for French publisher Les XII Singes. He has published a number of short stories and novels for Malpertuis, Le Carnoplaste, Critic, Trash and Rivière Blanche. For the latter, he has written two novels featuring the Hexagon group of super-heroes, *Dark Matter* and *The Immortals' War*, and assembled four anthologies devoted to the Hexagon Universe.

Born in 1970, **Jean-Marc Lainé** was editor at Semic (the predecessor of Hexagon Comics) in the late 1990s. He then edited a line of comics for publisher Bamboo. He has written several graphic novels including the *Omnopolis* trilogy, the second volume of the series *42*, and the two-volume *Grands Anciens*, which describes the meeting between Hermann Melville and H.P. Lovecraft. He has also written several acclaimed non-fiction books about the art and history of comics.

Jean-Marc & Randy Lofficier have collaborated on five screenplays, a dozen books and numerous translations, including *Arsène Lupin*, *Doc Ardan*, *Doctor Omega*, *The Phantom of the Opera* and *Rouletabille*. Their latest novels include *Edgar Allan Poe on Mars*, *The Katrina Protocol* and *Return of the Nyctalope*. They have written a number of animation teleplays, including episodes of *Duck Tales* and *The Real Ghostbusters*, and in comics, such popular heroes as *Superman* and *Doctor Strange*. Randy is a member of the Writers Guild of America, West and Mystery Writers of America.

Ghislain Morel discovered comics at age six in a box that belonged to a cousin of his, filled with French editions of Marvel titles. Born in 1971, he is old enough to have bought and read the original black and white mags which featured the heroes of the Hexagon Universe. He has written games, short stories, articles, played music in the groups Maigh Tuireadh, Skøll and Naheulband, and chaired the musical and literary collective, The Deep Ones.

Eric Nieudan has written comics, role-playing and video games, short stories and even advertizing copy. More than one publisher experienced doubts after having hired this ninja-like and dinosaur-obsessed freakazoid. When Eric is not writing he can almost seem normal. There are photos of him pushing a supermarket cart filled with exclusively bags of coffee. Lately, Eric has gone into self-imposed exile in Ireland but the authorities are monitoring his movements by reading his blog: *www.quenouille.com*. Eric won the Alain le Bussy Award in 2011 for his short story *Les octets de ma vie*.

Olivier Vignot grew up under the clouds of Tchernobyl, September 11 and Fukushima but emerged (almost) unscathed. He published a first short story collection, *Les Délétères*, in 2010, and had a stage play, *La Faute à Michel*, produced. He is associated with the musical group & workshop Slam and writes music articles for the website Music'ovores.

Jean-Hugues Villacampa, born in 1959, was thrilled from an early age by comics, popular literature and science fiction. As a kid, he was a big fan of Jules Verne's *Extraordinary Voyages* and the French adventure series *Bob Morane* by Henri Vernes. He also read all the digest-sized comics that became Hexagon Comics (as well as many others) and remembers envying Zembla's power to communicate with the beasts of the jungle. When editor Romain d'Huissier asked him to contribute to *Tales of the Hexagonverse*, Jean-Hugues gleefully went back to the Zembla tales of his youth and chose to locate his own story during the accession to independence of Karunda. Jean-Hugues has written numerous stories for and about role-playing game under various pseudonyms. He worked for a few years as a ghost writer and has had SF short stories published in several anthologies.

Antonin by Barbato

HEXAGON COMICS CATALOG

Barry Barrison, Ghost Detective: The Tarford Inheritance (novel) by Philippe Pinon translated by Nina Cooper & Jean-Marc Lofficier. 240 pages. $20.95.

Bob Lance #1: The Round Table. Carpi & Bernasconi. 64 pages b&w. $12.95.

Bob Lance #2: To Seek the Holy Grail. Carpi & Bernasconi. 54 pages b&w. $12.95.

Bob Lance #3: The Ghost of Rasputin. Carpi & Bernasconi. 54 pages b&w. $12.95.

C.L.A.S.H. Frescura & Trevisan. 248 pages b&w. $20.95.

Dick Demon: Vanishing Point. Lofficier, Arden & Peniche. 108 pages color. $26.95.

Dragut/Scarlet Lips. Lofficier & Macall. 68 pages color. $19.95.

The Enchanters. Lofficier, Mayorga & Castro. 88 pages b&w. $12.95.

The Frontiersmen/Codename: Glory. Lofficier, Peniche & Mayorga. 48 pages b&w. $9.95.

Galaor, Warrior of Mû. Lofficier, Macall, Xavier & Peru. 68 pages color. $19.95.

Guardian of the Republic #1. Mornet & Roncagliolo. 48 pages color. $12.95.

Guardian of the Republic/Barbarella. Lofficier & Ruiz. 48 pages color. $12.95.

Guardian of the Republic/Doctor Omega. Lofficier & Peniche. 48 pages b&w. $9.95.

Guardian of the Republic/Dragut/Scarlet Lips/Time Brigade. Lofficier & Macall. 48 pages b&w. $9.95.

Guardian of the Republic/Kit Kappa/Night Prince. Lofficier, Castro & Garcia. 48 pages b&w. $9.95.

Guardian of the Republic/Phenix/Super-Patriots. Lofficier & Macall. 48 pages b&w. $9.95.

Gun Gallon. Lofficier, Macall & Picard. 48 pages b&w. $9.95.

HEXAGON COMICS: THE FIRST 70 YEARS. Lofficier et al. 300 pages b&w. $22.95.

Hexagon Group #1: The Dark Hive. Lofficier, Roncagliolo & Ruiz. 76 pages b&w. $12.95.

Hexagon Group #2: Hexagon vs. Heptagon. Lofficier, Roncagliolo & Garcia. 96 pages b&w. $12.95.

Hexagon novel #1: Dark Matter. D'Huissier. 300 pages. $22.95.

Hexagon Spotlight on Alfredo Macall. 68 pages color. $19.95.

Kabur #1. Legrand, Lofficier & Bernasconi. 252 pages b&w. $20.95.

Kabur/Zembla. Lofficier & Ratera. 84 pages color. $24.95

Kidz. Lofficier & Macall. 52 pages b&w. $10.95.

The Lunatic Legion. Lofficier, Bouquet & Lafuente. 52 pages b&w. $10.95.

Morgane. Lofficier & Lirussi. 48 pages b&w. $9.95.

The Partisans #1. Thomas, Lofficier & Guevara. 48 pages b&w. $9.95.

The Partisans #2. Lofficier & Guevara. 64 pages b&w. $12.95.

Phenix #1. Lofficier, Bernasconi & Roncagliolo. 248 pages b&w. $20.95.

Scarlet Lips: Crimson Dawn. Wolfman, Lofficier & Guevara. 48 pages b&w. $9.95.

Starlock/Homicron. Lofficier & De La Torre. 54 pages color. $14.95.

Strangers Origins: Homicron. Buffolente, Lofficier & Dzialowski. 364 pages b&w. $24.95.

Strangers Origins: Jaydee. Grossi. 260 pages b&w. $20.95.

Strangers Origins: Starlock. Legrand & Bernasconi. 256 pages b&w. $20.95.

Strangers #0: Omens & Origins. Lofficier & Various. 128 pages color. $29.95.

Strangers #1: Strangers in a Strange Land. Lofficier & Various. 160 pages color. $34.95.

Strangers #2: Of Blood and Fire. Lofficier & Various. 160 pages color. $39.95.

Strangers #3: Of Gods and Men. Lofficier & Various. 160 pages color. $39.95.

Strangers #4: The Coming of Starcyb. Lofficier & Various. 118 pages b&w. $12.95.

Strangers #5: The Kingdom of Shivar. Lofficier & Peniche. 94 pages b&w. $12.95.

Tales of the Hexagonverse #1: Mutations (anthology). D'Huissier ed. 244 pages. $20.95.

Tales of the Hexagonverse #2: Family Business (anthology). D'Huissier ed. 244 pages. $20.95.

Tales of the Twilight People: Dr. Despair. Lofficier & Agapit. 148 pages b&w. $12.95.

Tiger and The Eye. Lofficier & Ruiz. 136 pages b&w. $12.95.
The Time Brigade: The Grail Wars. Lofficier & Green. 48 pages color. $12.95.
Wampus #1. Frescura & Bernasconi. 232 pages b&w. $20.95.
Zembla #1. Oneta & Oneta. 280 pages b&w. $22.95.

TO ORDER: Add $4 first book, $2 for subsequent books, for p&h. Pay by credit card/paypal direct from our website: *www.hexagon.comics.com/shop.html*
or pay by check to the order of BLACK COAT PRESS sent to: BLACK COAT PRESS c/o Mr. Greg M. Seigel, 18321 Ventura Blvd., Suite 915, Tarzana, CA 91356.
E-MAIL INQUIRIES: info@blackcoatpress.com.

Zembla vs Yatan by José Luis Ruiz Pérez